MISS DRAMATIC

MISCHEIF IN MAYFAIR—BOOK NINE

GRACE BURROWES

GRACE BURROWES PUBLISHING

To families of every description

CHAPTER ONE

"Are you two out of your happily married minds?"

Gavin DeWitt did not shout, nor did he pitch the nearest porcelain vase to the hearthstones. The acting profession taught a man to control himself before all audiences, as did life in Crosspatch Corners. "The only curse worse than a house party," he went on, "is a hen party, and you propose to gather up every clucking biddy ever to roost at a Mayfair ridotto."

"Remind me again," Lord Phillip Vincent drawled. "What exactly is a ridotto?"

His brother, Trevor, Marquess of Tavistock, lounged with an elbow propped on the library mantel. "The usual dancing and flirtation. Better food at a ball, better gaming at a ridotto."

"Ah." Phillip had taken to studying the niceties of polite society as Gavin might have applied himself to a Shakespeare soliloquy. "Interesting."

Gavin considered pitching the vase at the marquess, his brother-by-marriage. "'A learned fool is more a fool than an ignorant fool.' If you know polite society so well, Tavistock, then you know this gathering will only end in disaster."

"In finding you a wife, you mean?" Tavistock smiled in that urbane, self-possessed, annoying way of his.

Lord Phillip rose from the desk. "Stow it, Tavistock. Gloating is bad form even here in the shires. Just because you and I are the happiest of men, delighting in the affections of our darling wives, doesn't mean you should tease DeWitt about his lamentable bachelorhood."

Neither Molière nor the Bard offered a riposte worthy of that bit of inanity. "I like my bachelorhood very well, thank you, and I intend to enjoy it for some time."

Tavistock and Lord Phillip exchanged a look possible only between men who were both in the early throes of wedded bliss. Tavistock was fair, Lord Phillip dark-haired, but the pair of them were tall and rangy, and they shared a certain resemblance in their features.

And in their patient pitying of Gavin's bachelor state.

"I was like you once," Tavistock said, as if *once* had been ages and ages ago in a land far away, not the mere handful of weeks, and most of those weeks spent in Crosspatch Corners. "I was determined to avoid parson's mousetrap, but I had a reason: My father's example would have put any man off marriage. Phillip was concerned about his past overshadowing his future, which we can also lay at our late father's feet. What's your excuse?"

"Why do I need an excuse to enjoy my freedom? Phillip, you professed the self-same contentment until very recently."

Phillip's smile was sweet, and that hurt worse than Tavistock's smug condescension. "Then I met my Hecate, and mere contentment would no longer do, though I understand your hesitation. Women like Hecate and Amaryllis are rare."

Phillip had been raised in Crosspatch Corners, far from the madding crowd's ignoble strife—and its licentiousness. He was in some regards the most innocent of men, though in his understated, soft-spoken way, also quite shrewd.

"You could not possibly understand why the prospect of a lot of spinsters and meddlers congregating beneath my very nose gives me the collywobbles." Opening night on Drury Lane wouldn't have been half so intimidating. "These are the ladies who make up numbers, who pop up on short notice when more fashionable guests decline an invitation at the last minute. They aren't half so harmless as you might think. You have no idea..."

Phillip and Tavistock were looking at him as if he'd lapsed into Old English.

"You've been off racketing about the shires for two years," Tavistock said. "Doing your Shakespeare impersonation. How could you predict the sort of women Hecate and Amaryllis will favor with an invitation?"

The former Miss Hecate Brompton was not well known to Gavin, but he was better acquainted with his sister Amaryllis than with any other person living upon the earth. He could predict exactly what sort of ladies she'd invite to Berkshire for a few weeks of summer socializing.

Dragons in disguise, basilisks in bonnets, wyverns in white gloves.

"While I was on the stage," Gavin said, "my troupe was occasionally called upon to grace social gatherings."

Phillip squinted at him. "You were hired to entertain in private homes. Juggle for your supper?"

If only the expected entertainments had been limited to juggling. "We enacted selected scenes, delivered famous speeches, and assisted with the amateur theatricals. We were also expected to serve as supporting cast."

"Flirt with the dowagers?" Tavistock pushed away from the mantel. "So you rounded out the dance sets when you weren't mooning about the court of Denmark or preparing to storm Agincourt. What of it?"

Both men regarded Gavin with genuine puzzlement. If he told them the rest of it, that puzzlement might well turn to disgust or amusement. The situation wanted some thought, some rehearsal.

He'd find a way to explain, a way to say what needed to be said without making himself look like the ignorant bumpkin he'd been.

"For the good of all concerned," he said, "the only role I will be playing for the next few years is the country squire conscientiously minding his acres right here in Crosspatch Corners. Perhaps after Mama has Caroline and Diana launched, I will see fit to add a wife to the cast at Twidboro Hall."

"Wife is not a part to be acted," Phillip said, "any more than husband is a role to be put on and taken off. One fears for your understanding, DeWitt."

Better that than fearing for a man's good name.

"You won't run off?" Tavistock asked ever so casually. "Hecate and Amaryllis have quite warmed to the idea of a mostly ladies gathering, and if you were to absent yourself, they would be puzzled."

Amaryllis would be hurt, possibly furious. "I won't run off." Appending the word *again* was unnecessary. For the two years Gavin had performed on the provincial stages, his family hadn't known where to find him, through no direct fault of his.

The indirect fault had been and remained entirely his.

"Splendid." Phillip came around the desk and clapped him on the back. "You will enjoy yourself, and we might even let you do some of that to-be-or-not-to-be business. The guests we're expecting are a bookish lot, and they will doubtless appreciate some rousing speeches from a tall, dark, and brooding Hamlet."

"Not Hamlet," Gavin said, and brooding was doing it a bit brown. "The poor fellow went mad, committed suicide by duel, and left his kingdom ripe for plucking by a foreign invader. I don't suppose you have a copy of the guest list?"

Another shared glance that spoke volumes. *Got him!* from Tavistock, and *I told you he'd come around,* from Phillip.

Tavistock opened the desk's middle drawer and brandished a piece of foolscap. "Might not be complete, but these are the ladies who have accepted."

Gavin read down the list, recognized a few names, and allowed himself a gathering sense of relief. Formidable women, but none with a reason to wish him ill. No drunkards or hopeless gamblers, no prattling...

Oh spite. Oh hell. His dearest memory, his deepest regret lurked near the bottom of the list, gracing the space between Lady Iris Wolverhampton and Miss Zinnia Peasegood.

"You see some familiar names, I trust?" Lord Phillip sounded pleased with himself. "I know you and Mrs. Roberts are cordially acquainted."

"Rose Roberts was at the Nunnsuch house party, wasn't she?" Tavistock asked, overdoing the curious tone by half. "A widow, as I recollect."

"Mrs. Roberts was at Nunnsuch," Gavin replied, passing back the list. "An agreeable, sensible lady."

"And easy on the eyes," Phillip added. "Surely you noticed that part?"

How could Gavin have failed to notice that a woman who'd been luminous eighteen months ago despite her grief had bloomed in the wake of mourning? Hair between auburn and Titian that loved both sunlight and candlelight, a smile to intrigue even a saint—Gavin was not a saint—and silences that could bless or condemn. Then there were her hands, her eyes, the way she caressed the rim of her wineglass when her thoughts wandered...

"Quite pretty," Gavin said. "Also well-read and much enamored of her late spouse, if I'm to believe the Earl of Nunn. I can see why Amaryllis would enjoy her company. Unless you two have any more ambushes to spring upon me, I'm off to see Old Man Deever about a new pair of riding boots."

The bedrock of any successful role was in the details. Which hat would a rake wear to see his mistress? Which would he wear to take supper at his sister's house? The audience noticed those details, even if they didn't realize they noticed.

The mention of riding boots was such a detail—Gavin was notably fond of his colt, Roland—and apparently convincing.

"My regards to the Deevers," Tavistock said. "Amaryllis and I will expect you and the rest of the family for supper tomorrow evening."

Gavin assayed his best, harmless smile. "Wouldn't miss it for the world."

He knew not to rush his exit and denied himself a moment to tarry in the wings. He cared not one fresh horse dropping how Phillip and Tavistock parsed the conversation.

He knew only that this hen party could foretell his doom, but that he'd risk even his good name if he could once again escort Mrs. Rose Roberts into dinner.

~

Your brother and I have a past.

Rose Roberts could not say that in the face of Amaryllis DeWitt's gracious welcome—she was Amaryllis, Marchioness of Tavistock now, which made such a confession an even more daunting prospect. Her ladyship had always had presence, a certain calm self-possession, as had her brother.

In the past eighteen months, Gavin's self-possession had become the gravitas of a man who knew his place in the world, and that place did not require him to renew old flirtations. Though Rose could not call him Gavin here. He was Mr. DeWitt, just as he'd been Mr. DeWitt for the two interminable weeks of the Nunnsuch house party.

"Welcome to Miller's Lament," Lady Tavistock said, taking both of Rose's hands. "We are so glad you could join us. Hecate has been in transports to know you accepted our invitation."

Hecate, rather than *Lady Phillip.* The party was off to a very informal start, which made Rose want to turn right back around and climb into her traveling coach. At the Nunnsuch gathering, she had relied on the Earl of Nunn, an old and trusted ally, to ensure the decorum of the proceedings.

Though a gaggle of proper ladies could hardly turn into a summer bacchanal, could it? Then too, blowing retreat would inspire dear Timmens to new heights of I-told-you-so mutterings and looks, a penance not to be borne, even from a devoted lady's maid.

"I am delighted to be here," Rose said, giving her ladyship's hands a light squeeze. "An inspired idea. If the men must disappear to the grouse moors, why not enjoy the resulting peace and quiet in the company of female friends?"

Dane had never gone off shooting in the north. His expeditions in pursuit of sport had been to Town, always to Town. In late summer, he'd stayed home and pursued the manly art of canoodling with his wife in a duck blind.

"Mrs. Roberts." Lady Phillip offered Rose the same two-handed welcome Lady Tavistock had. While the marchioness was tall, with dark auburn hair and a few freckles across her cheeks, Lady Phillip was more compact and curvier. She wasn't a great beauty, but she had a compelling gaze and was said to be a genius with investments.

Rose curtseyed despite the two-handed grip. "A pleasure, my lady."

"We've put you in the Rose Suite, for which you must not scold us. You have the best view of the River Twid, and you'll have morning shade. You are among the first to arrive. Expect a tea tray before your trunks are carried up, have a stroll along the Twid, or indulge in a nap or a bath. Nobody will bother you until the buffet at seven. I trust all is well with Lord Nunn?"

The earl was an uncle of some sort to Lady Phillip. "His lordship is getting an education from his new understeward, and he seems to be enjoying the tutelage. I bring his fondest regards."

"And Mrs. Riley is thriving?"

"She and the baby are well."

Rose, by contrast, felt an increasing urge to flee, to plead a headache that could be cured only by an immediate return to Hampshire. The impulse was old and familiar, which made it no easier to resist. Timmens had been right—coming here was a mistake—but Rose need not admit the mistake quite so soon.

Gavin DeWitt did not dwell at Miller's Lament. His property lay nearby, also along the River Twid, and Rose held out hope that his path would not cross hers again.

She held out equal hope that it would. Frequently.

"Mrs. Riley and her daughter are thriving," Rose said. "Henry Wortham is making a respectful pest of himself, and Mrs. Riley is allowing it."

Widows were to remarry. This was an unwritten law at every rung of the social ladder. Widows who bore their late husband's posthumous child were most especially to devote themselves to recruiting a successor spouse, and Mavis Riley was making fast progress in the approved direction.

"That is wonderful news," Lady Phillip said, releasing Rose's hands. "Henry is a fine young man, and his prospects are good. Don't let me keep you here catching up on the gossip. Away with you. Travel can be so taxing. Mrs. Williams will see you to your rooms."

A sturdy, beaming housekeeper stepped forward. "This way, ma'am." She trundled up a curving staircase, and Rose followed, pretending to interest herself in the house's appointments. Miller's Lament, like many country manors, had endured centuries of habitation, alternately coming up in the world and then traveling in the other direction.

In good times, a wing was added in the normal course, an attic fitted out. In bad times, the damp got in, retaining walls subsided. Miller's Lament occupied a slight rise on an oxbow bend in the river. Human effort was doubtless necessary to encourage the river to maintain its course, else the house could find itself on an island after the next serious storm.

Colforth Hall lacked an encroaching river, but Rose's home had its own stories. A priest hole here, a tunnel built for smugglers rather than servants there. Dane had taken the place for granted, and Rose looked after it as best she could.

Miller's Lament was clearly enjoying an upswing. Every window sparkled, the carpets had the glow of new acquisitions, no cobweb dared lurk in a corner of the ceiling. All was light, quiet, and repose, with fragrant bouquets of sweet peas on the windowsills and sideboards.

"We're doing right by the old place," Mrs. Williams said. "Her ladyship has taken all in hand, and we're to have a conservatory too, by this time next year."

"The property is very attractive."

"That's the river for you. Gives the trees some purchase against the dry years, means the gardens and flowers will always flourish. This summer hasn't been too bad for rain."

"We should enjoy a good harvest in Hampshire as well."

Rose could talk pleasantly about nothing all day and for half the night. She could steer any conversation away from the fraught waters of politics and back into the safer channels of the weather, church-yard news, or art.

Art generally put everybody on good behavior, or kept their mouths shut lest they betray their ignorance on the topic. Dane assuredly hadn't troubled to take much interest in art.

"Here we are," Mrs. Williams said, opening a door carved with twining roses. "Fine view of the river, pleasant breeze. The east side of the house is downwind from the stable this time of year. His lord-ship says the conservatory ought to go on that side to take advantage of the morning sun. He's clever that way."

For a marquess to realize the sun rose in the east was clever, of course. "It would be a shame to interfere with the lovely view avail-able on this side of the house, wouldn't it?"

Rose crossed the room to French doors left open to catch the breeze. The land fell away in the usual progression. A wide flagstone terrace stepped down into walkways running between flower beds in full summer riot. The roses were done for the year, but lavender, hollyhocks, hydrangeas, and daisies bloomed apace, while formal parterres—privet and various white blossoms—held the ground between the bottom of the garden and the parkland that ended along the river.

Peaceful, pretty, predictable.

"Shall I send up a tray?" Mrs. Williams asked. "Your maid is doubtless tarrying in the servants' hall for a quick cup while we get your trunks sorted."

Timmens was on reconnaissance, of course. "A tray would be appreciated, and then I might go for a stroll."

"Lovely walks along the old towpaths, missus. Supper will be a buffet on the terrace at seven, weather permitting."

Of course it would. Followed by cards in the library for those so inclined, but nothing so protracted or taxing as a tournament on the first night.

Mrs. Williams bustled off, and the quiet was a benediction. Two wrought-iron chairs graced the balcony. Rose took one and tried to muster a lecture on all the progress she'd made since putting off second mourning.

Another lecture, though when Gavin DeWitt might even at that moment be somewhere on the same property, sermonizing was beyond her.

"Move," she muttered when the chairs whispered to her to *get off her feet*. She'd been off her feet for the past four hours. "Do something before Timmens invades and starts in with her suggestions."

Early in mourning, Rose had succumbed to the lure of inactivity. The attendant rituals of isolation and withdrawal made becoming one with a favorite wing chair all too easy. Not the bed—too many memories in the bed—but the couches, window seats, and reading chairs gracing nearly every room of Colforth Hall.

She'd stopped playing the piano, stopped riding out in the morning, stopped looking in on the tenants. Stopped living.

Timmens had been on hand then, too, always ready with a pillow for Rose's feet, a shawl against a nonexistent chill. Loyalty like that deserved to be appreciated, though the cosseting itself had eventually driven Rose to stop moping.

"Move, my girl," she muttered, turning her back on the chairs and the balcony with the pretty view of the Twid. "Put on your boots and sally forth." The towpath along the river would be shaded and private, and a pleasant stroll would be just the thing for shaking the lethargy of travel from a lady's mind.

Shaking Gavin DeWitt from her memories would be another matter entirely.

"The beauty of investing," Hecate said, "is that you need only a little coin to do it."

"Coin and a solicitor or agreeable male relative," Amaryllis replied. One also needed an *interest* in the subject, of which she was decidedly not possessed.

She and Hecate had hit a lull between arriving guests and had taken the opportunity to sit for a moment in the cool shade on the side terrace. The river made such a peaceful vista on three sides of the house, but Amaryllis's favorite view was this one.

Orderly, but colorful and bucolic too. Some of the beds would have to be redone—no country household was complete without a spice garden and a medicinal garden, but for now the flowers were lovely.

"We have agreeable male relatives," Hecate retorted, toeing off her slippers and putting her bare feet up on a hassock. "Phillip is as happy to learn about investing as I am to learn about management of Lark's Nest."

Phillip, whom Amaryllis had known for her whole life, was happy to do anything that allowed him to sit next to his new wife.

Amaryllis bestirred herself from a dragging temptation to close her eyes. "He's more interested in investing than learning the quadrille?"

Hecate's smile was impish, which Amaryllis would not have thought possible even three months ago. "Phillip has many fine qualities. If he never learns the quadrille, I will be content to partner him in other activities."

His lordship had grown up on a neighboring estate, a quiet, bookish man who nonetheless was passionate about his acres. Few in Crosspatch Corners had known much of his antecedents, and over time, his parentage simply hadn't mattered. Phillip was a good neighbor, an excellent farmer, and a generous friend.

He would bring the same focus and integrity to the business of being Hecate's husband as he brought to his agrarian undertakings, and she would make him the most devoted of wives—or Amaryllis would know the reason why.

"Trevor will invest for us if I ask it of him," Amaryllis said, "and I do mean Trevor. He might have Worth Kettering see to the details, or Ash Dorning, but we are done with old and respected firms of thieving reprobates."

"Amen. I do hope the ladies will be amenable to my proposal. Investing wisely will allow us to do good while doing well."

Hecate, when engaged on a topic, was like a girl in her first Season invited to discuss the ideal choice of fan. Inexhaustible, enthusiastic, and a fine soporific. Amaryllis was tempted to take off her own slippers, but nothing was more likely to inspire the arrival of the next guest than yielding to such an impulse.

"Some of the ladies will be interested in your scheme, some not. We will have a pleasant time nonetheless. Have you noticed how many of our guests have floral names?"

"Yours is a floral name," Hecate replied. "Better that than a goddess of sorcery."

"Phillip says you are the goddess of magic, and anyplace you bide becomes enchanted."

Another of those pleased, wifely smiles. "I am afraid I will wake up to hear my cousins squabbling, their mother demanding to discuss her allowance with me, and my London butler rapping on the study door in that tap-of-doom way that conveyed family calling. Crosspatch Corners is so peaceful, so..."

"So beautiful." The Twid made its placid meanders through the shire, the seasons wore their green, golden, and white finery by turns, and nobody could be bothered with who'd been denied a voucher to Almack's.

A notion to inspire a lady to catch forty blissful winks. Amaryllis mentally batted the thought away and instead wondered if putting Mrs. Rose Roberts in the Rose Suite was badly done. She'd be more or less isolated on that side of the house, and widows endured enough isolation.

"Phillip says Gavin took the news of our gathering calmly," Hecate observed. "You are Gavin's sister. What do you think?"

"I think our husbands are trying to be subtle, but their match-making is about as hard to miss as Mr. Dabney discoursing in praise of mules." A great fan of the mule was Mr. Dabney, proprietor of the local livery. His orations invariably inspired Vicar to counter with an exegesis on the virtue of the English hunter, whose stamina and bravery had brought the quality of British cavalry stock to near-Olympian heights.

"I think," Hecate said, "that Gavin is a highly skilled actor, one who could have moved on to the London stage after his provincial tours. If he appeared calm at the prospect of a dozen single women of respectable social standing invading his neighborhood, he was giving yet another virtuoso performance."

Amaryllis and Trevor had been spared the Nunnsuch house party by their newlywed status, but Gavin, Phillip, and Hecate had attended. For a few days, Gavin had been thrown into close proximity with Hecate as her informal bodyguard.

Gavin was a skilled actor, while Hecate had perfected the fine art of noticing more than she let on.

"A gentleman does not tread the boards," Amaryllis said. "Gavin would have declined a London offer even if one had been extended to him." She hoped, but then, if somebody had told her that her darling brother would run off to join an acting troupe without any warning to his family, she would have laughed.

"How do you know Gavin would have turned down a London offer? I realize you are his devoted sibling, and very astute, but how do you know what he would or would not have done?"

Amaryllis slipped out of her shoes and forced her sluggish mind to consider the question. Why did one think better when barefoot? Hecate had a point—she always had a point, bless her—but Gavin, as the only son, and then the only male, in the family, had been the epicenter of the DeWitt household. Impossible for his older sister not to know him, in other words.

"He wanted a wider world," Amaryllis said, "and what better way to experience that than to leave home and don a succession of roles in a succession of theaters before a changing audience from all walks of life? He liked the social aspects of university, the roistering and the books in combination, but what he enjoyed most was simply getting away from home. The time away did him good, though we are certainly glad to have him back where he belongs."

Mama, Grandmama, Caroline, and Diana were in transports to have all once again as it should be.

Hecate studied her toes. "I cannot imagine Gavin as a frivolous boy. Maybe the time away made him appreciate home?"

Amaryllis could not put her finger on what exactly had changed about her brother, but the difference troubled her. He'd been a blithe spirit as a youth, happy to entertain all and sundry with his stories, imitations, and recitations.

He still smiled, he still told stories, but an underlying somberness remained. Part of him had yet to come home and might never complete the journey.

"Gavin has always loved Crosspatch," Amaryllis said. "Now that his wild oats are sown, he can settle in here as he ought. I doubt he's ready to take a wife, though. He'll need more than a few pretty, sensible ladies to turn his head in matrimonial directions."

"Good, because our guests aren't looking for a husband. Perhaps you should tell your brother that. Set his mind at ease."

"If he gives me two minutes of his time to chat privately, I will. Who is that?"

A lone female figure had emerged onto the main terrace and was descending into the garden, a book in her hand. She wore a wide-brimmed straw hat and strode along with a sense of purpose at variance with the afternoon's heat.

"Rose Roberts," Hecate said. "Our latest arrival. Widowed, manages her acres very competently. Uncle Nunn likes her, and he is a man of few friendships."

"Are they more than friends?"

"I think not. He's many years her senior, which doesn't signify, but she was thought to be very much in love with her late husband. Nunn was much enamored of his countess, and that created common ground when Mrs. Roberts was bereaved."

"She appears intent on putting distance between herself and the house."

Hecate closed her eyes. "Coach travel is so confining. Doesn't your brother typically hack his colt along the Twid at this hour?"

Amaryllis surrendered to the languor and tranquility of the day, put her feet up on the hassock, and closed her eyes as well. "He does, and I expect today will be no exception. He and Mrs. Roberts are acquainted. They won't need us to hover about and make introductions."

"Suppose not. We will have such fun at this gathering. I can hardly wait for the rest of the guests to arrive."

Amaryllis didn't know about fun, but a pleasant time was a reasonable goal. She could also make some progress toward rehabilitating her husband's reputation in the eyes of Society. A young, handsome marquess who turned his back on Mayfair to marry a provincial spinster had some fences to mend.

And Phillip's attempts to learn the quadrille—and the minuet, and the country dances, and the rest of polite society's folderol—could advance among a bevy of friendly ladies who weren't too high in the instep.

If Hecate talked a few of the ladies into joining her investment schemes or supporting her charities, that would be all to the good as well.

Seeing Gavin married off, though, struck Amaryllis as tilting at a formidable windmill. He needed a wife—that was obvious—so she wished Lord Phillip and the marquess the best of luck in their roles as matchmakers. Then she succumbed to dreams that revolved around her husband, quilted slippers, and a private pleasure barge on the Twid.

CHAPTER TWO

"How is it possible that I am lonely in the village of my birth, surrounded by family and friends?"

Gavin put the question to his horse, though Roland, as usual, was keeping his own counsel. The summer marked a turning point for Gavin's steed, who was putting away the idleness of his foalhood and growing into the body of a horse of significant speed and athletic ability.

Roland's mind, though, was yet prone to coltish flights. He rarely bolted anymore, but he shied at nothing, bucked for joy or in token protest at his rider's requests, and had to carefully sniff over anything in his ambit that qualified as new or interesting.

He was vastly improved from a few months ago, when he'd gallop halfway to Windsor, entertain the whole village with his bucking sprees, and barely scramble over a low stile on flat, dry ground.

"You are growing up," Gavin said, patting his mount on the neck. Early in the mornings, he took Roland out for a long, hard gallop over hill and dale. Afternoon hacks were to work on manners and ensure the horse would acquit himself well if a racing career wasn't meant to be.

Also to allow Gavin to enjoy the shady seclusion of the towpaths along the Twid. Afternoons in high summer had a sweetness to them, a golden melancholy. Sunrise and sunset were subtly encroaching on midday as harvest approached, and the coming of autumn was most evident in the postmeridian.

The light softened, the heat began to lose its intensity, the undergrowth showed yellow and splashes of red, while the canopy remained green. Birds sang less, and the Twid ran at low ebb.

Gavin drew Roland to a halt on the towpath, waited a moment, then signaled the horse to back up a few steps. Roland wasn't keen on backing up. A fellow could not see what was behind him unless he turned his head, and thus some effort to modify Gavin's request ensued. A peek this way, a head toss that way, a tail swish, a hoof stomp that might have been necessary to dislodge a pesky fly, but was really in the nature of a protest.

"Back," Gavin said quietly, because sometimes Roland responded more willingly to voice commands than to nudging and tugging. Every actor had his own means of memorizing cues.

Roland took two steps back, a grudging concession.

"Back," Gavin said, because the effort had been late and prefaced with grumbling.

Roland took two more steps back—the stable wasn't far off, and protesting for form's sake was better done earlier in the ride, when a grassy paddock and a happy roll in the dust weren't so near at hand. Gavin had taken some time to realize the subtlety with which Roland timed his insurrections.

"Good boy. Walk on."

Roland hadn't gone four steps forward before he stopped, lifted his head, and peered intently in the direction of the Twid. No fish had leaped—not that Gavin had heard—and Roland wasn't reacting to the sort of imaginary horse-eating tiger that resulted in a dead run across the countryside.

Gavin followed the line of Roland's gaze. Not until the lady turned a page of her book did he see her down along the bank a dozen yards up the stream.

His body reacted before his mind told him that he beheld Mrs. Rose Roberts. The sensation was lightness, relief, peace, and even joy. *There she is.* As if he'd ridden this way day after day, hoping, always hoping, to catch sight of her, and at long last, she occupied the place his heart had sought to find her.

The Nunnsuch house party had taught him to get his bearings with that reaction. To wait for the joy to fade and the sadness to follow. He and Mrs. Roberts had managed two interminable weeks of civilities, of pretending not to know each other, of managing to never be alone in the same place at the same time.

Gavin had taken to toting around a fishing pole like a penitent's cross, signaling all and sundry that he was on his way... out, off to the great outdoors, bent on the important task of staring at quiet water while trying to stay awake.

Roland whuffled, the ruddy blighter.

Still, Rose remained fixed on her book. She made a lovely picture, a straw hat slipped down her back, her hair catching the sunlight. She was a woman of singular purpose, not given to dawdling, and yet, a book could bring her to a still point, to sitting quietly by the hour, all of her energies poured into her delight in the written word.

When Rose set her mind to a written passage, the rest of the world faded from her awareness. She had the same focus in other settings.

Gavin shoved that thought aside with his mental fishing pole. He should ride on, let her catch sight of him across a chattering crowd of Amaryllis's guests, let her decide whether to approach him.

Except he'd taken that tack at Nunnsuch, and she had remained steadfastly unwilling to seek him out. Not on any deserted streambank, not in a library full of whist players, not at the buffet meals, or even after he and Roland had bested a dozen other riders in an informal steeplechase.

"Good day." He spoke softly, knowing she couldn't hear him over the babbling of the Twid, but rehearsing the line for his own benefit. He was no longer a callow youth to run away when his troubles wanted confronting. Besides, Rose Roberts wasn't a trouble, and he'd rather they spoke their minds to one another here in private than go through more rounds of awkward courtesies.

He dismounted and loosened Roland's girth, which occasioned a curious look from the horse. Deviations from routine were always apparent to children, dogs, horses, and the ladies of Crosspatch Corners, according to Mr. Dabney.

"Come along." Gavin tugged on the reins—in-hand work was yet another area where more tutelage was needed—and Roland ambled forward.

"Mrs. Roberts," Gavin sang out, "good day."

She looked up, looked around, then focused on him as Roland clip-clopped along the path. She shaded her eyes rather than put her hat back on.

How to play his entrance? Gavin mentally sorted through options. In all the hours he'd spent pondering what he'd say to Rose, what his demeanor would be if they were ever again in conversation, he'd not envisioned being chaperoned by a horse when he encountered her on the banks of the Twid.

Though Rose Roberts was a widow. She needed no chaperone.

"Mr. DeWitt. And is that the famous Roland?" She nipped up the bank as nimbly as a goat, no need for gentlemanly assistance. "Greetings, Roland." She held out a bare hand to the horse, who sniffed as delicately as any courtier had ever complimented a damsel.

No formalities, then, which was a relief, but also... difficult. "I didn't know you'd arrived," Gavin said. "I trust the trip up from Hampshire was uneventful?"

"Dreadfully so. I borrowed Lord Nunn's traveling coach, and what it offers in comfort, it lacks in speed. Shall we walk?"

She liked to move, while Gavin wanted to remain in the shade of the path, taking in the sight of her. He'd not stood this close to her at Nunnsuch. Never close enough to catch that hint of lemony fragrance she wore—she refused to wear attar of roses—or to see that summer had brought out a few freckles on her cheeks.

"Roland and I were more or less on our way home when he spotted you," Gavin said, taking up the reins. "What are you reading?"

He should have offered his arm, should have offered to carry her book.

"Wordsworth. He knows the countryside, and I find his verse appropriate reading in summer."

"My youngest sister has developed a taste for Wordsworth in my absence. She fancies herself the first female contemplative."

"Caroline. She's what, thirteen now?"

You remembered. Gavin set a slow pace in the direction of Miller's Lament. "Going on forty-two. She reads voraciously, disappears into the woods by the hour, and shows no interest in putting her hair up. My mother and grandmother would be worried, but they are too preoccupied with Diana's wardrobe for next year."

"Diana is preparing for her come out?"

"The whole village is preparing for Diana's come out. What of you? How are you going on at Colforth Hall?"

She prosed on about the approaching harvest, some timber that was ready for coppicing, and a squabble over fishing rights, while Gavin was torn by a sense of unreality. They'd once been able to speak of anything and nothing, to share confidences, silences, looks, and touches with the ease of the devoted lovers he'd thought them to be.

To avoid each other as they'd done at Nunnsuch had solved nothing. To merely chat, to limit discussion to commonplaces, hurt, and yet, that was the sensible course. With Rose Roberts, Gavin was determined to be sensible—this time.

"And have you given up the stage?" she asked after regaling him with a story about a goose who'd wandered into the middle of divine services earlier in the summer.

He'd taught her that, taught her to tell a story when conversation wanted leavening. "I was never really on the stage in any meaningful sense. Having a lark, sowing wild oats, galloping off the fidgets. I'm home where I belong now, and my family is glad to have me here."

"Are you glad to be here?"

The old Rose, the Rose who'd woken up beside him and known his dreams before he'd said a word, might have asked that question. Gavin chose to answer honestly in honor of the old Rose.

"I am resigned to being here for now. My family has worked hard to make the leap from the shop to the ranks of gentry, and now Amaryllis has married a marquess. I must capitalize on that great accomplishment as Diana and Caroline prepare to join Society, or I am no sort of head of the family. I shall acquit myself as the wealthy squire I am, and it would be churlish to pretend the role is onerous."

A fine and mendacious speech. The jovial-squire part was worse than onerous, it was so very comfortably, smotheringly *all wrong*.

Rose walked along beside him, and he braced himself for more chitchat. How lovely Berkshire was, if one had to impersonate a squire anywhere. How silly Society could be. How happy Amaryllis and Trevor were—a love match for a marquess, who'd have thought it?

"It's not churlish to admit when an assignment doesn't suit one's abilities, Mr. DeWitt."

The *Mr. DeWitt* stung a bit, but the honesty soothed Gavin's soul. "My grandparents,

parents, and sisters have all expended considerable effort to ensure the DeWitts are respected gentry. I jeopardized their efforts with my ventures on the stage. I am well aware that this house party is an effort to rehabilitate my reputation by parading me before ladies of discernment."

"Is it? Here I thought Lady Phillip was determined that we should discuss investments, and Lord and Lady Tavistock wanted to give Lord Phillip a chance to polish his Society manners."

That was news to Gavin. "Phillip polished his manners—which

are quite above reproach to begin with—at Nunnsuch and came away engaged to an heiress."

They walked along, following the curve of the river. "It's good to see you," Rose said. "I probably shouldn't admit that, but two weeks of pretending at Nunnsuch put a strain on my nerves, and I thought my nerves had become nigh indestructible. You are looking well."

Why *not* admit that? Why *not* be glad to see him? "I am glad to see you too," Gavin said, because the words were the truth. He could have honestly said that the sight of her also baffled and saddened him and that he'd be much more careful with his heart around her in future, but to see her healthy, serene, nose in a book...

The sight still had the power to bring him joy, and that was mostly good. If he gave it time, the sad part might fade, as the hurt was slowly fading. He'd been a lark to her, wild oats, galloping off the fidgets, and she'd been the haven his soul had craved, his present joy, his future delight.

More fool he.

"You'll be at supper this evening?" Rose asked as the house came into view.

"I will bide at Twidboro Hall, but otherwise I am at Amaryllis's beck and call for the next two weeks. You will see me at supper, though I reserve the earliest hours of the day for schooling my horse."

"No breakfast sightings, then." She stopped and stroked a hand over Roland's nose. He commenced making sheep's eyes at her, for which Gavin could not blame him. Roland hadn't been gelded and consigned to the plow, after all.

"Do you suppose..." Rose said. "Do you think we might...?"

"Yes?" To see her at a loss was intriguing.

"At Nunnsuch, we avoided one another. I'm sure the other guests remarked it and were curious as a result. I loathe being an object of curiosity. I dislike center stage, Mr. DeWitt, and I hope that you..."

Ah. "You want me to pretend that Nunnsuch was our first encounter?" To forget the most glorious and devastating weeks of his life? To wear the role of genial country squire more convincingly than he'd ever done before?

"Wouldn't that be for the best?" She lifted her hat to replace it on her head, but some disobliging ribbon or hairpin got caught in curling locks. Holding her book, she could not untangle her hair properly.

"Allow me," Gavin said, taking the book and setting it on the ground. His intention was to be of use, as he'd be of use to his mother or sister in a similarly awkward moment. He pulled off his gloves and stuffed them into a pocket, then took the hat in one hand and went searching gently for the offending hairpin.

Too late, he realized his error. Rose stood still, suggesting she had also been ambushed by the proximity necessary when a gentleman's fingers sifted slowly through the curls at a lady's nape, when silky tresses and body heat and the quiet of a summer afternoon conspired to thieve his wits right out of his grasp.

Roland stomped at another imaginary fly, and Gavin mentally shouted at himself not to break role. He found the crosswise hairpin, carefully extracted it, and stepped back.

Rose was staring at him as if he were a particularly arcane line from Mr. Coleridge. He put her hat on her head and passed her the hairpin.

She shoved the pin into her hair. "Thank you." Her thanks were less than emphatic.

"You're welcome." The words were steady, Gavin's heart was not. "Shall I see you to the garden?"

"No need for that. About what I said earlier?"

He busied himself pulling on his gloves. "Earlier?"

"Can we not start afresh, Mr. DeWitt, or give that impression? What passed between us before—up north—was another time and place, and we are adults."

The next bit of stage business was tightening Roland's girth, which nonsense earned Gavin a double tail swish.

"You may rely on me, Mrs. Roberts, to comport myself as a gentleman. If you prefer that we ignore our initial dealings, I will oblige you. You need have no fear that I will presume on our previous acquaintance or spread untoward gossip."

She was giving him the same intent, puzzled examination. "Have you a different suggestion?"

Well, no, he hadn't. Suggesting that they be friends would put his feet on the same slippery slope that had led straight to a muddy ditch of humiliation and heartache. Suggesting they avoid each other would draw notice, and besides, the stupid, callow idiot part of him that had slid down that slope so easily once before didn't want to avoid her.

Gavin wanted to *understand* her, and in some small, stubborn part of his soul, he wanted her to admit that she regretted her treatment of him.

"We will be cordial new acquaintances," Gavin said, running the offside stirrup down its leather. He came around the horse to face her again. "But if you expect me to forget what happened in Derbyshire, I am bound to disappoint you."

She retied her bonnet ribbons and dipped a curtsey. "Cordial new acquaintances, then. Nothing more, nothing less. We cannot help the tenacity of fairly recent memories, Mr. DeWitt. Good day." She marched off with that singularly active walk of hers—Gavin did not stare at her retreating form for more than a few seconds—and then she was gone from sight around a bend in the path.

Roland gave Gavin the look of a horse who had been patient long enough.

"You were no help," Gavin muttered, prepared to vault into the saddle and trot for home—except he'd forgotten to run the nearside stirrup down its leather. "Bollocks."

He climbed into the saddle and tried to gather up the reins, but Roland was intent on sniffing something on the ground—or on being contrary. Gavin hauled up on the reins, and Roland rooted in response.

"You ill-mannered, contrary... Oh. Beg pardon, horse. My mistake. I humbly apologize."

Rose had forgotten Mr. Wordsworth's poetry. The book lay on the dusty path, looking forlorn and out of place.

Gavin dismounted and retrieved the volume, stuffing it into the tail pocket of his riding jacket. Even cordial new acquaintances didn't let each other's poetry lie about at risk of harm from the elements.

Then too, Rose Roberts would not have left her book behind unless she'd been *exceedingly* flustered. That thought cheered him immensely.

CHAPTER THREE

"Before we pick up the extra saddles, let's pop into the Arms and collect the mail," Trevor, Marquess of Tavistock, said, bringing the dog cart to a halt outside Dabney's livery. "Enjoy a pint, catch up on the news."

Phillip climbed from the bench. "You are avoiding your own home," he said as a lad came forward to stand at the horse's head. "The ladies aren't even all assembled, and you are dawdling in the village."

Tavistock leaped off the bench in a single athletic bound. "Not dawdling, brother dear. Allowing my marchioness to catch her breath before we gather for supper. She tasked us with picking up spare sidesaddles, which is her way of getting us out from underfoot. If you'd been married longer, you'd understand these things."

Phillip understood that his brother—who had but a few weeks' seniority as a husband—was in great good spirits. Even greater good spirits than usual. Obnoxiously good spirits.

"What scheme have you put in train, Tavistock? You are clearly up to something."

"Nonsense."

Dabney himself came out to greet them as the lad led the horse away. "Milords, a fine day to look in on our fine village. I have a half-dozen sidesaddles shined up and waiting for you."

Dabney spoke with the musical lilt of the Caribbean islands and stood perhaps five feet in his boots. He'd been a jockey in a former life and, at the slightest provocation, would regale all and sundry with a fence-by-fence account of his career.

"No hurry loading the saddles," Tavistock said. "We're off to the Arms to wet our whistles. Come along, Phillip."

Dabney's eyes danced, and were Phillip not now *Lord* Phillip, he might have cuffed Dabney on the back of the head and received a retaliatory back slap in return. Dabney had put him on his first pony, though, and deserved what entertainments his day offered.

Phillip caught up to Tavistock. "Dabney expects a report," he said as the marquess set a course across the green. "If you'd lived in Crosspatch Corners longer, you'd know that. He will want to hear that your guests are all safely arrived, that the grooms he sent over are giving a good account of themselves, that nobody's harness needs a quick—"

"Spies he sent over, you mean. I might not have lived in Crosspatch very long, but I understand how villages work. Amaryllis has waxed eloquent on Dabney's intelligence network. He can't quite rival Vicar or the Arms, but he keeps them on their toes."

The truth was more subtle, though Tavistock, if he lived in Crosspatch for decades—which he probably would, to the endless delight of all and sundry—might not grasp the complexities. Dabney, because he ran the livery, collected both local gossip and the news from any travelers looking to hire a temporary mount. He rented out spare teams. He maintained harness for all the farmers and country houses in the area.

His clientele was a cross section of local gentry, yeomanry, shop owners, and "foreigners," meaning anybody whose accent identified them as from another shire. Vicar's sources were mostly to be found in the churchyard Sunday mornings, and the Arms, as the coaching inn, prided itself on having all the news from Town.

Between the three institutions, each responsible for a different sort of news, Crosspatch had much to discuss. A favorite topic with the local denizens was the marquess and his determination to build a business around the brewing and purveying of fine beer and ale.

"The eminent citizenry are at their posts," Tavistock muttered. "Don't they have anything else to do besides sit outside the Arms and surveil the green?"

"Nobody else in all of Crosspatch would use the verb 'surveil.' Can't you say 'they watch the green,' 'they enjoy the view of the green'?"

"'Surveil' is from the French, and for several years, I spoke almost exclusively in that language, and the term applies. Granny Jones, Old Deever, Old Mrs. Pevinger, and their cronies don't simply enjoy the view, they are sentries on duty. Watchkeepers. Before we turn our vehicle for home, that lot will know why we came to the village, how many saddles we're borrowing, and what Dabney is charging us for the loan. I don't care for it. One has no privacy."

"Rather like life in Mayfair?"

Tavistock had the grace to smile. "Touché, but in Mayfair, I am a marquess, and nobody dares interrogate me to my face. Here..."

"Here, you dunderhead, you are *our* marquess." Phillip paused at the foot of the steps leading up to the broad front terrace of the Crosspatch Arms. "What you fail to grasp is that the eminent citizens, along with their grandchildren, nieces, nephews, in-laws, and friends, will move all in their power to see your brewing venture become a success. Your good fortune is their good fortune. Your sorrows are their sorrows. They have decreed it to be so, and even if you are 167th in line for the throne, you cannot gainsay their decisions."

Tavistock braced a foot two steps up and used a plain handkerchief to wipe the dust from the toe of his boot. That bit of vanity, which he probably considered simple good manners before entering another man's establishment, was the very sort of behavior that had won the Old Guard's approval.

The lad knows how to marquess, see if he don't.

Not at all like his father.

Phillip waited for Tavistock to shine up the second boot, while Granny Jones looked on approvingly. Phillip, to the village born, was not expected to put on airs, even if he was a lord, which Granny had known all along, but kept to herself for reasons having to do with sagacious nods, the old lord's temper, and a shrewd woman's inherent discretion regarding a titled family's business.

Or some such twaddle.

"While I appreciate the good wishes of my neighbors," Tavistock said, touching a finger to his hat brim and sketching a bow to Granny and her familiars, "they *are* my neighbors. If my brewing is to succeed, I must find customers far beyond the lovely surrounds of Crosspatch."

Dunderheaded, clodpated, backward, hopeless... "Granny has thirty-four grandchildren and great-grandchildren. At least six of the full-grown ones are in London, clerking, in service, and otherwise earning a living in the metropolis. One of them is now in Kettering's employ."

"I grant you, thirty-four tongues wagging is a lot, but six is not so many."

"You have a basic grasp of math. Always a boon for a man embarking on commerce. Say the fellow in Kettering's office goes to his local pub and asks for a pint of Crosspatch summer ale."

"The pub won't have it, because I lack the inventory to make inroads on the London market. When the weather cools off, and—"

Phillip started up the steps. "By the time you get the next batches made, six London taverns will be willing to at least sample your offerings. Old Man Deever has only twenty-three grandchildren, but seventeen of them are male, and four are off in Bristol working in custom- and countinghouses."

"One takes your point. Your dear wife would tell you that

investing among the aristocracy works in much the same fashion. An evening of cards at the club might be the most profitable investment a man can make."

Phillip preceded his brother into the inn, tossed his hat onto its usual hook, and bedamned to protocol. "So why aren't you making it?"

"Amaryllis does not care for Town, and nobody who is anybody bides in London over the summer. Mrs. Pevinger, good day."

Mrs. P, who was related to half the shire, nodded genially from her desk in the spacious foyer. "A pint and a pie for milords?"

Tavistock swept off his hat with a flourish that managed to be both playful and elegant. "Just the thing for a lovely summer afternoon. Have you any mail for us?"

She set a few epistles on the blotter. "Happen I do, from Town and from Oxford." When she'd watched Tavistock sort through the lot, she passed Phillip two letters. "Good news, I hope?"

Tavistock smiled. "Time will tell, dear lady. Phillip, to the snug."

Tavistock sailed off, letters in hand.

"Don't mind him," Mrs. Pevinger said. "He's not had a brother for long. Takes some getting used to."

You don't say. "Fortunately for the king's peace, I am a patient man and the best of siblings." *Even when my long-lost brother decides to invade my village, overrun my churchyard with his friendly manners, and take my market-day green by storm.*

Or by charm.

"Don't be too patient with that one, Master Phillip. We're relying on you to show him how to go on. How is the missus settling in?"

"Splendidly, of course." Though *settling in* wasn't quite the right phrase. Hecate had barely opened her trunks at Lark's Nest before she and Amaryllis were cooking up this gathering of ladies for their summer idyll.

Not how Phillip had envisioned spending his honey month. Not nearly. Ah, well. He and Hecate were managing a few private celebrations nonetheless.

"Your smile, sir, would make the cat in the cream pot envious." Mrs. P winked and bustled off, calling for her daughter Tansy to pull pints for a pair of thirsty gents.

That wink marginally restored Phillip's spirits, if not his patience. He joined Tavistock in the snug and took a sip of cool summer ale.

"Any news from Town?"

"The usual. My Dorning relations are being fruitful at a great rate. Step-mama sends her love. Dear Phillip must bring his new bride to Town when the weather is more agreeable, et cetera and so forth." Tavistock passed over a letter from his step-mother, which Phillip set aside.

Tavistock's Dornings were more numerous than the denizens of German royal houses, and Phillip couldn't keep them straight, rather like the steps of the quadrille, only livelier. That Tavistock might be finding himself a bit off-rhythm at having to share his family with Phillip was further reason for good spirits.

"What of the letter from Oxford? You attended there, I believe?"

"I did, for a brief and unimpressive time." Tavistock slit the seal on the second epistle and scanned the contents. "This is lovely news." Tavistock looked delighted—with himself and with his correspondence.

"Somebody is putting in an order for your ale? If anybody is fond of a pint, it's the college boys."

"Better than that. You recall that DeWitt was attached to a group of players in East Anglia when I hailed him from the shires?"

Phillip took another sip of ale, though something about Tavistock's question made him uneasy. "He was Galahad Twidham at the time. Darling of the provincial venues."

"Before he matriculated to East Anglia, Galahad was a member of Drysdale's Players, and his old troupe has agreed to grace us with their presence. They will be my guests starting Monday and available to enliven the house party by plying their art and making themselves generally agreeable."

Phillip mentally reviewed the marquess's proclamation. Why,

yes, Tavistock had just announced that he was *hiring* the cast of Gavin DeWitt's youthful folly to come haunt the man in person.

Before a dozen astute female guests, one of whom was Mrs. Roberts. "Tavistock, to quote a very astute man: Are you out of your happily married mind?"

Tavistock folded up the letter. "You're just jealous because you didn't think of it. The ladies will want for entertainment. They're a bookish lot, and some speeches and drama will appeal to them."

Tansy Pevinger brought two steaming, fragrant meat pies to the table. "Will there be anything else, milords?"

A cudgel to smack some common sense into the marquess's handsome head might have been useful. "No, thank you, Miss Tansy."

She peered at Phillip more closely. "Mind you take care in the heat, sir. You're looking a bit peaky."

"Newlywed pallor," Tavistock said, saluting with his tankard. "A common malady among happy husbands."

Oh, for pity's rubbishing sake. Tansy had sense enough to swan off without dignifying that bit of flummery with a reply.

"Did you discuss this brilliant notion with your marchioness before you hired these players?" Phillip asked.

"Of course not. It's a surprise. I realize she's getting her feet wet as a hostess, beginning in the shallows before she attempts deeper waters, but a husband needs to put his imprimatur on the hospitality offered under his roof."

Phillip wanted to put the imprimatur of his boot on the marquess's lordly arse. "What of DeWitt? Did you clear this with him?" *Say yes. Please say yes.*

"These are his old chums. Why wouldn't he be glad to see them?"

Tavistock meant well. He meant to perform some lordly legerdemain, produce a lovely surprise, and earn the goodwill of all. He was an outsider to some extent in polite society because he'd absented himself on the Continent right out of university, and he was an outsider in Crosspatch by virtue of his rank and origins.

Phillip marshaled his patience and attempted an explanation.

"DeWitt didn't intend to leave his family without means for two straight years when he decamped to indulge his theatrical interests. He didn't mean to risk scandal. He didn't mean to come dangerously close to losing all the standing his family has worked for two generations to establish."

"And he hasn't lost it," Tavistock said, setting down his drink. "High spirits, youthful folly, an extended lark. We no longer send young men on a grand tour, and DeWitt was just having a bit of a tame adventure."

Phillip had known Gavin DeWitt his whole life, and yet, he could not say what precisely had motivated DeWitt's histrionic episode. He was certain, though, that had Tavistock not made inquiries, DeWitt would still be strutting about in Elizabethan finery and stealing the show as Benedick.

"Perhaps DeWitt would rather put the whole business behind him, forget it happened." Phillip spoke quietly, though the common was deserted. "I have the sense our Gavin is ashamed of whatever transpired during those two years, ashamed of abandoning his family, ashamed of something. Now you will throw it all back in his face, and he might not be best pleased."

Tavistock picked up his fork. "He won't run off again. He promised us he wouldn't."

"Do I have your permission to at least warn him?"

Tavistock took a bite of pie, and drat the man for being able to *chew* elegantly. "I'll do it. He's my wife's brother, and he and I are family, and that means we must be able to have honest discussions."

Phillip was fairly certain that the boot went on the other foot. All the blood ties and legal connections in the world did not make two people family if honesty and respect weren't there to begin with. He sipped his ale and kept his opinions to himself, while Tavistock demolished food and waxed eloquent about the many fine qualities of Crown of Crosspatch summer ale.

~

Rose sipped her punch and listened with half an ear to Lady Iris Wolverhampton waxing eloquent on the topic of restorative tisanes. Lady Iris was passionate about her subject, while Rose wanted passionately to return to the towpath and make a far better job of her discussion with Gavin DeWitt.

Can we not start afresh, Mr. DeWitt? So polite, so uncertain. A supplicant when she should never have asked him for anything ever again.

Have you another suggestion? What had he made of that inquiry? Had he heard an invitation where none had been intended? Rose had spent months wishing she'd handled herself differently where Mr. DeWitt was concerned, and the two weeks at Nunnsuch had been wasted on the same exercise.

"And peppermint," Lady Iris said. "You never met a more agreeable herb for refreshing the mind or soothing the bowels. Sore muscles can benefit from peppermint unguent, and I firmly believe memory is improved by inhaling the scent."

Lady Iris had no business being so earnest when she was so pretty, but this gathering was rife with women who'd managed to eclipse beauty with a less agreeable quality—bookishness, a gift for rhetoric, a talent for ciphering.

Miss Zinnia Peasegood, for example, was brunette perfection with gorgeous azure eyes, and yet, she had the recollection of an elephant and trotted out her word-for-word memories of previous conversations with all the grace of an inebriated pachyderm.

Lady Iris was a traditional beauty—blond, willowy, blue-eyed, with the complexion of a Renaissance angel. Her voice was musical, her gestures graceful, and yet, Rose harbored the suspicion that Lady Iris had perfected the use of peppermint as a conversational tisane to counteract the impact of her good looks.

"We grow plenty of peppermint at Colforth," Rose said. "My herb gardens are extensive, and if you are ever in the area, you must take a tour."

"I would adore that above all things," Lady Iris said, with her signature guileless intensity. Her focus abruptly shifted, and without turning, Rose knew exactly what—or who—had captured her ladyship's attention.

Gavin DeWitt had raised making an entrance to a high art. Rose casually turned under the guise of setting down her glass. He stood by the door, not overtly calling attention to himself, but drawing every eye nonetheless. In his stillness, in his bearing, in the way he wore his very clothes, he commanded notice.

Also in the way he didn't wear clothing.

"Brother to Lady Amaryllis," Lady Iris said, as if cataloging a specimen. "Mr. DeWitt is certainly striking."

"Is he? I see some height, brown hair, regular features. A somewhat memorable nose, but nothing to rival Wellington's proboscis, and yet, here we stand, all but gawking." At a man who appeared to have no idea whatsoever that he was being gawked at—an actor's trick, no doubt. Gavin DeWitt's pockets were full of actor's tricks.

"You know Mr. DeWitt, Mrs. Roberts?"

The question had no biblical underpinnings, thank heavens. "We met at the Nunnsuch do earlier this summer. Mr. DeWitt, having been born and raised in Crosspatch, is friends with Lord Phillip, who was the ranking guest down in Hampshire."

"One needs a large fan with many sticks for gatherings such as these." Lady Iris brandished an article painted all over with flowers. "Some people scrawl dance steps on their fans. I use mine to keep social connections straight. Might you introduce me?"

"I'd be delighted." Introducing Lady Iris to Gavin would get the small talk over with, a consummation devoutly to be wished.

Rose and her ladyship made a leisurely progress across the terrace, and all the while, Gavin stood by the door as if awaiting his cue.

"Mr. DeWitt," Rose said, offering the requisite curtsey. "Good evening."

"Mrs. Roberts, and... Lady Iris, I believe?" His bow was elegance personified. "Might you do the honors, Mrs. Roberts?" He wore his gracious-gentleman smile, though on him the polite expression shaded toward genuine friendly interest. He did that with his eyes and with a slight inclination of his posture, regarding a lady not boldly so much as sincerely, as if he truly was pleased to be in conversation with her.

His sincerity was his most devastating magic trick of all. Rose reminded herself of that as Lady Iris reprised her fascination with native herbs. Gavin nodded, asked questions, and by a gaze that never strayed, by the cadence with which he conducted his conversation, he put forth every facsimile of rapt attention.

The third bell sounded, interrupting Lady Iris's panegyric to St.-John's-wort.

"I must find Miss Peasegood," Lady Iris said, snapping her fan closed. "I promised to dine with her. This has been a delightful conversation, Mrs. Roberts, Mr. DeWitt. Perhaps we can continue it another time. You will excuse me?"

She swanned off, as graceful as a sloop running close to the wind on a sparkling summer morning.

"I now know more about St.-John's-wort than I ever sought to learn," Gavin said quietly.

"I was treated to a discourse on peppermint before she asked to make your acquaintance. We should count ourselves lucky she didn't regale us with her views on the subject of purges."

Rose regretted that last remark. Lady Iris was devoted to her medicinals, and purges were hardly polite.

Gavin winged his arm and turned that enchanting smile on Rose. "I do count myself lucky. Exceedingly so. Shall we to the buffet?"

She slipped her fingers around his elbow. "You need not flirt, Mr. DeWitt. In fact, I'd ask you not to."

"Who's flirting? Lady Iris strikes me as a woman who has memorized an herbal's worth of soliloquys, but as soon as she spotted me by the door, she had her introduction. At the first opportunity, her inspection complete, she sailed away."

"She did, didn't she?" Interesting. "Is there anybody else to whom you'd like an introduction? I know some of these women from my few forays into London, but Lady Tavistock also ensured we were all acquainted over afternoon tea trays."

"The rest of the introductions can wait. I am famished."

He managed to imbue even an admission of hunger with the weight of a confidence. Rose resigned herself to a long meal, though perhaps it was best to endure that ordeal and be done with it. She'd avoided him for two weeks in Hampshire, and it had been a very long fortnight indeed.

They filled plates and found a table in the garden by the spent roses. Footmen lit torches, though darkness was better than an hour away, and other guests strolled past in search of their own tables.

"On the grouse moors," Gavin said, "the ratio of men to ladies is more unbalanced than this, and yet, in this context, I find the lack of parity unsettling. I feel as if I ought to have four arms and practice bowing *en croix*."

Rose buttered her bread. She should have known even Gavin's small talk would be more than idle chatter.

"I suppose it's a matter of setting. When you played in the Shakespearean casts, men's roles were more abundant than female characters. Did that strike you as odd?"

"The ratio is better than four to one, nearly eight hundred men's roles, and about one hundred fifty for women. But then, women were not permitted to act in the Bard's day."

"You *counted* the roles by gender?"

He took a spoonful of cold potato soup. "A great deal of idle time can befall an actor who starts off with the minor parts."

"Do you miss it?" Rose fashioned herself a butter-and-cheese sandwich. She did not care for cold soup even in summer. "You changed troupes, as I recall."

He paused between spoonfuls. "I joined a southern ensemble. The Black Country has its charms, but there's a reprise of feudalism taking hold up there. Here, Henry Wortham can move from the forge to the role of understeward, and that's a step up. Most families would consider such good luck every third generation to be a wonderful legacy. My own family has done quite well in recent years, from a humble start as chandlers. In the north..."

Rose had traveled enough to know of what he spoke. "The weavers are all out of work, after generations of being able to support their families with their looms. The sawyers are out of work as steam replaces them by the dozens. The wages available in the factories are a slow road to starvation and the working conditions horrific. True, some men have jobs maintaining the factory machines, but not nearly as many as had honorable work with the hand looms."

Gavin put down his spoon. "While the few families fortunate enough to own a coal mine, or have some blunt to begin with, become wealthier and wealthier. I'm sure the south is subject to the same trends, but we haven't the coal here they have elsewhere, and somebody still has to grow the crops."

Perhaps an actor was doomed to pay attention to the wider world. To notice that world because the stage had to represent life realistically, maybe not in particulars of dress or diction, but in themes and personalities.

"I prefer the south," Rose said, "though I avoid London." Had avoided Society generally until recently.

"I was in East Anglia when Tavistock tracked me down," Gavin said, taking up an orange and tearing off a strip of peel. "Has anybody acquainted you with the particulars?"

Rose shook her head. She'd watched the London newspapers for advertisements featuring Mr. Galahad Twidham among itinerant acting troupes, but actors changed names as easily as costumes, making the exercise doubly futile.

"I left Crosspatch Corners to join a group of traveling players," Gavin said, making short work of peeling the orange. "You know that much. I believed my family would be well cared for in my absence. Our means are abundant. Our solicitors had been chosen by my late father to handle our funds. The business, to the extent I was permitted to take any hand in those matters, was thriving."

"All should have been well."

Gavin tore the orange into sections and set three on her plate. "The solicitors were denying my family all but a pittance and keeping a great deal more than a pittance for themselves. They professed to my mother and sisters to know nothing of my where-abouts, all the while assuring me they had forwarded my every letter home most conscientiously. When I received no replies, I concluded my womenfolk were having a collective tantrum, but then, becoming an actor was something of a tantrum on my part, so I didn't feel I could take the ladies to task."

"And you were busy learning your lines." And disporting with widows, merry and otherwise.

"Tavistock owned Twidboro Hall, and he came nosing about to have a look at the property we've been renting for years. I thank God for Tavistock's conscientious stewardship, or who knows what might have happened to my family while I was having a great laugh over Aphra Behn's comedies?"

Rose reached across the table to half pat, half smack his hand. "Don't punish yourself for what's over and done with. Self-flagella-tion can keep us connected to what we've lost." Though what, precisely, had Gavin DeWitt lost? Given his antecedents, had he truly convinced himself he could have a career on the stage?

She hadn't known of those antecedents when they'd met before. She'd assumed he was the proverbial penniless actor, though she'd learned otherwise at Nunnsuch. He was about as penniless as Dane had been humble.

"You are correct," he said. "Ruminating serves little purpose now. I am home to stay and trying to put matters right with my family. Amaryllis has made a splendid match, Twidboro Hall has been deeded to my grandmother, and the DeWitts are prospering."

"All's well that ends well?" He sounded like a widow who'd looked very much forward to life improving when she could set aside her weeds, only to find no improvement at all.

"All is well," he said as Lady Iris walked by in rapt discussion with Miss Peasegood. "Or near enough to well as makes no difference. Tell me, what inspired you to accept my sister's invitation?"

Rose stuffed an orange section into her mouth. She'd accepted the invitation because... because she was an idiot. Because Timmens deserved to be proved wrong at least occasionally. Because two weeks of avoiding Gavin DeWitt had lodged his memory only more deeply in her mind. Because he'd treated her ill, and she deserved an explanation, or a chance to convey to him how hurtful he'd been.

Because she wanted an apology, damn him, and not merely three orange sections and more of his soulful self-reflection.

He excelled at soulful reflection—and kissing. "I like Lord and Lady Phillip," Rose said, "and sitting about waiting for harvest to begin grows tedious. Lady Phillip is known to be an astute manager of funds. She mentioned that we women might find time to discuss our investments while we're socializing."

All true, but nowhere near the whole truth.

I've missed you. That declaration of treason to her dignity sprang full-fledged into Rose's mind. She took another bite of orange, then followed up with a sip of punch. The punch tried to go down the wrong way, and then she was coughing while Gavin patted her back and offered his own libation.

"I'm fine," Rose said, resisting the urge to shove him away. "Please, no fuss, or we'll have half the guests here recommending tisanes and chiding me for not being more careful. *I am fine.*"

He subsided into his seat and retrieved his glass of punch. Eighteen months ago, he might have launched into a story about somebody else's unfortunate moment with a glass of punch, or offered a quote or quip appropriate to the moment.

Instead, he sat across from her, his gaze unreadable, his expression anything but genial. Rose's earlier thought—*I've missed you*—still echoed in her mind, and another notion resonated with it: *I've missed you, but who have you become since I thought myself in love with you, and did I ever truly know you at all?*

CHAPTER FOUR

On the towpath, Gavin had approached Rose, assuring himself that a private encounter was better suited to establishing civil relations. Rose had been amenable to that proposal—*can we not start afresh, Mr. DeWitt?*—and yet, he wasn't as relieved as he should have been at her willingness to dissemble.

As she buttered her bread and arranged her cheese, she radiated a reserve she hadn't had up in Derbyshire. She'd grown into her widowhood, which wasn't fair.

She should have been missing him with the same confounded lack of self-control he'd been missing her. Thinking of her, hoping she was happy, puzzling over her treatment of him.

"I should be taking another look at my investments," he said as Rose nibbled her sandwich. "Papa clearly did not choose wisely when he selected our solicitors, and now I'm trying to acquaint myself with the particulars of our situation without being too much of a bother."

Not a topic he should have raised with a lady he'd ostensibly met two weeks ago, but much on his mind, and Rose had no patience with chitchat.

"Be a bother," she said. "Be the most imperious, stern, high-handed... I vow until the Earl of Nunn accompanied me on a call to my late husband's solicitors, they treated me as if I were slow-witted. They recited Dane's wishes—as they interpreted those wishes—and expected me to sniffle and nod and dab at my eyes in meek surrender."

"You went to war instead?"

"I certainly took matters in hand. Nunn was a great help, though all he had to do was sit beside me looking unimpressed and late for an appointment with his tailor. My husband was vintage gentry and quite set in his ways."

That observation approached criticism of Saint Dane. How odd. "I am not vintage gentry. I am the first to qualify for the honor in my family, and yet, I haven't a manor of my own."

Rose finished her sandwich and dusted her hands over her plate. "Do you want one?"

No, he did not. A place to live, yes. A dwelling to house his family, of course. But not acres and acres, ditches and drains, flocks and herds...

No.

In Derbyshire, he and Rose had talked of books, philosophy, politics, and history by the hour. Long walks had been taken up with plays and poetry, morning hacks had been filled with debate on the Corn Laws and parliamentary reform. Late nights had been for the quiet language of the heart.

Or so he'd thought. In any case, he'd avoided any mention of the boring reality of his nonacting life.

"Grandmama has already told me that Twidboro is coming to me."

Rose took up her spoon and dipped it into a bowl of fruit compote. "That doesn't answer my question. You left Twidboro Hall to pursue the stage, and I gather your family disapproved. Now you are back where you started and where your family expects you to be. How are you finding the role?"

Tedious. Stifling—'cabined, cribbed, confined, bound in'—and Gavin was ashamed of himself for his ingratitude. One should cite the Scottish play only in cases of true tragedy.

"I love my home. I love my family. Why would I be anything but pleased to bide here?"

Rose sampled her cream, peaches, and blueberries. "You left this bucolic paradise for reasons, Mr. DeWitt, and you are very skilled on stage. I loved my husband, and I love Colforth Hall, but that doesn't mean I want to keep it as a shrine to his memory."

She would not have said that eighteen months ago. Then, every mention of her late spouse—and they had been frequent at first—had been glowing and wreathed in fond sentiment.

"Two years of my life spent pouring everything I had into the acting profession is supposed to have been a lark," Gavin said as, across the garden, Tavistock inspired four women to go off into whoops. "A frolic, a queer start. My version of the grand tour. A bit eccentric, but *you know how young men are.*"

He'd raised the pitch of his voice to imitate some Mayfair beldame and infused the words with amusement.

"I honestly don't know how young men are," Rose replied. "I married right out of the schoolroom, and Dane saw no need for me to incur the expense of frequent jaunts to Town. When I began exploring London at the conclusion of my mourning, the bachelors were after younger game. Eat your dessert. The fruit is luscious."

The forbidden fruit always was.

"You are young," Gavin said. "Also formidable, and that's why the fribbles have left you in peace." He didn't intend the words as flattery, much less as a compliment. He simply stated the truth. He knew how young men were—he still was one, and acting troupes were full of them—and women who could quote from the American Constitution and Blackstone's commentaries would freeze the guts of the average Town tulip.

And Rose thought *her age* had been to blame?

"I have sown my wild oats," Gavin said, trying for some lightness. "I shall now become the contented, conscientious squire."

Rose took another bite of compote, closing her eyes as she slipped the spoon from her mouth. Gavin sipped his punch, found the glass empty, and told himself to stop gawking.

"You will be a squire on a very fast horse," Rose said, setting aside her empty bowl. "You school your colt in the mornings?"

The change of subject was welcome. Too welcome. "Every morning. If the going is wet, I check Roland's speed, but he needs to sort out for himself how to negotiate a muddy track. Berkshire has afforded us many opportunities to practice keeping our footing. I'll begin competing him in the autumn, with a view toward some serious racing next spring."

"Where did you find him?"

Gavin let himself be led onto this safer ground, though Rose's earlier questions and answers stayed with him. His life would be the envy of most, and yet, he was restless and discontent. The feeling grew the longer he bided in Crosspatch Corners, no matter how many miles Roland galloped, no matter how many stiles they leaped.

That wasn't news.

That Rose had never had a London Season had escaped his notice, though. In Derbyshire, she'd been so self-possessed, so well adapted to the part of young widow bravely venturing back into Society that he'd never considered how little experience she might have been bringing to the excursion.

How unworldly she might have been. The idea fit poorly with what else he knew of her. But then, the notion of spending the rest of his days dithering over whether to plant barley or oats in the bottom field fit poorly with what he knew of himself.

"I like this way of having a supper," Rose said, glancing around the garden. "A buffet al fresco. A picnic without the ants and acorns. Shall we stroll a bit to settle the meal?"

They'd hiked, not strolled, over half of Derbyshire. "Of course."

Tavistock's harem went off into peals again. Over by the

hydrangeas, Lord Phillip sat with another bevy of beauties, and Gavin was reminded of the house party where he'd met Rose. The troupe had been hired in part because too many last-minute guest cancellations had left the gathering lopsided. Handsome young gentlemen had been in demand, and virtually any handsome young gentleman with acceptable manners would do.

Actors, often from good families, well-read, sociable, and competent to play genteel roles, had been an easy and entertaining solution.

Gavin had left the place feeling like a combination sacrificial goat and village fool.

"The path along the Twid is lovely at this time of evening," he said. "Let's enjoy it, shall we?" He held Rose's chair, as he had a hundred times in the past, but denied himself the pleasure of leaning over her for a moment, murmuring in her ear, and otherwise making a cake of himself.

And yet, a small, stupid part of him still wanted to. Wanted to pretend they were embarking on another flirtation, one that could end more happily.

His dignity alone ought to prevent such a catastrophe, ably assisted by his common sense.

Rose took his arm, and they wound down the garden path, greeting other guests and eventually leaving the formal parterres.

I've missed you. Gavin understood that sentiment—they'd shared considerable pleasure, and only some of it in bed—but he need not indulge it.

"If we go this way," Rose said, gesturing to the left, "we might come upon my book of poetry. A thorough search of my effects leads me to conclude that I left Mr. Wordsworth on the banks of the Twid."

"You left him on the towpath," Gavin replied. "I retrieved him. If you'd like to hack out with me tomorrow afternoon, I can return him to you then."

The words were out, unplanned and unrehearsed. Not really a disaster either. Entirely in keeping with starting afresh and consistent with the behavior of guests who'd met earlier in the summer. Rose would doubtless decline though.

"What time?"

Erm... "Four-ish. The heat is waning by then, and thunderstorms are unlikely. Roland needs to learn how to comport himself in company and how to behave when the outing is purely for the joy of the fresh air."

"I have my riding habit with me," Rose said, "and I would appreciate time in the saddle. One thing I do like about managing Colforth Hall is hacking out on my acres. I like knowing when the berries are ripening by the bridge and whether last night's storm yielded any deadfall. Tenants who would never approach me at the Hall will stop to chat with me on the farm lanes. Dane said his father had found the same thing to be true."

"You still miss your husband." Not a little of their previous dealings had been taken up with her reminiscences of married life. Dane Roberts had been affectionate, witty, devoted to his wife, and taken much too soon. Gavin could not resent even such a paragon as that, because the poor fellow wasn't on hand to bask in his wife's adoration.

"Not as I once did," she said. "Nunn told me that time would help, and it has."

Gavin had had no illusions about the role he'd been intended to play for her. He'd been her first venture into the terrain of the merry widow, her attempt to get back on the horse. That his ambitions had soon run far ahead of her stated agenda wasn't her fault.

For the first time, he wanted to ask her if she considered their previous venture a success. Not rail at her, demand explanations, and air his hurt feelings, but discuss the situation as two adults benefiting from hindsight.

He was entitled to rail at her, of that he had no doubt, but what would be the point? More sacrificing of his dignity, for no purpose.

"Shall we invite others to ride out with us?" Rose asked as the

Twid drifted by and a mistle thrush began singing his birdy vespers high up in a lime tree.

"I'd be happy to, though Roland hasn't much experience in company. Let's start with a duet, and if that goes well, he can graduate to larger groups over the next two weeks."

"A sound plan. Ah, we have company."

Lord Phillip and his lady strolled up the path, husband and wife holding hands rather than adopting the posture of an escort and his companion.

"DeWitt, Mrs. Roberts, a fine evening for a constitutional," Lord Phillip called. "In fact, I was hoping to run into you."

They had left the garden in plain view of the whole company, so *hoping* hadn't come into it. Phillip—who was as observant as he was decent—had planned this meeting, recruited his favorite accomplice, and abandoned his dinner companions to accost Gavin in relative privacy.

"The property is lovely," Rose said. "Makes me wish we had some abandoned towpaths on Colforth land."

"You must convey those sentiments to Lord Tavistock," Phillip said. "If I might impose briefly, I'd like to commend you to the company of my lady wife, Mrs. Roberts. I need a moment of DeWitt's time."

Phillip was shrewd, he wasn't always subtle, and he probably thought he was rescuing Gavin. "Mrs. Roberts, will you excuse me?"

"Of course, and my thanks for a pleasant meal."

So polite, so prosaic, and yet, honest too. They'd gone beyond small talk without stumbling into recriminations or—worse yet—doomed flirtations. Gavin watched the ladies retreating, arm in arm, and sorted through unexpected sentiments.

"What can you possibly be thinking?" Phillip said, taking Gavin by the elbow and steering him in the opposite direction.

"I'm wondering if Mrs. Roberts and I might aspire to become friends." Not lovers, not enemies, not allies, but... friends. Hmm.

"She strikes me as an entirely estimable woman, and the two of you clearly have a past. That's not what we need to talk about."

Clearly they had a past? "Clearly, how?"

"You all but bolted out the window whenever she came into the room at Nunnsuch. She developed a pressing need to head for the door when you made your appearances. Then there was all that fishing without a single trout to show for it. Hecate noticed the pattern right off, but that needn't concern you now."

"It doesn't concern me. Mrs. Roberts and I have found cordial footing." *Cordial.* An insipid, neutral word, but better than *acrimony* or *foolishness.* Friends were cordial, weren't they?

"Delighted to hear it." Phillip glanced over his shoulder, though the ladies had disappeared around the bend of the Twid. "You need to know that Tavistock is laboring under a series of unfortunate assumptions and that he has taken action on his mistaken beliefs."

Gavin stopped by the very spot where he'd come upon Rose earlier in the day. "How unfortunate are these assumptions?"

Phillip scooped up a handful of pebbles and began tossing them into the water. "I don't know, hence this conversation. Hecate said the sooner you knew, the better, because Tavistock means for you to know, but he's preoccupied with his guests. Heed me, DeWitt. I don't intend to repeat myself."

Gavin watched the succession of pebbles sink, one by one, and resigned himself to exhibiting still more patience.

"Evenings like this are the embodiment of peace," Rose said, mostly meaning it. "The crops are ripening, the lambs, calves, and foals have begun to grow up, and the very air feels benevolent."

"You truly do prefer the country, don't you?" Lady Phillip ambled along, arm in arm with Rose.

"I prefer the country in summer. Spring and autumn can be too busy, winter too bleak. Summer strikes me as a good balance of idle pleasures and industry. What of you? Do you have a preferred time of year?"

And what of Lord Phillip's private chat with Gavin? His lordship hadn't been rude, precisely, but he'd been determined on some pressing objective.

"I love the changing of the seasons," Lady Phillip said. "Just when I am out of patience with summer's heat or winter's chill, along comes a change in the air. When all the bustling about in Town in spring has driven me barmy, a few weeks of Nunnsuch in its summer glory will restore my spirits. I gather Mr. DeWitt was something of a change of air for you?"

Not fair that her ladyship should be so astute, but then, she'd seen all the awkwardness at Nunnsuch, and she was a surpassingly intelligent female.

"I am supposed to say that Mr. DeWitt and I are only recently acquainted, and he seems a very agreeable gentleman."

"He strikes me as a very honorable gentleman, but discontent."

"Honorable?" Not the first word Rose would have used to describe him. Or the third or fourth.

"When Phillip had to absent himself from Nunnsuch, he appointed Mr. DeWitt my bodyguard, for reasons on which I need not elaborate. Mr. DeWitt was at my side, or within earshot and keeping me in view, from first light to last. He didn't merely attend me, he directed my activities to ensure I wasn't bothered by those who would have vexed me. He executed thankless duties conscientiously and without a thought to his own convenience.

"After three days of that," her ladyship went on, "I was ready to wallop him for his devotion to duty, and yet, he would not be swayed. He was more tenacious than an overactive conscience."

They rounded the bend in the path, and through the trees, another manor came into view. "Is that Twidboro Hall?"

"The very one. The DeWitt ladies are likely enjoying the evening air in the garden, if you'd like to be introduced."

Rose beheld a modest manor on a slight rise. The place looked of a piece with its setting, contented, dependable, solid, the perfect home for that squire Gavin was trying to become.

"I would like to meet the DeWitts, but perhaps another time, when visitors are more likely to be expected." *When I have my wits about me and am not recovering from a verbal ambush.*

"It's not like that here," Lady Phillip said, taking a seat on a bench that had to have been built shortly after the Great Flood. The oak had long since silvered, and several sets of initials had been carved into the seat. "Neighbors drop in unannounced. They visit back and forth across the hedgerows and collect the day's news on the bridle paths. Unnervingly informal. Phillip says I'll become accustomed to it. It's not that different from London, except it is, and Phillip can't quite grasp that. People here are kind."

"You love Lord Phillip very much, don't you?" A woman in love was always willing to see the world in a benevolent light.

"Extravagantly so. I flatter myself that my sentiments are returned. I should not have asked about you and Mr. DeWitt, but I'm something of a co-hostess here. If you want to be thrown together with our Gavin, if you want him kept out of your way, you should tell me."

Rose settled onto the bench. He'd never been *her* Gavin, though she'd wished and hoped and wondered if he might be.

"We met early last spring. One of those house parties that tries to take advantage of the end of hunt season, but isn't a hunting party. I spent some time in London when I'd first emerged from mourning, but the whole business was too much. I am merely gentry and only comfortably well-off. What was I *doing* there?"

"Fending off offers of marriage?"

"A few. Widowers looking for somebody to manage their nursery and have their slippers warming at the end of every day. Older bachelors having second thoughts about their finances. I was appalled at first."

Crosspatch was blessed with an abundance of songbirds. The resident chorister on this stretch of the river was an enthusiastic robin, and his solo, while vigorous, struck Rose as sad. His babies were likely flown, and he was doomed to bide here through the harsh winter rather than fly off to gentler climes.

No warmed slippers for him or his missus.

Lady Phillip regarded her in the slanting evening light. "You were appalled by the offers of a practical match, until other sorts of offers began arriving?"

"Those other sorts of offers had likely been extended from my first week in Town, but I was too naïve to grasp what the flirtation and pretty manners were truly about. I was staying with a friend, and she found my lack of experience hilarious. I knew nothing of how to hold my fan, my parasol, my gloves. I was ignorant of half the meanings of flowers that arrived in bouquets. I was very much trying to fill a role without knowing the plot or my lines."

Lady Phillip stared at the river flowing placidly by. "Because you were not titled or an heiress, they all assumed you had come to Town to frolic. You had probably come thinking to catch up on the latest fashions, having put aside your weeds at long last."

"And to see some professional acting, to hear some opera, to take in St. Paul's and the Tower. Hampshire is lovely, but our entertainments are humble. My late husband always spoke so glowingly of Town, and I had never been for more than an occasional short stay. I wanted to know what he'd fallen in love with. I have concluded London is a very different experience for a young man of means than it is for his widow some years later."

"Doubtless true, and does that take us to Mr. DeWitt?"

Whose past with me is none of your business. "I mean Mr. DeWitt no harm."

And upon reflection, that was true. Rose had raged and railed and ruminated where he was concerned—and felt beyond stupid—but now, having seen him again, she could be more dispassionate. He wasn't a monster, nor was he irresistibly magnetic.

He was simply a man who'd behaved disappointingly.

"You mean him no harm." Lady Phillip's study of the river

became intent. "That suggests to me he left you with a less than favorable impression on an earlier occasion."

Rose flailed about in search of patience, humor, or any genteel spar in a sea of private and difficult emotions, but Lady Phillip was hectoring her past all bearing.

"Coming here was a mistake." Rose stood and sketched a curtsey. "Even my lady's maid could see that. Please excuse me, and I hope you will understand if my attendance at this gathering is brief."

"Run off, then," Lady Phillip said pleasantly. "Gavin ran off, and his family and friends are still at a loss as to why."

"Because he was *miserable*," Rose retorted. "Denied any hand in the family business lest gainful employment be seen as relapsing into the foul clutches of trade, expected to ramble around his acres for decades though nobody had bothered to tell him how to tend those acres, no friends despite everybody being friendly and *kind*, no control over his own funds... Why on earth would he have stayed where he was little more than a handsome tailor's dummy? On the stage, he was valued for so much more than good looks and pleasant repartee."

The robin had gone silent, and from the direction of Twidboro Hall, the notes of a pianoforte tinkled forth over the lengthening shadows. The tune was as sprightly as the robin's, jarringly so.

"Clementi," Lady Phillip muttered, rising. "Diana is in a taking about something. I suspect you are too. Keep your counsel if you must, and please do not swan off in high dudgeon because I have been graceless in my interrogation. Phillip is concerned about Gavin —Phillip is Crosspatch born and bred—and you were kind to me at Nunnsuch, very kind. I am concerned for you and Gavin both."

Why must you always make a Drury Lane production out of nothing, little Miss Dramatic? Dane's accusation still had the power to hurt. His wagering had been *nothing*, his temper had been *nothing*, his flirtations had been *nothing*, his increasing inebriated forgetfulness, and his leering friends...

All *nothing*.

"Mr. DeWitt and I did not part on friendly terms," Rose said. "Our expectations were at cross-purposes."

Lady Phillip for once held her peace.

"I went to Derbyshire thinking I would get in some reading, practice my pianoforte, put the whole confusing, unpleasant business in London behind me. Meet a few new faces in a congenial situation, but raise no expectations and have none put upon me. I was half right. My hostess—Countess Rutherford—assured me my wishes would come true."

Rose resumed her seat on the bench, while Lady Phillip remained standing on the path. Smart of her, to keep some distance.

"At the last minute, the guest list ran short by a few bachelors," Rose went on, "so the countess arranged for some members of an acting troupe biding in the area to join the gathering. Not quite guests, not quite servants. Gav—Mr. DeWitt told me that actors expect to inhabit the fringes of polite society, the outer reaches of low society, and everything in between."

"You might refrain from telling his family about the low-society part."

"Because they won't want to hear it, just as they didn't want to hear of him taking a hand in the family businesses, didn't want him joining the local militia, didn't think he needed an extra year at university. Those women were driving him half mad."

Lady Phillip worried a fingernail. "I ought not to admit this, but I am well acquainted with the frustrations family can engender. The DeWitt ladies are delightful, though I fear they were so comfortable with Gavin the youth that they couldn't see he'd become Gavin the man."

"Gavin the man is formidable," Rose said, resorting to the very word he'd chosen to describe her. "He reads voraciously in several languages, his grasp of politics is keen, he'd make an exceedingly effective member of Parliament, and when he chooses to be charming..."

"Yes?"

Rose felt an odd urge to cry. "I fell for him, my lady. I fell as I'd never fallen for my husband. Dane and I had grown up together. We'd known we were to marry from a young age. I was familiar with Dane, he esteemed me. We were happy, at least at first, and I was devoted. With Gavin DeWitt..."

The aggressively cheerful piano music came to a merciful cadence. "You were knocked top over tail? Phillip knocked me top over tail. All it takes is his smile across the breakfast table, and I'm back to doing aerial somersaults in my heart. Most bewildering."

"You are happily bewildered, though," Rose said, "and delighted with the notion that Lord Phillip is tumbling about in midair with you. Now imagine you are in the initial throes of those feelings, thinking that for the first time, somebody has *chosen* you, is enthralled with you, and would love to spend the rest of his life with you. Then you learn that it has all been a sham."

"You're saying Gavin was acting the part of the smitten swain?"

In for a penny... "Acting the part of the *lover*, my lady. The devoted lover. The first of his kind to grace my experience. Mourning was well behind me. I wasn't getting any younger, and he was nigh irresistible. I was ripe for the plucking."

"Oh dear. He played you false?"

Better if he had. "Not in the sense you mean. I never found him in any other lady's bed. He was never rude or overtly mean." Rose paused to consider what exactly she was about to reveal. "You will hold this conversation in confidence?"

"Of course. I am not a gossip."

By reputation, Lady Phillip had been the next thing to an antidote. Bookish, much given to managing her funds, not very well liked.

Deserving of trust, if anybody was.

In for a pound. "I was gently informed by another member of the troupe that actors *act*, and they expect to be *paid* for their performances. For all of their performances."

"Good God. Might you have misconstrued the innuendo?"

The urge to cry was shifting into an urge to throw rocks and shout and gouge a knife into sturdy old wood.

"I was not mistaken. Mr. DeWitt performed wonderfully, and then his behavior toward me abruptly cooled. No explanation and no overt rudeness. He became painfully correct. When I remarked the shift in his demeanor to a senior member of his troupe, the situation was explained to me. I could not bring myself to pay him—did not know what sum would have been expected and would not have been able to look him in the eye, as angry as the whole business made me."

Lady Phillip took the seat beside Rose. "Well, good. At least you were angry."

"I beg your pardon?"

"Consenting adults may do as they please, but Gavin should have been clear with you regarding the terms of the arrangement. He deceived you and had his pleasure of you—even actors cannot dissemble in some regards—and that is despicable. Heinous. Beneath contempt. He toyed with your trust and your affections, and I can assure you of one thing, Mrs. Roberts: Gavin DeWitt did not need your coin."

Lady Phillip's outrage was reassuring, but not as gratifying as it should have been. "He was a penniless actor. I'm sure he had need of every..." Except he hadn't been a *penniless actor*. Gavin DeWitt was heir to a thriving business and a pretty rural property... His older sister had been legendarily well dowered.

He'd bought a thoroughbred colt on a whim, simply because he liked the look of the beast.

"He didn't need the money," Rose muttered. "Then why not simply part from me fondly, allude to wonderful memories, and be about his next *role in the hay*, as it were? Why the chilly reserve and air of subtle disdain?"

She fell silent, the only sound the soft murmur of water lapping past rocks.

"Gavin DeWitt and I are of recent acquaintance," Lady Phillip said slowly, "but my husband considers him a friend and entrusted my safety to him. To have treated you so ill seems out of character."

"I could not fathom it at the time. How could I have been played for such a fool? *How could he do that to me?*"

Rose had never voiced the question aloud, but all the bewilderment and disappointment in the world filled those few words. How could he humiliate her, disdain her, he who'd heard her every confidence, dried her tears, and held her through hours of darkness? He who had been so patient, so kind, so *loving*?

"You have a chance to confront him," Lady Phillip said. "At the very least, you deserve an apology. Gavin is nobody's fool. He must realize that if you choose to alert the right gossips, you could ruin Diana's chances in London next year."

"I wouldn't do that."

Lady Phillip paced a few yards down the towpath, skirts swishing. "If you want to return to Hampshire, I will make your excuses, but I suspect Gavin DeWitt has haunted your nightmares and will continue to do so if you can't get him sorted out."

"We're to hack out tomorrow afternoon." Rose wasn't about to turn up as sniffy and distant as he had on her. They were *starting afresh*, by heaven. "I will stay another day or two at least, and I really am interested in your investment advice."

"And I am keen to give it. I plan for us to begin by discussing charities, which we ladies are usually left in peace to run as we see fit. When we confidently manage those, we are better schooled for taking on the profitable enterprises."

Rose stood and started off in the direction of Miller's Lament. "You've given this a good deal of thought."

"Years and years of thought. Women run households, budgeting to the penny. We run charities, and we inherit our husband's properties and businesses and keep them prospering, as you have with Colforth Hall. The notion that women aren't competent to handle financial matters is poppycock wrapped in nonsense tied up with a bow of balderdash."

Her ladyship held forth about a sailors' home in Bristol she wanted to open before Christmas and was as enthusiastic on her topic as Lady Iris had been regarding peppermint. All the while, Rose nodded and murmured and asked appropriate questions, but her mind was consumed with a different puzzle.

Gavin DeWitt hadn't needed her money.

Why did that realization matter so much?

CHAPTER FIVE

Phillip could be droll when tipsy.

Gavin suspected he was the only person in the whole world to know that fact about his lordship. They'd traveled this towpath on foot, on horseback, pushing barrows of rocks to build a sheep ford, and by moonlight after a few too many pints of Mrs. Pevinger's best.

Phillip wasn't remotely droll now.

"Tavistock means well," Phillip said as the last of the pebbles went into the Twid. "Only the best of intentions inspired him to hire this troupe of actors. One must give credit where due and make allowances where necessary. He cannot help that he's the marquess."

"*Our* marquess," Gavin said, because in Crosspatch Corners, one did not miss an opportunity to stress the possessive where the ranking peer was concerned.

Phillip took Gavin by the arm and resumed walking. "Tavistock is your sister's husband, too, lest you forget."

"How could I? Tavistock has turned a once-articulate, ferociously efficient woman into a lady who smiles pleasantly at the middle distance, who *wafts* when she used to march from room to room, and who gathers up a bouquet of wallflowers and calls it a house party."

Phillip's steps slowed. "Whatever else these ladies are, DeWitt, they are not wallflowers. I have no doubt Miss Zinnia Peasegood was reciting the royal succession without a single mistake by the age of two. Lady Iris has a prodigious grasp of medicinals. Lady Fern Linwood can describe for you, to the last tiara on the oldest dowager, what was worn at any social event she's attended. These women pay attention."

Phillip had always been the quiet neighbor, content to mind his patch, but he'd also read more widely on agriculture than anybody else in Crosspatch. He ordered books from Paris and London. He corresponded with botanists and horticulturalists from all over the Continent.

He would know astute observers when he saw them.

"Amaryllis is in love," Gavin said as a squirrel raced across the towpath. "She hasn't gone completely witless since marrying Tavistock. She would hardly surround herself with ninnyhammers and blockheads."

"Tavistock has turned blockheaded on us."

"He's in love too. I expect the condition is permanent, though the outward symptoms might moderate in another few decades. We need only be patient." Gavin did not envy Tavistock the foolishness of his infatuation, not much anyway.

Good God... actors in residence at Crosspatch Corners. *Professional* actors.

A soaking in the Twid was too good for *our marquess.* Any dramatist could see that Gavin was owed revenge upon Tavistock. Mandatory attendance at an extended Dorning family gathering might serve. Tavistock's step-mother's family numbered in the thousands, and they were all *lively.*

"Then you aren't annoyed that Tavistock has hired a troupe of traveling players to entertain the ladies?" Phillip asked, tugging Gavin to a stop. "Lady Tavistock has no idea of this plan. He thinks to surprise her."

The evening light turned the surface of the Twid variously

molten white, golden, coppery, and sable. The river sought the sea, and for one instant, Gavin's heart leaped toward his former profession.

"They'll do Portia's speech for the ladies."

"Beg pardon?"

"Act 4, scene 1." Gavin adopted the measured pacing of the barrister before a jury, and began with a gracious gesture toward the evening sky.

"'The quality of mercy is not strain'd. It droppeth as the gentle rain from heaven on the place beneath...'" He ceased his playacting. "Shakespeare was forever stressing the notion of forgiveness, particularly from those in positions of power." No *Taming of the Shrew* for this audience, though, and certainly not Kate's preachy and saccharine final monologue.

Even Shakespeare hadn't been above pandering to the drunks in the stalls.

Phillip scrubbed a hand through his hair. "Tavistock has hired your old outfit. He thinks to reunite you with your acting friends, entertain the ladies, and be the helpful husband. That you might not want to see your former confreres never occurred to him."

A bullfrog began his homely evening hymn.

"*Which... former... confreres?*"

"The first bunch you were with—up north. They typically spend summers in the spa towns, and Tavistock caught them between engagements."

Gavin had traveled two hundred miles to get away from them, left leading roles behind to take his chances once again with the bit parts. They'd witnessed his deepest humiliation and had box seats at his worst blundering. If he never saw them again—

In the next instant, it occurred to him that Rose would hate to see Drysdale's Players again. She'd probably leave the gathering, and maybe that would be for the best. Until she did, the awkwardness would simply have to be borne.

Nothing for it but some inspired acting. Philosophical detachment, a hint of amusement just shy of indifference.

"They're a good group," Gavin said. "Drysdale's Players make up
in enthusiasm what they sometimes lack in faithfulness to an original
script. A flair for improvising. Well suited to comedy."

He'd had no heart for laughter by the time he'd left the north, but
he'd had all manner of insights regarding the tragic roles.

"Then you are at peace with the notion that your station in life
parted you from them?" Phillip posed the question with far too much
diffidence.

Philosophical detachment, damn and blast. "Tavistock meant
well, and I can appreciate that. My station in life did not part me
from the stage, but my sense of responsibility to my family did."

Phillip started back the way they'd come. "And will Mrs. Roberts
take a similarly sanguine view of these professional entertainers?"

Gavin fell in step beside him. "Has somebody been talking out of
turn?" Or listening out of turn. Phillip was prodigiously skilled at
going unnoticed, or he had been before ascending to the status of
brother to *our marquess.*

"Nunn and I correspond. He mentioned that Mrs. Roberts had
spoken disappointedly of a house party last year in Derbyshire, one
involving some handsome, friendly actors who had shifted the tone of
the gathering in less than genteel directions. The Almighty sees fit to
visit the occasional coincidence upon us, but Nunn is not the
Almighty, and Derbyshire is not exactly crawling with acting
troupes."

"This is not of your concern, Phillip." It was nobody's concern,
save Gavin's and Rose's.

"My lady wife is my concern, and she noticed you and Mrs.
Roberts at Nunnsuch, circling each other like cats. Now you and the
widow are sharing supper beneath the stars. I won't have Hecate's
first venture as a hostess marred by drama and upheaval, DeWitt."

"Right. I'm to deal pleasantly with all parties under all circumstances, but not too pleasantly. I know my lines, Phillip."

"Something went wrong," Phillip muttered, as if Gavin hadn't spoken. "Something between you and Mrs. Roberts went egregiously wrong. You blundered, she presumed, somebody was mistaken. I know not which, but given the nature of our guests, I'd like to see the situation resolved."

"We had a misunderstanding," Gavin said, which was a line he had rehearsed, mentally, over and over. "We have agreed to start afresh."

And because Phillip was the closest thing he had to a friend, and because the whole situation would soon have him baying at the moon, he graced the night air with more truths.

"She paid me."

Phillip ambled on for another dozen paces, while Gavin hoped that additional particulars need not be elucidated.

"She paid you," Phillip said, "for comporting yourself in an ungenteel direction?"

"We were very genteel, for days on end. I recited more poetry to her than I've recited in the whole of my career in the common of the Crosspatch Arms. She ran lines with me. We debated everything. I thought we were courting."

"Picnics?" Offered with a blend of commiseration and dread.

"Two a day, weather permitting, and walks in nature, and sedate hacks, and shared jokes, and the whole smarmy bit. Falling into bed together was simply the next delight on an endless list of delights I'd experienced with only her. The elements, the other guests, the very birds of the air conspired to abet this great romance."

"Until Mrs. Roberts *paid* you?"

True darkness was falling, a mercy, that. "I was so... smitten, Phillip. So unsuspecting. She *listened* to me. By the day and the hour. I confided my every radical political stance and my most damning criticisms of the Bard to her. She did not care that I was a mere actor, and I doubt she would have cared had she known I was heir to the DeWitt candle fortune."

"You fell in love," Phillip said.

"I thought *we* had fallen in love, and I have never been more wrong, more humiliated, more mortified... She *paid* me. I rose from the most unspeakably awe-inspiring night of my life, thinking to gather up my clothing and steal down the corridor on permanently attached wings of joy. What should I find tucked into the folds of my cravat but a great, obscene pile of coins. She hadn't mislaid them, hadn't put them there by mistake. She paid me."

"And you left the money there?"

"Put it in her jewelry box with the rest of her coins. I avoided her thereafter and managed to finish out the week without making an even greater fool of myself." The moon was rising off to the east, though Gavin could navigate the towpath in pitch darkness. "I've spent the night with many women, Phillip. I'm university educated, after all. But Rose slept *with* me. If I stirred in my sleep, she'd touch my shoulder—simply that—and I could return to my dreams a happier man. She breathed with me..."

How to describe a sense of oneness that had little to do with copulation? A unity of body and spirit? "I have never found such a depth of repose in slumber, though I could sense whenever she stirred as well, and that pleased me."

Gavin left off trying to find more words, lest the last scintilla of his dignity go floating down the Twid.

"You came south shortly after that?"

"Started a-damned-fresh. I seem to be doing that a fair amount lately." Gavin could have some compassion for the callow fellow who'd gone north, now that he'd again been relegated to the status of family pillar.

"She heard all my dreams, Phillip. My hopes, even my homesickness. She listened, her attention inebriated me. To be *heard*. It changed how I acted, to be truly *heard*, changed how I comported myself before audiences. I became a better actor because of Rose Roberts."

"And you listened to her dreams and hopes?"

Gavin thought back to what exactly Rose had told him. "She

spoke of her late husband and said after a woman puts off mourning, she's apparently not to mention her late spouse again, other than in passing fondness. That was hard for her. She regretted not having children, not for herself, but because her husband had so wanted sons."

Not daughters. Dane Roberts had apparently been set on sons.

"She told you these things, which are tender, intimate sentiments, and then she *paid you* for your sexual favors?"

"Confusing, to say the least." Utterly, maddeningly bewildering. "But grief is an odd beast, and she was still very much a woman grieving." Less so now, though Gavin wasn't sure why he thought that to be true.

"I am no expert on the mind of a woman," Phillip said as garden torches came into view, "but I cannot divine why Mrs. Roberts paid you. Nunn reports that she'd had her turn swanning about Town and buying out the shops. She'd had her chance to be a merry widow where the Hampshire neighbors would take no notice."

"Rose—Mrs. Roberts—didn't care for Town. Said everybody was too much consumed with gossip, shopping, and indolence."

"You miss my point. If she was bent on a frolic, then you obliged her. A lovely idyll unlooked for by either party. She could have parted from you with a fond wave and a sigh. House parties lend themselves to such liaisons. Mrs. Roberts does not strike me as the sort of woman who'd repose her confidences in a man, then deliberately insult him. She had no need to pay you."

Gavin stopped short in the darkness. "That is the conundrum that has vexed me the most. She had no need to insult me like that. Such behavior was out of character, pointless. I would have taken my congé like a gentleman, albeit a brokenhearted one, if she'd merely... but she paid me."

"You promised you wouldn't hare off again, DeWitt."

"That was before Tavistock took a hand in the stage direction."

"A promise is a promise."

The torches winked in the gathering shadows, while guests moved beneath them in pairs and trios. *She had no need to pay you.*

"Mrs. Roberts and I are to ride out tomorrow afternoon. I have a book to return to her. After that, I make no guarantees."

"My dear fellow, life makes us no guarantees. Try to act surprised when Tavistock tells you he's hired some actors to entertain the company."

"Surprised and pleased," Gavin said, feeling instead exasperated and tired. "I am a thespian at heart and probably always will be."

The mounted nature of Rose's afternoon outing made dressing for the occasion simple, though Timmens had still managed a few long-suffering sighs and dubious glances as Rose donned her riding habit.

"You know I'm not one to judge, ma'am." Timmens passed Rose a tall boot. "But that Mr. DeWitt wasn't what he appeared to be. You don't owe him a minute of your time."

Rose shoved her foot into the boot and stood to anchor her heel, then sat to don the second boot. "We are none of us entirely what we appear to be, and it's a pleasant day for some fresh air. Are you getting on well with the other lady's maids?"

"They're a good lot," Timmens said, passing over the second boot. "They don't put on airs and don't gossip." But of course, Timmens would not be distracted from her sermonizing. "I hope you take this opportunity to tell Mr. DeWitt to mind his place. He was up to no good, pretending to be an actor. Deceptive, that."

"He was an actor, and a good one."

Timmens held out a fetching little toque adorned with peacock feathers, one of the guilt offerings Dane had brought back from London.

"I'll do without a hat," Rose said.

"But, ma'am, the sun is hard on a lady's complexion. It's *summer*, and you are no schoolgirl."

Timmens, who might have been two years Rose's junior, had a lovely complexion. She was quite pretty in a plump, blond, blue-eyed way and a favorite with the footmen, whom she disdained to notice. Timmens would flirt occasionally with a youngish butler, and to the Colforth steward, she was gracious.

A creature of standards, was Timmens.

"We'll be riding mostly along shaded paths," Rose said. "Hats are hot, and that hat in particular is silly."

"Fashionable," Timmens said, putting the millinery back in the dressing closet. "Ma'am, I do despair of you sometimes. You'd rather have a gent noticing your freckles or wrinkles than noticing a pretty little hat."

Even for Timmens, that was a bit much. "I'm not yet at my last prayers. If you lay out an ensemble for supper, I can dress myself."

"As if I'd leave you to manage on your own. For shame, ma'am. The aubergine silk for tonight. Gives you a youthful glow while emphasizing your dignity." She went off into deliberations about whether brown slippers would be overdoing the decorous theme, though white wouldn't do either.

Rose left her to her muttering and incantations. Gavin DeWitt was not one to be taken in by costumes and stage settings.

"I was taken in," Rose murmured, making her way to the stable. "By handsome manners and sweet kisses." Though that wasn't entirely fair. Gavin's articulate politics, his devotion to his art, his endless willingness to listen and to offer affection without sexual expectations had also come into it.

His nature was passionate in many regards, and that intensity had been attractive.

Still was attractive, for that matter.

By note, Gavin had informed her that he'd meet her in the stable yard at four of the clock. The other guests were enjoying the quiet hours before the dressing bell, and several had taken a notion to investigate the shops in Crosspatch Corners.

And there he was, seated on the ladies' mounting block, a book in his hands, his colt standing with a hip cocked, head down, eyes closed. They made a tableau of contentment, male specimens in repose, and yet, Rose would have bet her favorite slippers that Gavin was aware of her approach.

"Mr. DeWitt, good day."

He rose in no hurry, set the book on the mounting block, and bowed. "Mrs. Roberts, greetings. I've asked to have Sid saddled for you. He's a perfect gentleman and will set a good example for Roland."

Rose curtseyed and made a little fuss over the colt. "He's a handsome devil." All soulful eyes and sleek muscle, like his owner. Rose did not want to be aware of Gavin DeWitt in any physical sense, but such was his self-possession and so compelling were her memories of him, that she couldn't avoid making comparisons.

The Gavin over whom she'd made a fool of herself had been more prone to laughter, more playful. He'd had depths, but he'd also been pleased with his own ability to charm and entertain. The present incarnation had acquired gravitas as befitted the head of the DeWitt family.

Rose resented his new seriousness, because it made him yet still more attractive, which should not have been possible.

"Roland is a good lad at heart," Gavin said. "He wants to please, but he gets distracted. He doesn't enjoy a lot of native courage, and thus he's prone to assert his dignity when what's really in question is his confidence."

A widow understood that description. "You are patient with him?"

"We are learning to be patient with each other, to assume good intentions rather than treachery. Progress has been slow because I was away from my post when Roland might have more easily been taken in hand."

Some sort of self-deprecation lay in those words. Rose ceased stroking Roland's velvety nose, took her riding gloves from her pocket, and pulled them on.

"I don't care for the notion of rushing young horses into work," she said. "The plow stock is particularly abused in this regard because they are born large and gain size quickly."

"And because their lot in life is honest, hard work. The riding stock have it easier in many regards."

Rose wanted to ask what that comment was about, but a wizened stable lad led out a handsome chestnut gelding.

"Mrs. Rose Roberts," Gavin said, "may I make known to you Thucydides, affectionately known as Sid. I'll take him, Franklin, and we should be gone about an hour. We'll keep to the Twid, then have a turn about the village green, and come back by way of Lark's Nest and Twidboro Hall."

"Aye, guv. Sid will enjoy the outing." The fellow tugged his cap and shuffled off.

"You tell them your route in case you come to harm," Rose said. "That's wise." A rule Dane had scoffed at, though every equestrian was taught to follow it.

"Roland and I are often tearing neck or nothing over the countryside. A rabbit hole, a darting squirrel, a patch of mud could do us mischief, and so I take what precautions I can. Let's get you aboard, shall we?"

What are you running from when you gallop over hill and dale? Rose would have asked that question, before. She didn't need to ask it now. Gavin was being sewn into the costume of the country squire, and the part suited him ill.

Rose mounted her steed, Gavin swung aboard his, and they were soon ambling off in the direction of the Twid.

"Will you go to Town once the harvest is in?" she asked.

"My mother advises me not to. She is concerned that somebody who saw me prancing around in a provincial production of *A Midsummer Night's Dream* will recognize me prancing around Vauxhall Gardens. I'm to lie low until next spring."

"And somebody might still recognize you, because you excelled at your craft. What of it?" That his mother should bind him hand and foot to Crosspatch, when he had such talent...

They turned onto the sun-dappled towpath in the direction of the village. Sid was a seasoned lady's mount, happy to toddle along, and Roland seemed willing to follow his example.

"My talent, as you call it, doesn't signify," Gavin said, "except as it comes to bear on a new role. I have never been a country squire before, and Mama has never been an in-law to a peer. She is at sixes and sevens. One moment, she's awash in glee with high expectations for Diana and Caroline, the next she's poring over DeBrett's and scolding me for how I knot my cravat."

"You don't have a valet?"

"In a small theater troupe, we often had to change clothes from the skin out in less than three minutes, without assistance, several times in a single performance. I have a valet. He tends to my clothing, and I guard my privacy as best I can."

"I was to acquire a companion when I graduated to second mourning. As if having a stranger hovering about would somehow improve the situation." Timmens's words, and for once Rose had been appreciative of an outspoken lady's maid.

"But you managed without a companion quite well."

"I needed privacy more than I needed to appease the expert jury in the churchyard." And Rose needed to *not do this*. To not slip back into exchanging confidences with Gavin DeWitt and trusting him to exercise a loyal friend's discretion.

A lover's discretion. A lover who'd had no need of her coin, but had expected payment all the same.

"Good for you," Gavin said as a quartet of ladies came around a bend in the path. Roland shied, then recovered himself. Sid took barely any notice of the foot traffic or of Roland's lapse. "If you were missing your Dane, then all the companions in the world would serve no purpose but to impose on you a burden of pleasant manners and agreeable behavior."

That was the sort of honest, kind, socially suspect response she'd learned to expect from him. He'd forever been encouraging her, putting her at ease with her own feelings.

All part of the service?

"Ladies." He tipped his hat. "Good day. You've plundered the shops to your satisfaction?"

"We conquered the ladies' parlor at the Arms too," Miss Pease-good said, nodding earnestly. "Miss Tansy Pevinger tried to warn us about her mama's cider, but we were heedless of caution. This is a frequent failing on our parts."

"We left not a hair ribbon unpurchased in the whole of Cross-patch Corners," Lady Iris said. "Your local maidens will be tying their tresses with purloined yarn."

Her admission provoked peals of merriment, a sound Rose had also heard the previous evening. Women laughing, truly enjoying one another's company. Being a bit silly and possibly even tipsy in broad daylight.

She wanted to join in the banter, and she wanted to gallop all the way back to Hampshire.

"Then you must stash your booty in yonder smuggler's cave," Gavin said, nodding in the direction of Miller's Lament. "If the Sheriff of Nottingham and his *posse comitatus* come looking for you, Mrs. Roberts and I will direct them to London."

"Robin Hood is mine," Miss Peasegood said, nose in the air. "Lady Iris, you can have that Alan fellow if we spot him in his Sher-wood green." The women trundled off, arguing with good-natured vehemence over the fate of Little John, who fought so well *with pike and staff*.

"What's wrong?" Gavin asked when the horses were again plod-ding along the path. "You look as if the expert jury just found you not guilty by reason of insufficient evidence."

The Scottish verdict, condemnation without capital conse-quences. "They are happy," Rose said. "Unmarried, aging, and entirely pleased with themselves. They will never be widows."

"That upsets you."

Gavin stated what to him was likely obvious, but came as something of a revelation to Rose herself.

"I went to London when I first put off mourning," she said. "I should not be telling you this, but when has that stopped me from confiding in you? I saw Dane's mistress, the woman who'd drawn him back to Town over and over. I kept the Colforth books, and the first time a jeweler's invoice ended up with the monthly bills, I paid it, thinking my Christmas token would be very fine indeed."

Gavin kept his peace. Rose had always appreciated his way with a silence, damn him.

"Dane gave me a set of earbobs for Christmas. Pearls, quite nice. Understated. They matched the bracelet he'd given me the year before. I've managed to since misplace the lot. The jeweler had sought payment for emeralds. Emeralds can cost more than diamonds. She looked like me. Emeralds would have suited her."

A fish leaped, the sound a little punctuation of an otherwise placid summer afternoon.

"I am sorry, Rose."

"Dane wasn't. He tried to jolly me past my outrage—what was a bit of frolic when he was far from Hampshire? Surely the fact that he put a roof over my head signified more than his passing fancies ever could."

"Emeralds are not a bit of frolic, and emeralds weren't the point."

"Precisely. My settlements pulled Colforth Hall back from the brink. My dower properties are why that estate is profitable even now. My mill, my leaseholds... Dane no more put a roof over my head than I presented him with triplet sons. Why can't I put this behind me?"

Why did the sight of happy, unmarried women upset her so? Why could she manage to keep these thoughts to herself until she once again saw the author of her greatest recent humiliation?

"You are still vexed by your late spouse, because marital betrayal matters," Gavin said, "and you honor me with this honesty because your confidences have always been safe with me. They will remain so."

He was being a gentleman, which made no sense, because a gentleman did not expect payment for sexual favors, particularly not payment he didn't need. Rose hadn't been able to let that go either, but she intended to give it a good try.

"In Derbyshire," she said, "something went wrong between us. I don't want to revisit ancient history, but I want you to know I regret how we parted." She refused to apologize to him when she was the wronged party, but she could offer an olive branch.

They took a turn away from the towpath, and some of the tumult Rose had been feeling subsided. She'd wanted to extend that olive branch, to conclude the old business and put it behind them.

"I have regrets about that interlude as well," Gavin said, holding back the limb of a birch sapling and allowing her to precede him. "Regrets about how we parted, not about the time I spent with you. I agree we need not dwell on prior mistakes, and despite whatever missteps were committed then, I am glad to see you now."

Was that an apology? A reciprocal olive branch? He'd admitted to missteps. Whatever else Gavin might have intended, those words were an expression of goodwill, and that was a relief.

An enormous relief.

"You came upon me reading Wordsworth," Rose said, "or so you thought. Dane gave me that book the last Christmas before he died."

"And you were considering pitching it into the Twid?"

She nodded. The temptation had struck her as monstrous at the time. Half hysterical, half juvenile. Such impulses had been common during first mourning—she'd nearly pitched her whole jewelry box down the jakes—much less so recently. She had other copies of those poems, but none signed in Dane's hand, *with all good wishes from your devoted husband.*

"I have a suggestion," Gavin said.

He'd been full of suggestions as a lover. Excellent, interesting, naughty, wonderful... "Unburden yourself, Mr. DeWitt."

"Let's trot to the stile on the far side of this field, hop over, and then let them stretch their legs on the lane into the village. It's about three-quarters of a mile, and Sid could use the exercise. Roland tested his speed this morning, and this will be in the nature of a pleasant little reprise for him."

A pleasant... little... reprise. *No, you don't, Rose Constance. Don't even think it.*

"Trot, hop, canter," Rose said, gathering up her reins. "You're on." Sid all but leaped forward at the touch of her heel, and when he landed the stile, she sent him onto the lane at a brisk gallop, then a dead run.

She could hear Gavin laughing half a length behind her, and thus she thundered in the lead, all the way to the Crosspatch green.

CHAPTER SIX

Gavin assisted Rose to alight from her horse with more decorum than if they'd been in the churchyard. He and she were making a fresh start, and that meant best behavior for the sake of all concerned.

No lingering slide of his hands at her waist. No standing too close for just one instant too long. No bending near as if some imaginary nearby fife and drum corps made conversation in close proximity a polite alternative to shouting.

If the past hour had told him anything, it was that he truly had missed Rose. Missed her tart tongue, her fierce honesty, and her courage in the face of uncomfortable emotions.

"You'll join us for supper tonight?" Rose asked as Gavin loosened Sid's girths.

"I will. My younger sisters, mother, and grandmother will come as well. I decline this evening's invitation at peril to my continued habitation in the earthly sphere." And he would find a quiet, private moment to alert her to the impending arrival of Drysdale's Players. The outing to Crosspatch had been too sweet, too pleasant to mar with such an announcement.

Rose took to stroking Roland's neck. "Will you introduce me to your mother?"

"Of course, and to my sisters, but be warned that Diana chatters and Caroline blushes. Grandmama is a delight, though she's slowing down of late." Had slowed considerably during the two years Gavin had been on the stage.

"I'll look forward to that." Rose gave Roland a final pat and stepped back. "Thank you for a lovely outing, Mr. DeWitt. Until this evening."

Roland turned limpid eyes on her.

"Your book," Gavin said, retrieving Mr. Wordsworth from the mounting block. "Pitch him into the Twid if you must, but Caroline might fish him out. She's a particular fan of the nature poets."

Rose plucked the book from Gavin's hand. "No dunking for Mr. Wordsworth today. I have galloped off my wayward impulses. Good day, Mr. DeWitt, and again, thanks."

She didn't curtsey, which was some consolation, and she did stride off with that particular sense of purpose she brought to any undertaking—every undertaking, in fact.

Roland sighed.

"I saw her first," Gavin murmured. "You'll have to find your own filly, my lad."

Roland lifted his tail and, as was his wont, broke wind at length.

"Behave like that in the presence of a lady, and I'll gallop you straight to the knacker's yard." Gavin swung back into the saddle and turned his steed for Twidboro Hall. The outing had been sufficiently lengthy and athletic that Roland was content to walk, though he did give a prodigious shy at nothing when Gavin turned onto the towpath.

Well, not nothing. "Caroline, good day." She occupied the same notch in the same maple Gavin had often preferred for memorizing sonnets. "Will you join us for the walk home?"

She studied him for a few moments, while the Twid babbled past, and Roland's ears flicked in all directions.

"Roland, it's only me. You mustn't be in a taking every time you find a girl in a tree. Contemplatives love trees." She climbed down rather than leaping, doubtless in deference to Roland's delicate nerves. "See? It's your own Caro, silly beast."

She held out a hand, which Roland tentatively sniffed. They had a relationship involving carrots and curry combs. Gavin suspected Caroline had turned to his horse for comfort when she'd found herself deprived of a resident big brother.

And maybe the horse had been comforted too. "Shall you ride up before me?"

She wanted to. Gavin could see the longing in her eyes, the wistful yearning for a pleasure they'd shared when she'd been small, and he'd been—to her—the older, wiser, adult brother who'd always made time for her and her troubles.

"I'm not a toddler to be riding astride on my pony," Caroline said, scratching beneath Roland's chin. "You hacked out with Mrs. Roberts."

"You spied on us."

"I was in plain sight. You were too absorbed to see me."

Caroline was clearly unhappy about that. Gavin dismounted. "Up you go. Sit aside if you must, but please don't grow up any sooner then you have to. Adulthood, I assure you, is vastly overrated."

Still, Caroline hesitated, and Gavin wanted to howl. She'd been a little girl when he'd left, a small, sprightly, curious person who over-heard much and said little. Now she was too tall, too dignified, and lost to him in some awful, permanent way.

"A leg up, if you please." As imperious as the Queen of the May.

Gavin obliged, and Caroline was soon perching aside in his saddle, which she accomplished with surprising grace despite the lack of a horn around which to secure her knee.

"Will you marry Mrs. Roberts?" she asked, taking up the reins as Gavin ran up the offside stirrup.

"We rode out together, Caroline. To the village and back for a pint of cider at the Arms. That is hardly a romantic interlude."

Roland daundered along as placidly as an old pony, Gavin in step beside him.

"Lately," Caroline said, "you have the same look in your eyes that you had before you went away. I thought going to the Hampshire house party might agree with you, but the look was still there when you came back. Now Amaryllis is married, Diana is planning her come out, Mr. Heyward is married *and* he's Lord Phillip now, and you have that gleam in your eyes again."

Gavin walked with his horse, recalling many such chats he'd had with Caroline when teaching her to ride. Put a quiet little girl on an equine, and she gained confidence in more than just her seat.

"What gleam would that be?"

"Restless, unhappy. I don't care for it. Trevor says you need to indulge your manly humors, and I know what that means, Gavin, but you aren't calling on Tansy, which would address *that* problem, if it even is a problem."

Stop growing up. Just stop. "You are trying to shock me. That is usually Diana's tactic, when she isn't murdering everybody's peace in the key of C major."

"Diana is a talented musician. Why do we all pretend she's only making noise? I could practice until Domesday and never be half as good as she is."

Gavin heard the unspoken lament: *I'm not good at anything. I'm not grown up and brilliant like Lissa. I'm not pretty and charming like Di. I'm not sweet and kind like Mama. I can't recite all the plays by heart like you.*

"I suspect Di fortified herself by controlling the keyboard when she couldn't control anything else," Gavin said.

"Like you ride Roland hell-bent all over the shire?"

Caroline sat atop the horse, to all appearances just a girl enjoying an impromptu pony ride, not the oracle of Crosspatch Corners she'd apparently become.

"If Roland trains carrying my weight, he'll have an easier time with a lighter jockey on the race courses."

Caroline drew Roland to a halt and glowered at the person she'd once called her favorite sibling in the whole world. "Are you planning to leave again? Will you one day ride Roland straight to Bristol and take ship for America? I bet he'd win every race in every colony if you did."

They call themselves states now. "I thought you all knew where I was, Caroline. I believed you were refusing to reply to my letters, that you'd closed ranks against me. I envisioned you larking about Bath and Lyme Regis and buying out the shops in London. The lawyers lied to me as skillfully as they lied to Mama and Lissa. I am sorry, and it won't happen again. They aren't our lawyers anymore, and I'm not going anywhere."

She urged Roland to resume his progress. "See that you don't."

A world of injured feelings lurked in those words. If Gavin hadn't spied his youngest sister in her tree, how much longer would she have nursed that pain in silence?

"You look like Lissa when you're in a temper." Gavin hadn't noticed the likeness before.

"My hair is too red. Her hair is Titian. I have freckles."

"Because you don't bother with a bonnet, and red hair is unique. Of all the guests Lissa has invited, I've seen none with red hair."

"Grandmama keeps telling me it's time to put my hair up. She says that as if putting my hair up won't send Di into fourteen takings and three fortissimo F minors. Do you know, Diana has a calendar counting down to Easter of next year? She crosses off the days, one by one, and makes Trevor speak French with her. She's getting quite good at French too."

Gavin saw with painful clarity how badly Caroline's universe had been knocked off its pins and that he'd delivered the first, hardest blow to her sense of security. And no, he hadn't known about Diana's calendar, though he'd conversed with her in French enough to have seen that change sitting in plain sight.

"As the head of the DeWitt family, I declare you old enough to put up your hair if you want to, Caroline. I will even insist upon it if you ask it of me. Diana can take out her F minors on me for making the decision. Do you want to put up your hair?"

Say no. Say you are much too young to put on such airs.

"I've been practicing," Caroline said, turning Roland onto the path to Twidboro Hall. "I can manage a bun, provided I use a thousand pins. My hair is so thick."

"Amaryllis started off with two thousand hairpins. We had to send a wagon to London for them, and when she made her come out, her slippers alone required a pack train."

The smile Caroline bestowed on him broke his heart. Part girl, part former girl. Not a grown woman, but some fey, fetching creature who'd once been Gavin's baby sister.

"You should write a comedy," she said. "Di could pen you an overture, and you could cast me in the boy parts. I'll tell you something else for free, brother of mine."

Nobody else called him that. "You'll tell me I have the smartest, kindest, most wonderful sisters in the world?"

"I'll tell you that when you came back from your pint of cider with Mrs. Roberts, you didn't have that restless, unsteady, getting-ready-to-bolt look on your face."

Ye gods, Mayfair Society was in for a shock a few years hence. "Was I making sheep's eyes at her?"

"No, and she wasn't making them at you, but you both rode right under my tree, twice, and you never saw me, even though I waved at you and Roland shied. I think Mrs. Roberts likes you, but you mustn't marry her if that means you move to Hampshire and I will never see you again."

Caroline had tried for a teasing tone, but Gavin's heart knew better. "If I did marry Mrs. Roberts and moved to Hampshire, you would always be welcome to visit, and if you decided to disdain my company, I'd kidnap you by dark of night and spirit you away on my fire-breathing steed."

"You are so silly." Relief lurked behind a fine showing of sibling exasperation.

"That is no way to address the head of your family, Miss Caroline."

She stuck her tongue out at him, tapped Roland lightly with her heel, and—sitting half aside in a man's saddle, only one foot in a stirrup—cantered off without a backward glance.

In another year, she might be too adult to attempt that bit of mischief. Gavin desperately hoped not, and he made a promise to himself that he'd ride out with Caroline and with Diana, separately, at least once a week.

Assuming they had the time to spare him.

As for that bit about manly humors being out of balance, the reasons to toss *our marquess* into the Twid just kept adding up.

"I don't understand why Mr. DeWitt didn't warn you, is all." Timmens spoke around a pair of hairpins, both of which she then jammed into Rose's chignon.

"Ouch."

"Sorry, ma'am, but we can't have you coming undone in company."

The implication, that Rose had come undone in private, was surely not intentional. Rose surveyed herself in the vanity's folding mirror and silently pronounced her appearance above reproach. Demure, widowly, boring.

She stood and took her bottle of lemon scent to the window. "Perhaps Mr. DeWitt does not know that traveling players are to join the house party."

"He knows," Timmens muttered, tidying up the vanity and extracting a gold bracelet from Rose's jewelry box. "If I can believe the housekeeper, who had it from the Lark's Nest housekeeper, who had it from Lord Phillip's Frenchie valet, Lord Tavistock has hired the self-same bunch Mr. DeWitt went off with when he left home two years ago. Dryden's Players. I hoped to never see that lot again."

Drysdale's Players. One didn't correct Timmens over trivialities when she was sharing intelligence from belowstairs.

"I wasn't aware the acting troupe had given offense among the servants." Rose dabbed scent on her wrists and, because she was feeling a bit defiant, applied a touch behind her ears as well. She had also hoped never to see Drysdale's Players again, but how did Gavin feel about this development?

"They get above theirselves, actors do. Don't argue with me on that score, ma'am. Little better than strolling strumpets, I always said. You'll want this bracelet to give that dress a bit of color. Aubergine is so somber, though the color flatters you."

Aubergine had been Rose's first step beyond mourning, a substantial, pretty shade that could stand up to black or go nicely with cream and gold.

"If I'm to wear the bracelet, I should probably wear the locket as well," Rose said, though the locket—small and heart-shaped—was nearly girlish in its simplicity.

"Sorry, ma'am," Timmens said, holding the bracelet open between two hands. "I wasn't able to find that particular bauble. I'm sure it will turn up once we're back at Colforth Hall."

"I dearly hope so." Rose held still while Timmens fastened the bracelet around her wrist. The bracelet had been a gift from her departed mother, the locket—complete with a miniature of Dane's profile—had been another one of his peace offerings. The two items didn't match exactly, but Rose wore them as a set anyway.

Mama had doted on Dane, and he'd flattered her shamelessly.

"Your shawl," Timmens said, stepping back and retrieving a black lace article Rose hadn't asked to have packed.

"Let's have the cream instead," Rose said. "For a summer evening, with gold jewelry, the lighter color appeals."

Timmens wrinkled her nose. "You're sure? That Mrs. Booker is a widow too. She might like to know she's not the only one who lost the love of her life."

Dane had not been the love of Rose's life, but Timmens was loyal to his memory. "Mrs. Booker's spouse died at least five years ago. I haven't seen her in anything approaching weeds since we arrived. The cream shawl, please."

"Aye, ma'am." Timmens draped the requested article around Rose's shoulders. "You stay up with the ladies as late as you like. I'll be waiting."

"No need for you to go short of sleep. I can undress without assistance, one of the beauties of this ensemble. You are to seek your bed and enjoy a pleasant night's rest. I'll ring in the morning when I arise."

Timmens made a great production out of refolding the black shawl. "If you say so, ma'am." A world of judgment lay behind that seeming politesse. In Derbyshire, Rose had all but forbidden Timmens to leave the servants' hall, the better for Rose to enjoy privacy with Gavin DeWitt. Timmens had repaid Rose with months of baleful lamentations.

If only you hadn't gone so peculiar on me, ma'am.

If only you hadn't taken such odd notions, missus.

If only you'd let me give that actor fella a piece of my mind.

"Timmens, Gavin DeWitt doesn't even bide here."

"A man can get up to very great mischief indeed when off his home turf." Timmens disappeared into the dressing closet on that parting shot, and Rose let her go. Scolding a maid for loyalty and protectiveness was bad form, and Timmens would simply retaliate with silent recriminations and forced good cheer.

She does a good job. She's loyal. Dane's defenses of Timmens still rang in Rose's ears, and in this case, Dane had been right. Somewhat right.

Not entirely wrong.

Rose made her way down to the terrace, where guests were assembling prior to supper, which was being served under a long white tent set up in the park beneath the formal parterres.

"Punch, ma'am?" The footman was older than his London counterparts, and homelier, and his smile was friendlier too.

"Is this Lady Phillip's signature raspberry recipe?"

"Champagne with some raspberry cordial, I believe. We're certainly enjoying our portion in the hall."

Rose took a glass. "If you come across my lady's maid, Timmens, please exhort her to try some. I vow raspberries were never put to a better use."

"I'll do that, ma'am." The footman assayed a slight bow, even holding his tray, and glided off.

Rose was considering joining the circle around Lord Phillip, whom she liked insofar as she knew him, when Gavin DeWitt appeared at her elbow.

"What a wonderful color on you," he said, "and you have dressed to match the punch. Good evening."

"Mr. DeWitt." He made a fine picture himself in his evening attire. Rose kept that thought to herself. "No punch for you?"

"I know to go slowly with Hecate's brew. In warm weather, it's easy to overdo the libation." He offered his arm. "Shall we admire the privet, or whatever one does while waiting to be seated al fresco?"

The privet hedges had all been trimmed to waist height or below, which showed off blooming beds of salvia, geraniums, hollyhocks, and daisies.

"Let's tarry among the lavender borders," Rose said. "The scent is marvelous, and soon enough those borders will be trimmed back."

"Harvested, you mean," Gavin said, escorting Rose down the terrace steps. "*Tempus fugit.* I gave Caroline permission to put up her hair today. That she needed my approval makes me feel antediluvian."

"That you gave it without teasing her, pretending to dither, or mocking her made her feel special," Rose said. "You took her situation seriously."

"She's taking it seriously. Caroline was biding in one of the maples by the towpath, and I rode right past her without seeing her."

They'd been able to do this in Derbyshire. Talk about anything and everything, no preliminaries, no bantering for the sake of establishing positions. Why hadn't Gavin mentioned that Drysdale's troupe was soon to arrive at Miller's Lament?

Did he not know? Not care?

He bent to snap off a sprig of lavender and held the buds to his nose. "I have learned of a development hatched up by my brother-by-marriage to enliven this house party. Tavistock intends that his surprise provide entertainment for the guests and impress his lady with his husbandly devotion." He passed over the lavender sprig. "I thought you deserved a warning."

Rose gave the lavender a sniff—what a magical, complex, bracing aroma—and recalled many similar informalities from *before*.

Timmens was doubtless watching from the window, and Rose resisted the urge to turn around and stick her tongue out in the general direction of the second-floor balconies.

"You refer to the impending arrival of Drysdale's Players," Rose said, more than a little relieved that Gavin had brought up the topic. "My maid mentioned this as I was dressing for supper."

"The estimable Timmens?"

"The same. The servants have been alerted, doubtless because beds must be readied and so forth. I don't particularly care to cross paths with Mr. Drysdale and his underlings again. What of you?"

"I'm to regard my time onstage as a misguided frolic, to gaze upon my youthful errors with a fond dismay. I was the best Shakespearean lead Drysdale had ever seen, as he himself admitted, but that was all so much folly."

Gavin was the best Shakespearean lead Rose had seen too. "Will you resent having Drysdale and his confreres paraded before you now?" Or did Gavin dislike rubbing shoulders with those who'd known him when he'd been dabbling in the role of male strumpet? Why was there no word for a *male strumpet*, because they apparently existed in life?

"I left Drysdale's group under something of a cloud," Gavin said as they crunched along the crushed-shell path. "I wanted more serious fare, and Drysdale wasn't about to demand that from his players, when they'd spent so much time and effort perfecting their farces and comedies. We remained civil, but there was a strain. Mrs. Drysdale in particular will likely have little use for me."

No mention whatsoever of having sought coin for intimate favors, but then, what had Rose expected? A full confession? An apology between the herbaceous borders? That Gavin had slunk off to the south in a fit of self-disgust?

Apparently, a fresh start meant a *fresh* start, complete with convenient lapses of memory.

Very well. "So you miss the stage, but not these players. I miss marriage, but not my husband as he was before he died."

Gavin came to a halt. "You adored your husband. His death devastated you."

If Gavin had been playing a role up north, so had Rose. In part because of her experiences in Derbyshire, she could—in some circumstances, at some times—put the role aside. She'd come to that realization only recently and was still pondering its significance.

"The manner of Dane's death was lamentable," she said. "An overturned curricle while galloping down his own driveway, two days without regaining consciousness, and no heir of the body left behind. He was nonetheless in that curricle and three sheets to the wind, again, because what gave him joy lay in London and not in Hampshire with me."

Gavin snapped off another sprig of lavender and twirled it between his fingers. "He was drunk at the ribbons?"

Rose abruptly felt ancient and exhausted. "By then, he was always drunk. He was bitterly disappointed, and spirits offered him oblivion, or so my mother claimed. He and I had quarreled—he was in no fit state to manage a vehicle, and I begged him not to make the attempt."

Mama had also said that Rose should take the shame of her marital failings to her grave, to confide in no one, and tend to Colforth Hall as conscientiously as possible in Dane's memory.

Mama hadn't been married to the man. "You need not say

anything," Rose went on, "but I wanted the truth aired between us, lest you... be deceived."

Gavin tucked his sprig of lavender into his lapel. "To guard one's dignity, and the dignity of a departed spouse, is not a deception. You were and are entitled to your privacy, and you deserved much better from your husband."

She'd expected him to offer some polite platitude made substantial by his sincere gaze and beautiful diction, not... not understanding. Not judgment of Dane.

"For the most part, I can manage well enough. I'm fine. I understand what's expected of me, and I know my lines. But sometimes..."

Gavin's smile was wan. "You want to curse and rail at the night sky, to fling profanities to the heavens, and tempt the wrath of fate with your honesty."

Also to throw a few slippers at Dane's portrait. "Very Shakespearean, Mr. DeWitt."

Whatever Gavin might have said next was obliterated by the third dinner bell. Rose lined up at the buffet, her partner for the evening to be Miss Peasegood, while Lady Phillip appropriated Mr. DeWitt, who politely winged his elbow.

He'd meant to warn Rose about the invitation to Drysdale's Players, but Rose had not meant to admit the truth of Dane's passing to anybody. Why confide that to Gavin DeWitt, of all people?

A fresh start, indeed.

But upon what?

CHAPTER SEVEN

"I gather Phillip told you?" Hecate murmured as Gavin accompanied her to a small table on the river side of the supper tent. "Your old chums will be doing a few scenes from *A Midsummer Night's Dream* for us, among other offerings. Tavistock meant to see that you were warned, but he's busy playing host."

Gavin did not know Hecate well, but he'd had several days in Hampshire to observe her at close range. She had a thespian's ability to control her features, voice, and posture such that what information she gave away, she usually meant to convey.

Not always. The softness in her gaze when Phillip was in the room was likely beyond her control, as was the genuineness of her smile. She was dignified, but honest, and Gavin liked that about her.

"Phillip mentioned that Drysdale and his troupe would be providing some entertainment," Gavin said, assisting the lady into her chair. "I'm sure your guests will enjoy the diversion."

He took his seat, which allowed him a view of the other diners. He and Hecate occupied an open corner of the tent, while Rose and Miss Peasegood were about halfway down on the same side. Without doing anything fancy to her hair, in the plainest frock, wearing only a simple bracelet, Rose outshone all the other women. The contrast had to do with that indefinable quality of *presence*, which actors coveted above all other traits.

"Whatever passed between you and Mrs. Roberts," Hecate said, whisking her table napkin across her lap, "you still care for her."

The situation was much, much worse than mere caring. "Mrs. Roberts is an estimable lady, and our views march on many matters. I take it Lord Phillip has been telling tales out of school?"

"Don't be fanciful. Phillip would never betray a confidence. I watched you and Mrs. Roberts in Hampshire. She could have wrangled a marriage proposal from Uncle Nunn, a cordial and platonic union, but it was you she watched when nobody was looking. Let's have some of that punch, shall we? This batch turned out exceptionally well."

Punch, indeed. Hecate's Uncle Nunn, known to any outside the family as the Earl of Nunn, was an upright fellow of significant self-regard and even more significant acreage.

Gavin passed over one glass and held up the second. "To successful gatherings." *That ended soon and without drama.*

"I expect this gathering will be successful," Hecate said. "The guest list all but formed itself." She cut a slice of rolled-up ham and commenced eating.

"How does a guest list form itself?"

"Amaryllis suggested we start with Lady Iris and Miss Peasegood, who are cousins. They expressed great fondness for Mrs. Booker, who was married to another cousin, and opined that Mrs. Booker was particularly close to a neighbor in Mayfair..."

"Lady Duncannon?"

"The very one, and so it went. The guests know each other better than their hostesses know the guests. A curious situation, but off to a congenial start."

Gavin surveyed the food on his plate, the usual artful presentations of cold meat, cheese, two slices of pale bread, some sort of peach-garnished crème brûlée tart. Simple, delectable summer fare for which he had little appetite.

Rose had not loved her husband as Gavin had believed she had. She had esteemed Dane, clearly, but she'd also... resented him. His death had left her with guilt and more resentment, and all that romance up in Derbyshire had been about more than a first attempt at merry widowing.

When she'd served up that confession, Gavin had wanted to take her in his arms and... what? Comfort her, of course. He knew what it was to resent close ties that one also valued, but he'd also wanted to—

"You should eat something," Hecate said. "At supper, one usually partakes of the food. Mrs. Roberts will still be there if you happen to look away for a moment."

Gavin put a cube of cheese into his mouth. Lark's Nest cheddar. He recognized the nutty undertones and the smooth tang on the tongue.

"You are smitten," Hecate said. "No shame in that. I am so smitten with Phillip... I thought romance diminished us, and diminished women in particular. I have no patience with gushing ninny-hammers and bad poetry. But when I contemplate the vast generosity of a universe that put my husband into my life... I am humbled and invincible both. I gather you feel vanquished rather than invincible?"

Rose had been able to converse for hours on so many topics. She was well-read, she'd taken a keen interest in her husband's estate, and she followed politics, not only in England. The ongoing national French spectacle fascinated her—could a monarchy ever develop fresh roots in soil where a republic had been planted?—and she was an avid student of natural philosophy.

And more impressive than all of that, Rose had the gift of silence. Long intervals of simple affection, of lying hand in hand on a blanket and watching stars wheel slowly across the firmament. Long, quiet walks. Peaceful hacks.

Good God, I've pined for her.

"I was smitten," Gavin said. "I got over it. How are the plans coming for Phillip's conservatory?"

"He and Tavistock argue regularly over design, because they are both adding conservatories to their homes. They will purchase the glass and frames and so forth together, the better to save money. I don't suppose Twidboro Hall would like to expand its conservatory?"

"You would have to ask Mama." She had commanded Vicar's company at supper and was in fine good looks. Caroline—hair in a lovely coronet—was at the table graced with Phillip's presence, while Diana was in an earnest, if somewhat awkward, French conversation with the good-natured Lady Duncannon.

"And your mother," Hecate replied, starting on her tart, "would refer me to you, because Twidboro Hall will someday be yours. Have you considered buying your own place rather than wait for that day?"

"I have, but biding with my family is a priority now. Grandmama is getting on, they've missed me, and I've missed them."

"And you don't want the bother of tending yet still more acres. Phillip delights in making Lark's Nest prosper. Tavistock is enthralled with the possibilities here at Miller's Lament, while you...?"

"Confer regularly with my steward, gallop the countryside by the hour, and try to avoid any discussion that focuses on bonnets or calf scours. The idea of having more land to manage... I can't say it appeals."

Hecate treated him to a frown, which presaged more keen insights Gavin was in no mood to hear. When he'd fortified himself with another sip of punch, she swiveled her focus in the direction of the back terrace.

"Who is that?" Her question was semi-annoyed.

Gavin watched the figure coming down the steps and knew, at a distance of thirty yards, precisely which personage was making an entrance now, when all the guests were seated, well before the buffet was sent back to the kitchen and while plenty of golden light slanted across the gardens.

"That is Hammond Cicero Drysdale the Third, scion of a great acting family, consummate thespian, and all-around gracious addition to any party."

"You don't care for him?"

"It's impossible not to like him, but think carefully before you trust him. Cissy, as he's known to his familiars, will upstage his own wife—I've seen him do it—and then apologize so graciously in the green room that you almost forget you wanted to strangle him by the end of the first act."

"Almost," Hecate muttered. "He's a good-looking devil. Going distinguished without losing his roguish dash."

Drysdale made his entrance according to the time-honored formula of leading men. Pause in three-quarter profile a few steps onto the stage, or into the tent, in the present case. Peruse the audience with friendly dignity, perhaps even nod by way of a bow at large, then be about the business of sweeping up to the hostess and graciously capturing her attention.

Cissy was still looking very much the part—a touch of gray at otherwise dark temples, jaw still firm, figure trim, muscular, and tallish. His eyes were a startlingly vivid blue, and his smile would have given Helen of Troy reason to doubt her devotion to Paris.

"He works at being a good-looking devil," Gavin observed. "Diana never fussed over her coiffure as carefully as Drysdale polishes his appearance on opening night, and the rest of the company swears he married Mrs. Drysdale not for her fine ability onstage—she is very talented—but for her skill with a needle. She can turn the proverbial sow's ear into a silk purse." And where was dear Gemma? She rarely let Cissy out of her sight for long, though he appeared to be a faithful, if not always loyal, husband.

Drysdale made a very pretty fuss over Amaryllis's hand, and a footman was sent scurrying off in the direction of the buffet and punchbowl.

"She'll introduce me," Hecate said, patting her lips with her napkin. "Has anybody ever told you that your sister is a devious wretch?"

"Nobody had to tell me," Gavin said as Amaryllis gently steered Drysdale between tables on a path toward their table. "Prepare to be unrelentingly charmed, my lady."

"Heaven defend me."

Gavin stole one last look at Rose, who remained in conversation with Miss Peasegood. The expression of polite interest, the slight smile, the way Rose appeared to consider what Miss Peasegood was maundering on about—that was all playacting.

By the set of her shoulders, by her unwillingness to spare Drysdale so much as a glance, Rose conveyed displeasure in his presence. Drysdale hadn't noticed her yet, and he would not pass up an opportunity to convey that he had friends and acquaintances among the guests.

Gavin would spare her that nuisance. He'd spare her any inconvenience or trifling bother, because he was an idiot and a fool. He'd missed her, he was protective of her, he desired her, and worst of all, he was still beyond smitten with her.

"How did you meet?" Miss Peasegood asked.

Rose took a bite of her cream tart rather than stare at Hammond Cicero Drysdale slobbering over Lady Tavistock's hand.

"I was a guest at a Nunnsuch house party earlier this year, and Lord Phillip and his prospective bride were also in attendance. I'd crossed paths with Miss Hecate Brompton in Town, though we weren't at that point what I'd call friends."

Rose wasn't sure how Lady Phillip regarded her now, but friends was becoming a possibility.

"Not her ladyship," Miss Peasegood said. "How did you meet Mr. DeWitt? You have taken every opportunity to glance his way without appearing to do so. He has barely taken his eyes off you, if it's any consolation."

The assembled guests were of that strata that spent half the day tending to correspondence, and if Rose lied to Miss Peasegood, she'd likely be found out. Somebody's cousin kept in touch with somebody else's neighbor in Town, who was always exchanging letters with somebody else's friend from finishing school...

"I crossed paths with Mr. DeWitt at another house party," Rose said. "Lady Rutherford was our hostess, up in Derbyshire the year before last. I was reading, or trying to read, Wordsworth, because one is supposed to read and quote him, though at the time..."

"The poet struck you as self-absorbed and pretentious. What woman has time to *wander lonely as a cloud*, for pity's sake—except in the symbolic sense? Few of us are even permitted to walk in solitude, but do go on. I can wax very opinionated. I trust you find that nearly impossible to believe."

Miss Peasegood was poking fun at herself, though she'd hit upon the very points that had annoyed Rose so much about Wordsworth's verse.

"I was in the music room, where I hoped nobody would have thought to look for me. I'd taken a window seat, the better to enjoy the natural light, when Mr. DeWitt came in. The door was open. There was no reason for him not to spend an hour or so practicing his pianoforte or harp or whatever."

"But he invaded your sanctuary?"

"No, he did not." Rose thought back to that cool, blustery morning, the occasional leaf smacking softly against the panes at her back, while the house itself remained quiet. "He waited for me. Stood by the door in silence while I finished the stanza I was trudging through. He knew to wait. To spare me apologies, greetings, any sort of interruption, until I'd completed the poem."

"Patience is a virtue. I have a cousin named Patience, as it happens. I enjoy a surfeit of cousins. Did you and Mr. DeWitt embark on a great literary dialogue?"

"We did not, not then. When I looked up, he was smiling at me. We'd been introduced at some point." Rose did not say that he'd been a traveling player. "His gaze held such... such sympathy. As if he knew I'd been imposing some duty poetry on myself, and he understood how easily even one imbued with literary fortitude can be distracted from such a task. He offered a smile of commiseration, humor, and understanding."

"I'll grant you Mr. DeWitt is attractive, but I haven't seen him smiling much."

Rose hadn't either. "You'll know the smile I mean if he ever graces you with it. He becomes an ally with that smile, against all the foibles the flesh is heir to."

At the end of the tent, Drysdale was making a fuss over his introduction to Lady Phillip. Gavin, standing next to Drysdale, did the pretty, looking gracious and handsome and nearly bored.

He was such an accomplished actor. Too accomplished.

"Did Mr. DeWitt bow and withdraw on that rascally smile?" Miss Peasegood asked.

Not rascally. Understanding, self-deprecating, humorous. Almost... *tender*. "He did not. I put Mr. Wordsworth aside and smiled back."

"House parties do offer opportunities to form new friendships, don't they?" Miss Peasegood finished her punch and set the glass down. "Let's ride to the rescue, shall we?"

She was on her feet and wending between tables before Rose could retort with a hearty, "I'd rather not." Gavin DeWitt was the equal of Hammond Drysdale, at least when it came to opening scenes and public introductions.

Rose nonetheless followed Miss Peasegood to the end of the tent, where Drysdale still had Lady Phillip's hand in his.

"... for this wonderful opportunity to renew our acquaintance with our dear Galahad," Drysdale was saying. "Though I suppose he's DeWitt now, isn't he? Gavin DeWitt."

"I never did care for the stage name," Gavin replied. "I always felt

I was inviting dragons to pop out of dungeons with a name like that. Mrs. Roberts, I believe you know Mr. Drysdale. Miss Peasegood, might I see to the courtesies?"

The moment called for simple adherence to social protocol, but Miss Peasegood refused to oblige. She turned her azure gaze on Drysdale, and her demeanor, so amiable a few moments earlier, turned glacial. Not all dragons emerged from dungeons, apparently.

She did not extend her hand. "You may."

"Miss Zinnia Peasegood," Gavin said, "might I make known to you Mr. Hammond Drysdale, principal and manager of Drysdale's Players. He joins us in the capacity of both guest and entertainer, as I understand it. Drysdale, Miss Zinnia Peasegood, late of Mayfair, I believe."

Lady Phillip, who as a co-hostess might have intervened for the sake of the introductions, remained seated. Lord Phillip was watching from three tables away, while Lady Tavistock was in close conversation with her husband.

Lady Tavistock was not smiling. Miss Peasegood was not smiling. Even Drysdale had put away his smarmy ware, while Gavin was looking relaxed and preoccupied.

"And what repertoire do you intend to grace us with here in Berkshire?" Rose asked before the whole tent went silent.

Drysdale affected a quizzical air. "I have yet to discuss that menu with my hostesses. Every gathering is different, every audience is different, and this is a unique assemblage, if I understood Lord Tavistock's invitation. Perhaps Galahad, I mean, DeWitt, will have some suggestions?"

Gavin put his hands behind his back. "I wouldn't think to trespass on that terrain. Lady Phillip and Lady Tavistock will have ample guidance for you, I'm sure."

Lady Phillip popped to her feet. "I should alert the household staff that Mr. Drysdale has arrived. You come as something of a surprise, sir, though I trust we will enjoy adding you to the guest list."

Lady Phillip, in what amounted to near rudeness, swanned off, collected her husband, and walked with his lordship up into the formal parterres.

A footman hovered one table away, tray in hand. Rose was on the point of offering to share a table with Mr. Drysdale—Gavin assuredly should not have to suffer that chore—when Miss Peasegood took Mr. Drysdale's arm.

"While our hostesses adjust to what will undoubtedly be a near doubling of the guest list, why don't I find you a table, Mr. Drysdale? You can regale me with tales of your misspent youth and impress me with your literary acumen."

Mr. Drysdale looked to Gavin, who was absorbed with consulting his pocket watch.

"I'd be honored." Drysdale managed to make the platitude sound sincere, and Rose felt nearly sorry for him. The rest of the guests watched as he and Miss Peasegood settled at an empty table, while Rose wondered what that little exchange had been about.

"Humor me," Gavin said, putting away his watch and winging his arm. "I am in the mood to hit something. Hard."

"Drysdale?"

"I will settle for a wooden ball. The pall-mall court is on the west side of the house."

Rose accepted his escort, glad for any pretext to leave the tent. "You knew he was coming."

"I did, you did, Phillip and Hecate did, but somebody apparently forgot to tell my sister. Tavistock might find he has a hammock to himself tonight."

"I gather Drysdale arrived early?"

Gavin glanced back at the tent, which gleamed white in the evening light. "He must be the advance party. He will decide on rehearsal spaces, what scenes will be performed, whether and how guests will participate, and which footmen and maids can be bribed."

Money again. Always money. Coin had featured in Rose's marriage, and coin was never far from Society's mind.

"What need has Drysdale of bribes?"

"He might not, but he believes that a good performance is ninety-nine percent preparation. Having allies and enemies sorted before opening night is simply how he thinks. I don't believe Miss Peasegood cares much for actors putting on airs or making entrances before their proper cue."

Gavin led Rose from the path bordering the garden and took a walkway around to the side of the house. A wooden cart sat near a low fountain, mallets, balls, and wickets neatly stacked. Sheep or goats had trimmed the grass nearly to carpet smoothness, and a few wickets had already been set up.

"The thought of smacking the daylights out of something does appeal," Rose said, hefting a mallet. "I thought you handled Drysdale's posturing with a nice blend of amusement and boredom."

"I was aiming that direction. If I never hear the name Galahad again..." He chose a mallet and selected a ball. "Ladies first. A few practice swings."

He set the ball on the grass, and Rose considered options.

"Miss Peasegood muttered something when Drysdale made his bow to Lady Tavistock." She swung the mallet back and forth at nothing, then took a stance an appropriate distance from the ball.

"Something you overheard?"

"I don't know as I was meant to, or meant to understand what I heard, but yes: '*Hic incipit pestis*.'"

"Here begins the plague. A tomb inscription from Stratford-upon-Avon, but I forget who the poor wretch was who earned it."

"Not a tomb inscription, but written in the church register to mark the burial of Oliver Gunn in July of 1564."

"The Bard would have been a newborn about then. Right now, I don't give a Shakespearean insult for what troubled Miss Peasegood."

"Something displeased her." Rose sank her weight into her heels, took a steadying breath, and fixed her eye on a spot about ten yards distant. In another half hour, the shadows would be too dense to allow for play, but this notion of smacking a few balls had been inspired. "One minute, Miss Peasegood and I were chatting easily. The next, she was charging off."

"Rose?"

"Hmm?" She took aim, let the weight of the mallet amplify her backswing, and—

"I want to kiss you."

The mallet connected with a gratifying whack. The ball flew past its intended mark and barreled through the tall privet marking the boundary of the yard. Rose watched her trial shot disappear and desperately hoped—and feared—she'd heard aright.

"Say something," Gavin muttered.

"Let's find the blasted thing lest it roll all the way down to the Twid." She marched off in search of her lost ball.

Gavin, swinging his mallet, followed after.

CHAPTER EIGHT

I want to kiss you. What sort of opening line was that? A fresh start should be characterized by honesty and decorum. Gavin's mouth was apparently fixed on the honesty part at the expense of the decorum.

For the benefit of any maids and footmen lingering at the windows, he ambled in Rose's wake, exuding the nonchalance of a man humoring a lady at her diversions.

Rose disappeared around the end of the privet hedge, her mallet propped on her shoulder.

Her walk gave away nothing. She always moved with a certain confidence, a brisk sense of intention that put Gavin in mind of generals before battle and hostesses before a ball.

She could kiss with the same sense of purpose. "We can pretend I did not just say that." He came around the end of the hedge and began poking about the greenery. The ball might have hit a root and bounced anywhere.

"I am much less tolerant of pretending than I used to be." Rose jabbed at the hedge a few yards away. "Do you resent this longing to kiss me, or are you hoping I will resent it for you?"

Poke, jab. *Swat.*

Gavin spied the ball, sitting innocently in plain sight ten feet behind where Rose was menacing the shrubbery.

"I am hoping that we can be truthful with one another." He pretended to search for the ball, because the hedge afforded them privacy, and if nothing else, this ridiculous conversation should be private. "I spent half of supper trying not to watch you slip a spoon between your lips and the other half hoping you'd take another bite of your tart."

"Where in blazes could that ball have got off to?"

Gavin moved along the hedge a few feet in Rose's direction. "We'll find it, though it's no great loss if we don't. I take it my sentiments are not reciprocated."

Rose shifted her search by two yards. "What sentiments? Desire is not a sentiment. It's a... a physical business, like hunger or fatigue. It's not supposed to mean anything."

Gavin peered through a thinning in the hedge. The supper gathering was breaking up, the guests wandering into the garden or down to the towpath.

"Did your husband tell you that desire was like scratching an itch? Like sneezing?"

The hedge suffered a particularly energetic jab. "Perhaps for him it was. We're losing the light, and the footmen will not thank us for adding to their duties in the morning."

Gavin closed the distance between them. "Rose, for me it's not like scratching an itch. When I say I want to kiss you, that is a wish of the heart, not simply of the body. I've missed you. If we are making a fresh start, you need to know that. I can play the part of Mr. DeWitt, your new acquaintance, but between the two of us, I want there to be honesty."

She left off abusing the hedge and studied him in the waning light, then brushed his hair back from his brow. A tidying rather than a caress. "There it is." She dodged around him and fetched the ball. "I gave it a good, hard whack, didn't I?"

"A veritable drubbing." As Gavin's nerves were taking a drubbing.

Rose set her mallet down next to the ball. "I want to kiss you too, Gavin DeWitt. This... this... preoccupation is not consistent with my plans. I had intended to stay good and disappointed in you, to put you in your place at least once a day, and then forget you."

Put him in his place for refusing her coin? Her words bewildered him, but he'd ponder them later. "I had intended to be civil, dignified, and indifferent," he said. "I find I cannot *be* indifferent to you... Not for all the leading roles on Drury Lane could I be indifferent to you."

She took his mallet and laid it in the grass. "If we yield to these feelings, it can't be like before, Gavin."

"Then you have them, too—the feelings?"

She grimaced. "It's as if the feelings have me. I didn't know you as well as I thought I did in Derbyshire, though of course, how could I? I made assumptions. I don't want to err like that this time. If we choose to enjoy each other's company now, we do so without expectations or conditions."

"No money." The very words were distasteful, but they needed to be said.

"Right. No money. No pretending. Honesty or nothing."

"A fine policy." Had she been embarrassed by the coins she'd left for him? Did she regret that course now? He could ask her that later —perhaps. "I honestly long to kiss you."

"There's something I want more, Gavin, though I'm sure we'll get to the kissing directly."

Could she possibly want a proposal of marriage from him? "Name it."

"Please hold me. I missed... Please just hold me."

He opened his arms. She came to him, standing very near, then leaning a little, then a little more, until she was secure in his embrace, and he was hugging her with all the gratitude and tenderness his heart could hold.

And while darkness stole over the land, and small creatures began their nocturnal explorations, she hugged him back.

Gavin waited, hoping Rose would initiate the kissing, and his patience was rewarded with a soft, easy buss of her lips on his cheek. He went still.

"Again, please," he said.

"You."

He obliged by kissing her cheek, as fencers greeted each other with matching salutes. In the kisses that followed, Gavin tasted caution and confidence, hesitance and hope.

He wanted to tell her to *let go*, to give him a drubbing in this regard, too, but he was also going carefully, matching this Rose with the more reckless woman he'd met months ago. Whatever had driven her boldness then, she'd mastered it, and the result was maddening.

She offered deliberate, nigh tactical kisses that inspired him to hold her more closely and explore the curves and hollows that had so fascinated him on first acquaintance. The angular jaw, the rounded hips. The silky hair and muscular shoulders.

"Don't be so careful," she whispered. "I won't break."

"I might." His control was growing more tenuous by the moment, and thus he eased his mouth from hers and gathered her to him. "I might shatter into a thousand pieces of warmth and joy and float away on the night breeze."

"None of that shattering business please. We haven't enough privacy."

Warmth and joy filled him as he rested his cheek against her temple. "We have just the right amount of privacy. Not enough to be foolish, but enough to be safe. You kiss differently."

"I'm out of practice." Her sigh sounded a bit aggrieved.

"Whether you've been practicing or not is your business. Your kisses are more serious."

She peered up at him. "Interesting that you should choose that word." She brushed his hair again, and this time her touch bore an element of intimacy. "You are more serious too. I'm not sure what to make of it. We were heedless before."

"I am not heedless now, Rose, but if we stay out here much longer, I won't answer for the consequences. I don't want to be precipitous with you. That way did not serve us well."

"No, it did not." She stepped back. "I can see that now. At the time... I was like that ball, sent flying along the ground, onward through the hedge, to fetch up heaven knew where. The landing was so very hard, and I thought my marriage had taught me all about hard landings."

"I'm sorry for that." He collected the ball and mallets. "I want to hear whatever you choose to share about the years you were married. You deserved better."

"I did." She fell in step beside him. "It's so much easier to admit that—I deserved better—than to try to make excuses, conjure up explanations, or pretend it wasn't so bad. Toward the end, it was awful. Then for him to die..."

"Dane was an adult," Gavin said as they came around the end of the hedge. "He brought his end upon himself. Got stinking drunk, called for his curricle, took up the reins, and whipped up his cattle. If you'd behaved like that, Rose, I guarantee you, your grieving husband would not be blaming himself for your death."

"But I wouldn't have behaved like that. I was too meek and proper and guilty and sad."

"Also too sensible, responsible, and honorable."

She stopped walking, gaze on the garden, where footmen were lighting torches. "You forgot stubborn."

"Determined. Determination is an estimable quality in anybody." Thank heavens the mallets and ball meant he could not reach for her hand, though he wanted to.

Rose smiled at him. "Right. I'm determined, not stubborn, head-strong, mulish, contrary, difficult, or dramatic. Determined. Just so. Are you still planning to introduce me to your mother and sisters?"

"Of course."

Amaryllis, Marchioness of Tavistock, née Amaryllis DeWitt, considered herself a patient woman. She'd had to be as the oldest daughter of a family making the difficult transition from shop to gentry and now—thanks to her recent marriage—to the peerage.

She'd learned to never put a foot wrong, never make the wrong comment, never say the right words in the wrong tone of voice or at the wrong moment. Perfection had been tedious and tiring, and marriage had changed life very much for the better.

Mostly.

"You meant to be helpful," she said again as she walked arm in arm with her marquess along the towpath. The guests had all turned back, while Amaryllis wanted to keep walking, all the way to Windsor. Perhaps to Bristol.

Whose idea was this blasted house party, anyway?

"Entertainments are the soul of a house party," Trevor replied. "I was sure nobody in Crosspatch had seen much Shakespeare."

"More than you think, thanks to Gavin, but our guests do not hail from Crosspatch, my lord."

Trevor took her hand. He was tall—Amaryllis was politely deemed statuesque—so the fit remained comfortable whether they were hand in hand or arm in arm. His height was one of many reasons why Amaryllis had been desperately smitten with him.

They *fit*, and they were temperamentally suited. Trevor valued brains and integrity, most especially in his wife. He wasn't a snob, though he'd been to snobbery born, and he'd exerted himself to the utmost to be a good brother to Phillip.

"You are my-lording me, madam. I'm truly in your bad books, aren't I?"

He had been, for about five minutes, and that apparently disconcerted them both. For the sake of the common weal, Amaryllis knew she should not let him off with a wifely demurral.

"You sprang not just one surprise guest on me, but a dozen of them. The players can't be treated like extra servants and expected to make do in the garrets or on cots in makeshift dormitories. These people have a profession." One Gavin had shared with them.

"We could put them up at the Arms."

"Even the Arms hasn't that many extra beds on short notice, and their custom would suffer if they had to turn away their regular coaching guests." Amaryllis was tired in body, but her mind was like an overwound clock, ticking madly away. "We can place the distaff with Hecate and Phillip, and I'm hoping Gavin can take in a few of the younger men. The Drysdales will bide with us, of course." But where to put them?

Miller's Lament was a work in progress, and while a great deal had been done to restore the old place to its former glory, it barely qualified as a stately home.

"I'd switch those arrangements," Trevor said. "Put the fellows with Phillip and Hecate, the ladies with your family."

"Because of Diana and Caro?"

"And because Twidboro Hall is more suited to housing females—you had the running of it, after all—while Lark's Nest was a bachelor abode for years. The staff, the kitchens, the amenities will all reflect the differing owners."

Off in the distance, a hound began a desultory barking at odd intervals. Fortinbras belonged to Lawrence Miller, and when Lawrence lingered at the Arms, Fortinbras stood guard on the inn's front stoop. Regardless of his billet, the old dog cried the watch when the mail coach was a mile from the village.

I love this place, and I love my husband. "That sort of thinking," Amaryllis said, "is helpful. You are right—Twidboro Hall is better suited to housing ladies—and you make this observation in private, when I have a chance to ponder its particulars. Springing a troupe of actors on me... Trevor, what were you about?"

A piano joined the hound, not Diana's usual fiery Clementi, but rather, a slow movement. Herr Beethoven. Diana was growing up, and Amaryllis was on hand to see it. She owed that to Trevor. She owed much to Trevor.

"I thought," Trevor said, "if I informed Gavin that his old friends had been invited, he'd tell you, and that would spoil my surprise. I let a few details slip to Phillip, who insisted we tell your brother, and then Drysdale made devilish good time out from Town—or so he claims—and here I am, with an unhappy wife and a brother-by-marriage who likely wants to toss me into the Twid."

Trevor stopped walking and faced Amaryllis. "Now that I think on it, the element of surprise might have been suggested by Drysdale. We corresponded at some length on dates and prices and possibilities."

"Unbeknownst to me." Amaryllis took the side path that led to Phillip's gazebo, which was more of a hermit's-grotto-cum-tree-house. The moon had risen, but she hardly needed illumination to find her way.

Trevor followed, and she heard a muttered French curse when he tripped over a tree root.

Good.

"Your *surprise* is like that root," she said. "Unexpected, troublesome. The tree means no harm, sending that root right across the path. Just the opposite—the tree is simply trying to find sustenance and stability. But you nearly went sprawling nonetheless."

She climbed the steps and settled on the bench facing the river. The gazebo had been Phillip's retreat, built on the bank of the Twid such that the front looked out over the water. The interior was mostly private, being open only on the Twid side, and provided some shelter from the elements.

"I read in here by the hour," she said. "Took naps, daydreamed. Phillip never once chided me for trespassing."

Trevor ducked his head to enter. "Did he ever join you?"

The smell was piney—cedar formed a good portion of the structure's interior—and the darkness made the moonlight on the water brilliant.

"Not in the sense you mean. In case you haven't noticed, your brother is shy. He was all but a recluse before you came upon him. Do have a seat."

The benches were padded, the night peaceful. Amaryllis's upset was fading—between Lark's Nest and Twidboro Hall, there really was no problem housing the players—and thus she could think more clearly.

"I never once consulted you about the guest list," she said.

"Or the menus, though I know all the latest French dishes."

Oh dear. "Or the entertainments, the sleeping arrangements, the appointments."

Trevor kissed her fingers. "The *anything*. You know every variation on my recipe for ale. You test the batches with me. You helped me choose where to start planting the hops and barley because you know this shire better than I know my own family tree. Your contribution is central to our success. I wanted to help with your success."

Amaryllis's husband had wanted to help and also to *be appreciated*. His father had had no use for him. Polite society had seen the young Marquess of Tavistock as nothing but a good catch. Trevor's brother had been a stranger to him, and the village merely wanted bragging rights to *our* marquess.

"I need you," Amaryllis said, resting her head on his shoulder. "I need you not as I need sound sleep and good food. I can manage on bad sleep and poor rations, but I need you if I am to be myself. To be whole. This dependency unnerves me."

"Ah." He looped his arm around her shoulders. "Bit of a change of plans?"

"A change of worlds."

"Would tossing me in the Twid make you feel less unnerved?"

A dip in the Twid would be heavenly, particularly with Trevor as a swimming partner, but the hour was growing late, and the whole business of dressing when damp...

"My nerves settle when you kiss me," Amaryllis said. "Or when I kiss you."

"My own nerves have grown a touch unreliable. I've bungled with my wife, you see, and her good opinion of me defines the best part of my happiness. I am sorry, Amaryllis. No more surprises, unless they involve boxes wrapped in silk ribbon or perhaps a lovely new mare who's up to your weight for heart and courage. I'd be most grateful if you'd demonstrate this business of settling the nerves with kisses."

How she loved him. Loved his humor and patience and affection and...

Amaryllis's nerves were on the way to being well and truly settled when a sound caught her ear. "Voices," she whispered.

Trevor's hands disappeared from her person. "Miss Peasegood," he whispered back, "and Lady Iris."

The women were speaking softly, but clearly unaware of Phillip's hideaway behind the rhododendrons.

"Mrs. Roberts prevaricated," Miss Peasegood said. "I asked when they'd met, and she at first regaled me with some tale of a Hampshire gathering at the Earl of Nunn's. I had to ask very directly about when she'd met DeWitt."

"One doesn't forget a man like that," Lady Iris muttered.

"He's apparently forgotten you."

"He was never supposed to notice me. Nobody was. That was the point. What did Mrs. Roberts say about him?"

Miss Peasegood sighed, as if preparing to recite her signature verse for dear old Auntie Patricia at Sunday supper. "She said, 'I was reading, or trying to read, Wordsworth, because one is supposed to read and quote him, though at the time...' and I commiserated, and then she went on, 'I was in the music room, where I hoped nobody would have thought to look for me. I'd taken a window seat, the better to enjoy the natural light, when Mr. DeWitt came in. The door was open. There was no reason for him not to spend an hour or so practicing his pianoforte or harp or whatever.'"

"Zinnia, get to the point."

"Be patient. I asked if he'd invaded her sanctuary. She replied,

'He waited for me. Stood by the door in silence while I finished the stanza I was trudging through. He knew to wait. To spare me apologies, greetings, any sort of interruption, until I'd completed the poem.' Then she went into raptures about his smile. She clearly does not suspect him of thievery, or worse."

"I'm not sure *we* suspect him. Delphine says his finances are quite in order."

They moved up the path, and the rest of their words were lost to the night.

"What on earth was that about?" Amaryllis murmured, rising. "Those are my guests, and they all but accused my brother of thievery. Gavin would no more steal than he'd come to divine services drunk."

Trevor rose as well and wrapped her in his arms. "Give them a chance to get back to the house. We can ask Gavin what he makes of this."

"He'll be insulted. He can't call Miss Peasegood out, but I certainly want to."

"Somebody's bracelet went missing, perhaps, or a few coins were mislaid. Let's not take on the armada over some unintentional eavesdropping. We'll keep an eye on those two and consult with Phillip and Hecate."

Amaryllis stepped back and studied her husband in the moonlight. "You don't like this any more than I do."

"I like it less. I heard some of the original exchange between Mrs. Roberts and Miss Peasegood—a trick of the evening breeze, a lull in the general hubbub. Have you ever before known somebody who could quote a supposedly casual conversation word for word without a single mistake?"

"Children quote their parents at the worst possible time. Caro is also something of a mimic... but not word for word, not a whole conversation. I do believe I am unnerved all over again."

Trevor, devoted husband and nobody's fool, set about thoroughly calming his marchioness's nerves, and she generously returned the favor.

"Beloved, I am wrestling with a conundrum." Phillip had returned from his nightly venture to the river without having bathed. Whatever conundrum vexed him, Hecate concluded that it troubled him still.

She joined him behind the privacy screen and perched on the stool in the corner. "What sort of conundrum?"

He worked up a lather on a square of wet flannel with a dollop of lavender soap. "There I was, in all innocence, making my way to the riverbank, intent on my nightly ablutions, only to find that my gazebo was occupied."

"You should keep it locked. Some naughty boy will take a notion to dive off the front and come to grief."

"The Twid is fairly deep there, part of the reason I chose that spot. Besides, we haven't any naughty boys in Crosspatch Corners, only devoted husbands, handsome swains, and devoted husbands-to-be."

He'd taken off his shirt, and when Hecate ought to have been attending to his words, she was instead focused on the gorgeous, muscular expanse of his back and shoulders.

"You truly are a work of art, Phillip."

"Then I'm a work of art not yet fit for his slumbers. Shall I shave?" He caught her eye in the mirror, and naughty did not begin to attempt to approach what Hecate saw there.

"Don't you dare shave." She adored the piratical air he acquired with a day's beard.

"I am your servant in all things. I made it halfway down the riverbank before I realized my gazebo was occupied by the marquess and his lady. I became an unwitting eavesdropper to an exchange of marital confidences."

"Awkward." Phillip was nothing if not shy.

"Touching, enlightening, and yes, a bit... Amaryllis and Tavistock sorted matters out nicely, muddling through the situation with Drysdale's surprise arrival. I was proud of them, but one cannot *say* that. They were making a fine business of a marital reproachment when Miss Peasegood and Lady Iris came along the towpath, deep in conversation."

"While you lurked in the bushes?"

"Half dressed and beset by the most persistent mosquito in all of Berkshire."

"You poor darling."

Another look, this one promising a very different sort of persistence. "Miss Peasegood recited her supper conversation with Mrs. Roberts word for word. I do not mean a close approximation, Wife, I mean better than any actor reciting rehearsed lines. She interrogated Mrs. Roberts about her impressions of our Gavin."

Phillip scrubbed his face, under his arms, and the back of his neck. Hecate had watched this ritual any number of times, and it still made her heart beat faster. She'd joined Phillip for his nocturnal swims occasionally, and a tin of soap became a vehicle for marital sorcery in his calloused and capable hands.

"Recounting chitchat over supper is idle gossip, Phillip. You missed a spot."

He sopped the flannel and wrung it out. "Any assistance would be greatly appreciated." He slapped the cloth gently into her hand.

Hecate rose and began slow passes across his shoulders. "What else did the ladies say?"

"They suspect Gavin DeWitt of being a thief. I was left with the impression Lady Iris has met him before. He did not recognize her. I believe we have a pair of lady thief-takers in our midst. When I scrub off at the end of the day, I am getting clean, a pleasant undertaking. When you do that... I want to be the cleanest fellow ever to crawl between the sheets."

Hecate reached around him and undid the drawstring of his

pajama trousers. "Gavin DeWitt is not a thief." She wore only a summer nightgown, which meant that little hug she bestowed upon her spouse pressed her breasts intimately close to his freshly washed —and damp—back.

"I would stake five acres of wheat that you are right, my dear: Gavin is not a thief, but I'd also have said he wasn't the sort to decamp without notice, having arranged a position for himself with a troupe of traveling players, in whose company he whiled away two whole years. He is a talented actor. Who knows what roles...? That feels..."

Hecate pushed the trousers over Phillip's hips to pool on the carpet. "Gavin is not a thief, but I have no doubt something was stolen. Something valuable. Why shouldn't women be thief-takers when women can be thieves?"

"Valid point. You are stealing my wits at this very moment."

"We can consult with Lady Duncannon. She knows every scandal, on-dit, and whisper passing through Mayfair. If some valuable necklace was purloined, she will know."

"I'm not sure we... can." He braced himself on the washstand, his shoulders rising with each inhalation.

"Almost done," Hecate said, leaning close to delicately swab Phillip's jewels. "You were saying?"

"God alone knows..." He stood straight. "Lady Duncannon's given name is Delphine?"

Another slow, gentle pass of the cloth. "It is."

"She was quoted as having had a look at DeWitt's finances. If you do that again..."

"Yes?"

"Please do that again. As often as you like."

He let her torment him for some moments before taking the cloth from her, muttering about revenge, and tossing her onto the bed like a laughing sack of wifely grain.

"We must speak more about what you've overheard, Phillip. This could be a problem."

"A far more pressing problem plagues me, your ladyship." He came down over her and gave the word *pressing* particular emphasis. "Did you know that a husband's unsettled nerves can be remedied by his wife's kisses?"

She drew her toes up his calf. "One hears rumors to that effect. Kiss me. We'll test the theory."

The theory was well and truly proven, and Hecate was drowsing blissfully on Phillip's chest when his earlier comments came back to her.

"If Lady Duncannon, Lady Iris, and Miss Peasegood are all involved in this thief-taking business, we ought to confer with Amaryllis and his lordship. They doubtless overheard much of what was said."

Phillip's hand, which had been caressing her hip in a delicious, slow rhythm paused. "Somebody ought to tell Gavin. I built that gazebo for him."

"What...? Oh, by the river. Why did he need a gazebo?"

"After his father died, he needed a place to escape his women-folk. He was little more than a boy, with a man's expectations thrust upon him overnight, and yet, he was not master of his own household. Nobody is at that age. I built the gazebo so he'd have a place to retreat and ponder the world. He took the Bard with him, as well as the philosophers, lurid novels, and a few poets. I suspect he learned to tipple and smoke there and caught more than a few naps."

Hecate kissed her husband on the mouth. "You are so kind, Phillip. Did Gavin ever thank you?"

"He thinks I built that gazebo for myself. I had the whole Lark's Nest manor house to rattle around in, not to mention miles of bridle paths to wander, and more solitude than one man needs in a lifetime. We'll let this be our secret, shall we?"

She subsided into the warmth and security of his embrace. "Somebody else is keeping secrets at this house party, maybe several somebodies. I object strenuously to the notion that Gavin is being spied on, but if we say anything..."

"First, I cannot imply to Amaryllis and Tavistock that I overheard the same conversation they did, or endless mortification will ensue, at least on my part. Tavistock appears to have no shame. Second, we know the spies are among us, and much insight might be gained by spying upon them."

"I don't like it, Husband. A house party is to be full of good company and enjoyable diversions. Not intrigue and whispering."

"I don't care for conniving and scheming either." Phillip resumed stroking her hip. "Nonetheless, Gavin is innocent. He has no need to steal, no history of stealing. Telling him that he's suspected of thievery will only add to his troubles, and for all his pleasant good cheer, he strikes me as a man with troubles enough."

In his usual fashion, Phillip had seen to the bottom of matters. Gavin was unhappy. Hecate didn't need to know him well to sense that, but he was also making some sort of progress with Mrs. Roberts. To imperil that budding romance with nasty rumors and insults... not done.

Not at my house party. Hecate fell asleep after making a slight correction to her silent vow. *Not at our house party.*

CHAPTER NINE

"Whacking balls about on the grass," Timmens said, giving Rose's pillow a thump. "The very sort of nonsense to while away a summer morning, though some prefer to play pall-mall in the evening."

Rose's joy in the day dimmed slightly. "Were you spying on me, Timmens?"

"I don't spy, but all manner of fine personages from fine families are here, ma'am. They all brought their fine servants. You'd best recall that the walls have ears and the windows have eyes. More tea?"

Somebody had seen Rose disappear behind the hedge with Gavin last evening and remarked that fact in the servants' hall.

What of it? She was a widow, Gavin was more than of age and eligible, and the ball had gone missing.

Rose sipped her tea and waited for an internal voice that sounded like Mama, or Timmens, or occasionally Dane, to reproach her. Instead, somebody tapped on the door.

"At this hour," Timmens muttered, giving the pillow a final smack before answering the door. "My lady." She curtseyed, and not just a hasty dip of the knees.

"Lady Duncannon." Rose set aside her tea and curtseyed as well. "Good morning."

"Let's have no more of that bobbing about like chickens, shall we? We must plot our strategy, Mrs. Roberts. I've chosen you for my team, and we'll want to get in our practice rounds before the other teams are stirring. Besides, I'm famished. I'm always famished, and I want first crack at the breakfast offerings."

Her ladyship was, like Rose, a widow. The similarity ended there. Rose considered herself of medium height, medium coloring, medium good family. Lady Duncannon was a countess, a peer in her own right, statuesque, with flaming-red hair, a soft Scottish burr, and a hearty laugh.

She did not put on airs, though she was not a woman to cross lightly.

"I am ready for breakfast," Rose said. She was also ready to quit Timmens's company.

"Excellent." Lady Duncannon slipped her arm through Rose's and set a brisk pace for the steps. "So what did you think of that Drysdale creature making a grand entrance and taking half the dessert course to do it?"

"I hadn't thought of it like that, but he did give the company a very long moment to appreciate his approach."

"Like cavalry charging infantry squares. My late husband was retired military. Excuse the battlefield analogy before breakfast."

They rounded the landing, and Rose heard a door close on the floor above.

"I do believe your pretty maid was eavesdropping," Lady Duncannon said, continuing their descent. "To be expected, I suppose. Somebody should tell her to close doors more quietly when she's about her surveillance. Drysdale did not impress me favorably. He should have taken a room at the inn for the night and come by in the morning. He's not expected until tomorrow at the earliest."

The advance guard, Gavin had called him, though how did Lady Ducannon know when Drysdale had been expected?

"And if the Crosspatch Arms hadn't any room," Rose replied, "then he should have begged a tray here and taken any available cot, until greeting his hostesses in the morning. Perhaps actors anticipate disrespect and must take evasive maneuvers."

Lady Duncannon crossed the foyer at the same purposeful gait. "Now I have you doing it, too, with the army talk. Let's blame my sainted spouse, shall we?"

"You've been widowed for some time?"

"Five interminable years. I've grown particular in my dotage, though my family insists I must take another husband. I agreed to marry Archie because he was a known quantity. We rubbed along well, and I was confident I could handle him. He had one job—to get me with child, boy or girl, made no difference—and he went to his grave without having achieved that goal. Not for lack of trying, mind. Archie was the determined sort."

"Not headstrong, obstinate, stubborn, or dramatic?"

Lady Ducannon grinned. "Of course not. He was a man. I, on the other hand, qualified for all of the above plus a few Erse terms generally reserved for goats and donkeys. You?"

"Mulish," Rose said, smiling back. "Ungovernable."

"Infernal," Lady Duncannon said, sailing into the breakfast parlor. "Unnatural, because keeping a lot of fat, bleating sheep and a few grouse moors from the crown's paws doesn't strike me as a pressing duty any more, though I suppose I will remarry one of these days. That is a gorgeous ham."

Rose made her way down the sideboard, though her portions paled beside Lady Duncannon's. Perhaps her ladyship viewed husbands and hams as occupying similar categories—both for assuaging appetites, both expected to meet certain criteria regarding quality.

"Let's eat on the west terrace," Lady Duncannon said, opening a cabinet in the sideboard and producing two trays, to the apparent consternation of the footman who'd just come through the door. "Plenty of shade there at this hour, and my antique complexion requires shade. We won't have to put up with Lady Iris rhapsodizing over herbs, or Miss Peasegood trying to correct her, though they are, of course, both very dear."

"Of course." And old King George was invariably described as good, though he was more than a bit mad. "I take it your family is concerned for your holdings if you leave no heir?"

"They are concerned for themselves," Lady Duncannon said, leading the way out of the breakfast parlor. "First, the shame—the unbearable, unspeakable shame—of a title reverting to the crown, isn't to be borne. I will be dead on that dark day, so what do I care? The second consideration is more important: The loss of my title will mean my siblings, in-laws, cousins, nieces, nephews, tenants, neighbors, and passing acquaintances can no longer trade on the reflected glory of association with the peerage. Can't have that."

"This matters to you."

They emerged into the terrace, into the gilded splendor of a summer morning. "Of course it matters. We're still clannish in Scotland, still look to our own of necessity. I thought this house party would be a respite from the usual polite whirl."

"Isn't it?"

Lady Ducannon set a course around to the shady side of the house. "With only the one bachelor to speak of, yes, it is. Mr. DeWitt is devilish good-looking, on the threshold of his prime, and quite well-heeled. He also doesn't have the sort of sniffy pretensions all the heirs, spares, and nabobs adopt, though he's a candle nabob as sure as whisky is good for the digestion. Ah, my compliments to our hostesses."

Lady Duncannon set her tray on a wrought-iron table on the narrow terrace that overlooked the pall-mall court. Rose did likewise and took a seat facing the hedge behind which she and Gavin had... reached a new and better understanding.

As if her thoughts had summoned him, a tattoo of distant hoofbeats signaled the progress of a rider galloping along the towpath.

Roland thundered into view across the park, a dark streak against the green foliage, his rider bent low over his neck.

"Mr. DeWitt cuts quite a dash in the saddle," Lady Duncannon said, spearing a bite of ham. "That colt is a fine specimen, though I must say his form is unusual."

"Roland runs best like that, a loose rein, nose low. Not how I'd like to approach a jump, but Mr. DeWitt knows his mount."

"And you know Mr. DeWitt."

Rose busied herself applying jam to her toast. Lady Duncannon had taken her time, but her approach to this topic had been as strategic as Drysdale's grand entrance the previous evening.

"I do, to some extent. We've crossed paths at various house parties. What of you? You seem quite congenial with all the ladies."

Lady Duncannon waited until Gavin and Roland had disappeared around a bend in the river. "We are half of us cousins, the other half friends and neighbors, of the sort you allude to. Our paths cross at house parties, in London during the social Season, in the spa towns, that sort of thing."

Lady Duncannon was lying and doing it well—with a liberal garnish of truths and half-truths. Dane had had the same gift, which he'd used to cover his Town expenses, his gambling debts, and his flirtations with the ladies of the neighborhood.

He'd lied for the usual self-serving reasons. What inspired Lady Duncannon's prevarications?

"You mentioned that Mr. DeWitt is quite well-heeled," Rose said. "Have you had occasion to consider becoming more closely acquainted with him?"

Lady Duncannon's smile for the first time acquired a hint of calculation. "I own part of a bank, Mrs. Roberts. The stereotype of the thrifty Scot is based on grim necessity. English ports were closed to us for far too long, and we nigh bankrupted ourselves trying to gain our own foothold in Central America. Then we wasted more coin in Jacobite uprisings—you notice I do not call them rebellions—and supporting our banished relatives on the Continent. I am in the habit of paying attention to who is well fixed and who is pockets to let. Then too, ladies in our situation must be wary of the fortune hunters, aye?"

Was that a reference to Dane? More prevarication? "Mr. DeWitt is not a fortune hunter."

"I agree, and yet, he remains something of a puzzle. I like puzzles. I also like winning at pall-mall, and my short game is nigh untouchable. My aim is wanting for the longer strokes, though. What of you?"

Rose let the subject of Mr. DeWitt drop and chatted amiably about pall-mall, straw hats, grades of wool, and the Marquess of Tavistock's budding brewery. Lady Duncannon allowed as how she might be persuaded to invest in such a venture—"You'll ne'er part an English mon from his ale, Mrs. Roberts"—but Rose wasn't fooled.

The purpose of this meal tête-à-tête had been to bring up Gavin DeWitt, cast him in a questionable light, and see how Rose reacted. Last night, the interrogation had come from Miss Peasegood, and Rose suspected Lady Iris might have a go at luncheon.

Which was just too blessed bad. Rose expected to share her lunch with Gavin himself and, when the occasion allowed, to share more kisses with him as well.

"Is Drysdale truly so inept at pall-mall?" Rose asked, "or is this, too, one of his performances?"

Gavin considered the question as the great actor pretended to sight down the handle of his mallet.

"Probably some of both," Gavin replied, just as Lady Iris sent a ball bouncing onto the terrace. "Cissy Drysdale plays a convincing fool, though those roles fell to me initially. Drysdale came down with a cold a few months after I joined the troupe, and as I was his understudy, I stepped into a lead. Things began to change after that."

Lady Duncannon had demanded that Gavin play for her group,

there being one fellow on each of the four teams, and Gavin graciously consented.

"Change how?" Rose asked.

Gavin bided with her and several other competitors in the shade of the tall privet while play rotated through the teams. The day wasn't oppressively hot, but he liked being near the hedge that had afforded him and Rose such lovely sanctuary the previous evening.

"For one thing, the audiences noticed me," Gavin said. "The other players noticed me too. I went from being the new boy twitted for form's sake to one of them who might move on to better things and remember them fondly." Though Gemma Drysdale in particular had gone sullen and watchful on him.

"Did you?"

"Move on to better things? When I left Drysdale's Players, I took on roles more suited to my abilities." He'd also traveled far from memories both sweet and bitter in Derbyshire. "Buffoonery and farce take skill. One must be silly but maintain a bit of distance from even the silliness, the better to laugh *with* the audience, to be in on the joke *with* them. I can do that, but I'd rather take up the difficult issues that dramatists can put before us. Then too, there's the challenge of making the language of Good Queen Bess's day intelligible. I relished that challenge."

A fuss ensued over where exactly Lady Iris's ball should be returned to the court. Much measuring of mallet lengths and considering of angles followed. Lady Duncannon, several yards off, discreetly nipped from a flask, and Tavistock defected from his team long enough to whisper something into his marchioness's ear.

Her ladyship laughed and brandished her mallet at him.

"My sister is in charity with her spouse again. One is relieved for the peace of Crosspatch Corners."

"Let's stroll a bit, shall we?" Rose said, offering him a suspiciously bland smile. "The referees will soon be quoting Marcus Aurelius over by the terrace."

Gavin happily obliged. In this situation, he would not take Rose's arm, much less her hand, but something troubled her besides the tedium of play. She'd been sending glances at the windows since choosing her ball and mallet.

"The ladies have been asking me about you," Rose said, pausing as if to admire a torch stand surrounded by thriving red salvia. "Asking me what I think of you. It happened at supper last night and again at breakfast."

"I'm the only bachelor in sight. Of course they'll ask about me."

"Not that sort of asking. Lady Duncannon has looked into your finances. She and Miss Peasegood both wanted the specifics of how I'd met you. Their interest did not seem benign."

"They aren't showing me any special attention." Or were they? Gavin thought back to the initial buffet, when Lady Iris had insisted on being introduced to him, then swanned off. Miss Peasegood had intruded on Drysdale's introductions at supper, and Lady Duncannon had dragooned Gavin onto her team.

Over by the terrace, Lady Iris had adopted the politely anxious air of a woman who didn't want to hold up play, while Drysdale and Lord Phillip again measured a mallet length below the single step that raised the terrace. Gallantry won over strict protocol, and her ladyship's ball was placed at an easy angle for her next wicket.

Her smile was self-conscious and convincing, but also...

"She's acting," Gavin muttered. "And that hesitant, bashful air... I have the sense I've seen Lady Iris before." In a different costume, in a different role.

"If you frequented Town between terms, you might have come across her. Could she have attended one of your performances?"

"Not likely."

Her ladyship, under the guise of tilting the brim of her straw hat, looked directly at him. Her smile shifted, and she waved politely in a manner that included Rose.

"She was watching us," Rose said, "and trying not to get caught at it. Gavin, what in blazes is going on?"

"Maybe nothing more than a little perfunctory nosiness." They had reached the far end of the hedge, and the temptation to nip around, out of sight of the other guests, to steal a hug, a kiss, even a clasp of hands... "Would you *mind* if the ladies were matchmaking?"

Rose's gaze went again to the house. "We were seen, last night. Somebody spied us taking our practice shots. My maid remarked it. I am the only guest on this side of the house, and Timmens implied she'd not been the one keeping watch. Vigils at darkened windows don't usually characterize matchmakers."

"If somebody's maid wanted privacy with one of Tavistock's footmen, they'd seek it on the west side of the house. Are you sure Timmens wasn't simply being protective of your reputation? She's something of a dragon where your good name is concerned." Gavin kept to himself the notion that Timmens herself might have been trysting. Those overly preoccupied with decorum in others were often the first to bend rules on their own behalf.

"Timmens does like to scold, you are right about that," Rose said, starting toward the court. "We'll be up next. Can you arrange to stroll the towpath with me this evening?"

That did not sound like a romantic invitation. "Of course. We're scheduled for a picnic supper if this tournament ever concludes, then Drysdale has agreed to entertain us with a few choice speeches. He was made for the speeches, for short recitations with all eyes upon him."

Rose swung her mallet idly as she walked along. "What were you made for, Gavin DeWitt?"

Loving you. He knew better than to speak the words aloud, but they resonated in his mind with an authenticity he hadn't felt since he'd last been on the stage—oddly enough. A rightness. A substance and truth that sprang from his soul.

"To hear my family tell it, I was made for respectable squiredom. My steward thinks I was made for repetitious weekly lectures about the approach of harvest. At the Arms, I'm to give a good account of myself on darts night, and Mr. Dabney would tell you my purpose is to heed all of his sage and antiquated wisdom regarding horse racing."

None of those burdens was onerous in itself, and try as he might, Gavin could find only goodwill and best intentions aimed his direction. And yet...

"As I am to appreciate Timmens's frequent displays of disapproval. You miss the acting, don't you?"

They stopped at the edge of the court while Lady Duncannon deflected her shot off Tavistock's ball to make a nearly impossible angle through a wicket. She curtseyed dramatically to the smattering of applause and blew the marquess a kiss.

"We are all acting most of the time," Gavin said. "I miss being able to choose my roles."

"You miss the stage?"

He gave her his best green-room smile. "I've put all that behind me, exorcised a youthful demon, put away childish things."

Lady Ducannon took her extra shots and yielded the court to Miss Peasegood.

"I've seen you act, Gavin," Rose said quietly. "There was nothing childish about it. You personified madness when you toyed with the notions of revenge and suicide as Hamlet. You embodied benevolent enchantment when you delivered Puck's closing speech. Your performances compel *belief* from your audiences. You make the truth of the stage more real than the world itself."

"You don't have to say these things, Rose." He wished she wouldn't, actually.

"You have a rare gift. I'm sorry your family can't see that."

He'd never act again, unless he was cast as one of the wise men alongside Vicar and Mr. Dabney in St. Nebo's Christmas pageant. George Pevinger would have to retire from the role of Gaspar, which he'd likely do in a mere twenty years or so.

"I miss it. You're right." A gloomy thought, when the day was anything but gloomy. "I've missed you more."

"Flatterer." She shouldered her mallet and strode onto the court, then used her shot to roquet Lord Phillip's ball halfway to Windsor.

Rose had a hidden streak of ruthlessness. Gavin liked knowing that about her—she could be downright ferocious as a lover—and he wondered what other gifts she'd been expected to keep hidden away in the wings.

"Make us proud, laddie!" Lady Duncannon called. "The honor of the team rests upon your broad and handsome shoulders."

Hooting and whistles followed as Gavin saw the opening Rose had left him. Drysdale's ball reposed in innocent vulnerability about two yards from the next wicket. Gavin could brush that ball out of alignment and clear the wicket, if he was careful and lucky.

He made the shot to more applause, and Drysdale twirled him an elaborate court bow, then shook his fist at the sky.

Overplaying the moment, as usual.

Lady Duncannon's team eventually prevailed, but Gavin felt no sense of victory. The whole business had been like a first dress rehearsal. Trudged through. Stops, starts, missed cues, bungled entrances, garbled lines. Then finally over.

He shook hands with Tavistock and Phillip, but when he would have exchanged that courtesy with Drysdale, he caught his former employer studying Rose with a speculative eye.

Oh no you don't. Drysdale, though married, considered himself something of an at-large consoler of widows. Rose had barely noticed him in Derbyshire, and that might well have inspired Drysdale to fix his interest on her now.

Gavin finished accepting congratulations from the losers, set aside his mallet, and waited until Drysdale had joined the buffet line under the tent at the foot of the garden.

"'Smooth runs the water where the brook is deep,'" Gavin murmured, slipping into line behind his former employer.

Drysdale turned, signature roguish smile in place. "Twidham, or rather, DeWitt. Greetings. *Henry VI*, part 2, act 3, scene 1. The Duke of Suffolk. My turn. 'False face must hide what the false heart doth know.'"

"Interesting choice," Gavin replied, taking a wedge of cold cheese quiche. "*Macbeth*, act 1, scene 7. Spoken by Macbeth himself. I gather pall-mall does not number among your many accomplishments?"

Drysdale pretended to shudder. "Nor will it ever. To perfect skill at that game takes ample free time and an expanse of manicured lawn, when I can claim neither. You are looking... well."

That slight hesitation was the easiest way to make a line of dialogue imply its opposite. "As are you." Gavin added a serving of peach trifle to his dish. "When will the rest of the players arrive?"

"Possibly tonight, more likely tomorrow, depending on how effectively Gemma can chivvy them along. We've missed you."

In all the time Gavin had been traveling with the East Anglia troupe, and in all the months he'd been home, he'd received not a single letter from Drysdale.

"I have fond memories of the north," Gavin said, which was true. "I look forward to seeing what repertoire you'll present for the guests. They are ladies of discernment and varied tastes."

Drysdale took three beef pastries and two servings of trifle. "Know them well, do you, the ladies?"

"Lady Tavistock is my sister, as you no doubt are aware. Lady Phillip is married to my good friend."

"Your sister did well for herself," Drysdale said, adding two strawberry tarts to his already full plate. "On the tall side for a woman and a bit long in the tooth to be newly wed."

To criticize one's hostess in any regard was beyond rude. "The marchioness's generosity of spirit is in proportion to the rest of her. We get our height from our late father."

Drysdale took three French chocolates from the epergne at the end of the buffet. "You also inherited a fortune from him."

What business was that of Drysdale's? "You knew I had a good education. My clothing and luggage were well made. My books well cared for. Obviously, I came from some means."

"Oh, obviously. Is your sister trying to get your attention?"

She was, but being discreet about it. "Drysdale, what are you doing here? Berkshire isn't your usual territory, and Crosspatch Corners is hardly a hotbed of enthusiasm for light theater."

"You're smart to be curious." Drysdale popped one of the chocolates into his mouth and took a fourth from the buffet. "I always said you were smart, though too much intelligence in an actor is never a good thing. We'll talk, you and I, about what I'm doing here. For now, I'll be providing the entertainment, just as I was hired to do."

He winked and sauntered off, and Gavin was reminded of Rose's earlier question: *What in blazes is going on?*

CHAPTER TEN

The evening was gorgeous, the best of high summer. Slanting beams of the dying sun gilded a towering pillow stack of clouds. Soft breezes sent foxgloves and daisies bobbing gently at the edge of the park. A doe and fawn nibbled the grass a few yards up from the riverbank, despite the guests milling about in the garden across the park.

The peaceable kingdom made fashionable.

Rose was seized with a melancholy that sprang only partly from thoughts of her late husband. Dane had never loved the countryside, never loved his birthplace, as Rose had come to love it. An evening like this, overwhelmingly sweet in its passing beauty, would not have touched his heart as it touched hers.

Gavin might resent his weekly sermons from the steward, but he understood what a difference a well-managed harvest made. He understood that home and hearth, acres and forests, deserved protection.

"Are you pensive?" The inquisitor was a young lady in that ephemeral stage between adolescence and young womanhood, poised to leave the last echoes of childhood behind, but not yet fully surrendered to adulthood. "You're Mrs. Roberts. Gav introduced us.

I'm Diana DeWitt. Shall I sit with you, or would you rather have a good bout of the blue devils in lovely solitude? Caro is always going off by herself, but I daresay the child is a stranger to low moods."

Diana chatters, and Caroline blushes. Offered with fraternal affection.

"You must sit with me," Rose said, scooting over on her bench. "I'm told you are quite the musician."

Diana took the place beside her. "I love music. I can be loud at the pianoforte, and nobody can scold me. Where else can a young lady be thunderous with impunity?"

That observation suggested Diana might chatter, but she was no featherbrain. "You can also be morose, furious, ominous, hilarious... I never realized that music can be put to subversive ends." As theater could be and regularly was.

"We'll let that be our secret, shall we? Amaryllis is impressive in all regards, Gavin is brilliant at the theater, and Caroline will be a famous poetess, mark my words. I took up music in defense of my pride in such company. Do you play?"

"A few party pieces, and sometimes when I'm restless and the weather won't allow me to hack out."

"Do you suppose that's why Gavin is so devoted to Roland? Because he's restless? I shouldn't like to see Gav hare off again, but he's unhappy. Even Mama admits he hasn't really settled in yet. Grandmama says to give it time, but she says that about everything. What was Tavistock thinking, adding the players to his house party? I'm not supposed to ask that, but Trevor is my brother-by-marriage, and I would like to understand him."

This was not chattering, but rather, the questions that arose in an alert and observant mind in a world controlled entirely by others. Rose had once asked such questions and been told to read a bit more of old Fordyce rather than trouble her pretty head.

"Promise me something," Rose said.

"Ma'am?"

"Promise me that if anybody ever tells you to go read some musty old sermons just to get rid of you or have the last word, you will instead take up some thunderous Beethoven."

"*La Passionata*. I made myself start with the andante, and I'm getting better at the allegro, but the presto is yet beyond me. One cannot rush when learning fast music, and I love to rush. F minor does not suffer fools."

And neither, someday, would Gavin's middle sister. "Are you glad your brother is home?"

Up on the terrace, footmen were moving potted camellias and benches and chairs, while beneath the supper tent, guests were making final passes along the buffet. Gavin was in conversation with the local vicar, and a small, dapper fellow of African descent had joined them.

"Am I glad Gav is home?" Diana undid the ribbons of her straw hat and removed her millinery. "Not exactly. Relieved, of course. We had no idea what had become of him, but what's the benefit of being wealthy if your coin only binds you to the family seat? We don't even properly have a family seat—Grandmama owns Twidboro Hall—and yet, Gav is supposed to kick his heels and look tame and content when he's not. He's the reason I play the piano, you know."

"I didn't know."

Drysdale took it upon himself to direct the footmen on the terrace, and he was apparently being less than gracious about it, based on the looks he was getting.

"Gav is the one who told me that I could be loud on the pianoforte wherever the composer had jotted an f for *forte*, and very loud with the ff, or *fortissimo*. You never saw a girl hunt through a stack of simple tunes with more focused intent. I could also go as swiftly as I pleased when I found a presto, or *prestissimo*, none of this limiting myself to the trot or the canter on the keyboard. I can gallop as fast as Roland does. That's the Drysdale creature on the terrace, I take it? Gav never says much about him."

"Maybe that alone tells us something. Does your brother speak much of his time on stage?"

Diana twirled her hat on her finger. "He tells stories. Gavin tells stories like other people wear clothes. To conceal, to impress, to please, to distract. He's very good at it, and that's why I think he's unhappy. The theater is the most magnificent storytelling there is, and instead, he's supposed to content himself with..." Diana gestured generally toward the park. "Mama says I'm to keep these thoughts to myself, but refusing to state the obvious doesn't make it any less so."

"Sometimes silence has the opposite effect." Such as when Dane would mention he'd be off to London at week's end. For the intervening days, neither he nor Rose would mention his plans, much less the reason he was again fleeing his home.

She'd kiss him farewell at the mounting block. He'd promise to write, and he would write—to tell her that he was extending his stay in Town another fortnight. *Keep well, darling wife, and my regards to the neighbors and your dear mother.*

"You *are* melancholy," Diana said, returning her hat to her head. "I have intruded. I shall leave you in solitude, shall I?"

"You will not abandon me, Miss DeWitt, lest one of those ferocious blossoms affix herself to my side and interrogate me on my views regarding the French succession."

"I haven't any views on that topic, but I don't think the French people can be cowed back into putting up with the expense of a monarchy for long. Louis's best hope is good harvests and plenty of them. We do have an abundance of guests with flower names, don't we?"

"You do have opinions," Rose said, "and they are sensible. Flower names aren't so bad, once you get used to all the jokes about having thorns or smelling sweet or your proper place being in the garden."

Diana tied her ribbons in a loose bow and left the ends trailing over her bosom. "Who said such a dreadful thing to you?"

Dane, when in his cups. He'd been a tedious and sullen drunk. "Nobody in particular. Shall we find a place on the terrace? I believe Mr. Drysdale's recitations will soon start."

The light was waning as the sun dropped behind the increasingly impressive bank of clouds, celestial beams piercing through rose and gray. More footmen, augmented by a complement of gardeners or grooms, were lighting torches and moving the punchbowl from the buffet tent to the terrace.

"I'm sure Mr. Drysdale is very talented," Diana said, rising, "but he won't hold a patch on Gav, I can promise you that. My brother's gift is magical."

Rose resisted the impulse to hug Diana and instead accompanied her up the steps. Other guests had taken the same notion, and the benches and chairs were soon full of a rustling, chatting audience.

"Everybody's here," Diana whispered. "The whole village wanted a chance to look over Lissa's fancy guests. The blossom ladies have been to the shops, but Mrs. Pevinger, Mrs. Dabney, and Mrs. Vicar wanted to form their own impressions."

"Your leading lights?"

"After Amaryllis and Lady Phillip. We've never really had leading lights in Crosspatch before. Now we have leading lights and professional players. Who needs London?"

"I have little use of the place, though the shopping is impressive."

Diana patted her arm. "I like you. I knew I would. Gav likes you, and he's very discerning, for all his charm."

That exchange banished the last of Rose's lingering doldrums, though she couldn't put her finger on what exactly Diana had said that was so cheering. Perhaps the girl's general admiration of her brother or her acknowledgment of Gavin's talent had done the trick, or her simple, unaffected company.

Diana hadn't grown up doubting her own worth, certain in her bones that only by marrying the man of her mother's choosing could she justify her existence.

Rose paid Drysdale only passing attention as her thoughts meandered along paths old and new. She joined in the applause at the appropriate moments—Portia's speech, rendered in something of a falsetto, followed by the predictable Saint Crispin's Day maunderings offered with much elaborate gesturing to the imaginary ramparts of Agincourt.

As Drysdale took his bows, Diana leaned over. "He's not very good, is he? Not compared to Gavin."

"Drysdale is the humbler talent, I agree."

The clapping subsided, and Lady Tavistock announced that refreshments would be served in the library for all in attendance. She offered a particular welcome to her guests from the village and encouraged people not to stand on ceremony lest the tea get cold.

"I'd like to hear a speech or two from our Master Gavin," Mrs. Pevinger called as people began to rise.

"Go on, Gav," somebody cried. "Show 'em how we do it here in Crosspatch!"

The guests hovered, clearly wanting to see if Gavin would accept the challenge, but also willing to enjoy more food and drink.

"I must refuse the honor," Gavin called. "Drysdale himself taught me that to perform without rehearsing is a recipe for disaster, and I am very much unprepared. Shall we withdraw to the library?"

Tavistock soon had Mrs. Vicar on his arm. Lady Duncannon, the ranking guest, was relegated to Lord Phillip's escort, and the rest of the company milled and shuffled and chatted their way into the house, while Rose remained on the terrace with Diana.

"Gavin was being polite," Diana said. "He could do Saint Crispin, 'To be or not to be,' plus 'Friends, Romans, countrymen' by heart in his sleep. He probably has."

He did mutter the occasional line while dreaming. He'd startled Rose half out of her bed the first time that had happened.

"I'm glad he demurred," Rose replied. "Upstaging Drysdale would have been inconsiderate of the man himself and of our hostesses. Was that thunder?"

"Oh, probably. Mr. Dabney's knees never lie, and he said the weather would soon turn. Come along, and we can make Gavin fetch us some cake. He would have done 'But soft! What light through yonder window breaks' for you, Mrs. Roberts. Depend upon it."

She'd heard that one from him, to devastating impact. "But would he have done it for himself?"

"No, he would not, and more's the pity. Oh blast, I felt a drop. Last one into the library is a muddy slipper." She darted off and left Rose on the terrace.

More raindrops speckled the flagstones, and another rumble of thunder rolled from the west. The footmen and gardeners were once again scurrying about, moving chairs and benches under balconies, and still, Rose did not want to join the crowd in the library.

"Come along." Gavin had appeared from a shadowed overhang. "You can catch your death in a summer downpour, and I'll not have that on my conscience." He draped a man's cloak over her shoulders, did up the frogs, and plunked a plain straw hat on her head.

"Where are we going?"

"I promised you a walk on the towpath, but I think we'd better make it more of a dash." He took her hand and set off at a fast trot down the garden steps.

"What if this rain turns serious?" Rose asked as the footmen extinguished the last of the torches. "We could get a soaking."

In Gavin's present state, cold water dashed over his head might be welcome. "I get a regular soaking in the Twid this time of year when I enjoy the privacy to do so. Having three sisters left me with a certain caution in that regard. This way."

He led her down a track near where the doe and fawn had been grazing and soon had his lady trundling along the towpath.

"Diana will make your excuses," he went on. "A bit too much sun while vanquishing your pall-mall competitors."

"Oh right. We had plenty of shade, and I am country born and bred. What excuse did you give for your own absence?"

"I'm off to Twidboro Hall to send the carriage back for my

womenfolk. Because I am up at first light to exercise my horse, I'm the early-to-bed sort."

"A lie and a truth. You have already arranged for the coach, haven't you?"

Now that they were out of sight and sound of the house, Gavin slowed his pace. "Every soul in Crosspatch can navigate the farm lanes and bridle paths in this area blindfolded, my mother and sisters included. But rain can make the way muddy in patches, and I am a considerate brother and son."

"Except when you run off to join a theater troupe and leave your family to fret over your absence for two years."

Rose stated the self-same thought Gavin battled at least a dozen times a day. "I had informed the solicitors of my plans and my where-abouts, but I didn't want the arguments and messy good-byes. The recriminations and lectures."

The rain amounted to a whispery drizzle, as much mist as precip-itation this close to the river.

"And given how things turned out," Rose said, "you have likely been lecturing yourself ever since—when your steward isn't sermo-nizing at you."

"I bungled badly, Rose." To say that to her lifted a burden of some sort from his conscience. "I trusted the same wrong people my father had trusted, and while the DeWitts are still quite wealthy, I have jeopardized my mother's dreams for me."

"My mother had dreams for me," Rose muttered, "and I wish to God somebody had jeopardized them straight to perdition."

She seized him in a hug. Not a lover's embrace, more of a ship-wreck survivor's desperate clasp of a fellow passenger when both had staggered, sopping and shivering, to shore.

Gavin held her and mentally rearranged his expectations for the evening. "I'm sorry, Rose. You deserved better from your family and from your husband." *I'm not like Dane* begged to be said, but Gavin *had* been like her late husband, turning his back on home and family, indulging his own whims, convincing himself that nobody was harmed by his selfishness.

"It's the time of year," Rose said, stepping back. "Harvest approaches, and that brings difficult memories. Where are we going?"

"Not far. Phillip built me a retreat before I went off to university. He knew I'd need a place of solitude, where my mother and sisters could not intrude when I was home between terms. I was supposed to believe he built it for himself, though Phillip no more needs a retreat than Roland needs to be addled by darting bunnies. The gazebo is through here. Watch out for the root."

Even as he spoke, Rose stumbled and pitched into him. "Sorry." She righted herself and brushed down her skirts.

"That root even gets me when I'm distracted, and I think the tree put it there on purpose. We're not supposed to barrel onward without pausing. We're to stop and reflect on the beauty and tranquility of the spot, and our great good fortune that we get to enjoy it."

"The tree decided all of that?"

"I believe so, or I did before I became such a sober and upright fellow. You mustn't tell anybody how fanciful I can be." So fanciful, he'd like to kiss her, with the rain building into a steady patter on the leaves and the darkness acquiring a density unusual for the relatively early hour.

"Perhaps that's what's amiss with Mr. Drysdale's acting," Rose said. "He lacks imagination. It's all technique and calculation with him. We'd best get out of the rain, Gavin, or we'll both end up with a lung fever."

"Your wish, and so forth." He led her around a turn between the rhododendrons, and Phillip's gazebo loomed as a darker shape against the towering trees. "Three steps up, and they might be slippery. The door is unlocked."

Rose preceded him, and Gavin waited a moment to join her. *Steady on, you. No rushing fences or shying at imaginary rabbits.*

"This is cozy," Rose said, hanging her cloak and hat on a peg on the back of the door. "Who left the lantern?"

"I did, and I packed the hamper. This afternoon was half day at the Hall, so I had some room to maneuver in the kitchen and pantries. You are sworn to secrecy."

"Dane maneuvered in the kitchen and pantries at will."

While Rose had likely respected the privacy of her staff. "Did he try to maneuver with the women in his employ?"

"I assume so, but they were all local women and more than capable of putting him in his place. I don't want to talk about him, to be honest."

"I don't want to talk about how precisely an orchard should be harvested, but it's a topic I'm well advised to cover at least once thoroughly. Were you trying to play Dane false in memory with me up in Derbyshire?"

Rose settled on the bench at the back of the structure, facing the river. "Oh, probably, or that's how I started out. Getting back on the horse, hoping for a better ride. Also..."

Gavin took the place beside her. "Also feeling frisky? Ready to exercise the womanly humors?"

"There aren't any such things as womanly humors."

He nudged her, shoulder to shoulder. "In your case, I beg to differ. You can be ferocious, Rose Roberts. I adore that about you." Ferocious in bed, despite all the bland pleasantries she could manufacture by the hour over a formal supper.

Despite the subdued fashions, the demure coiffures, the lack of flashy jewels. Rose Roberts in the flesh was a one-woman tempest of passion.

"If I was ferocious on certain occasions, I was provoked." She nudged him back. "I love that sound, rain upon water. I never heard it in London. There, it was rain on cobbles, rain on tin roofs, rain on mud. Never rain on leaves and rivers and the good earth."

He looped an arm around her shoulders. "I don't mind London, in small doses. Drury Lane alone excuses much else about the capital."

"The shops," Rose said. "I went a bit mad in the perfumeries with sachets and soaps. Madder. Widowhood delivers a blow to the nerves."

Marriage had dealt her nerves plenty of blows before that, in Gavin's estimation. "Tell me the worst thing, the worst blow."

Rose kissed his knuckles. "This is not a gazebo, it's a confessional."

"I'll go first, then, and you can be inspired by my example." He sorted through his inventory of heartaches, a modest list, but weighty enough if he allowed it to be.

"The worst thing about coming home was knowing I would never again be plain Master Gavin. I'd gone off and seen the world without permission, and that was a betrayal of not only my family, but of the whole village. I'm banished now, to manners and propriety. Everybody is still friendly, still fond of me, but I occupy a different place, and I'm lonely here in a different way."

"You were lonely before?"

"Terribly. No brothers, no cousins—half of Crosspatch is related to the other half—no real friends because I was neither village boy nor gentry born and bred. Phillip was kind to me, but he's solitary by nature, or he was until Miss Brompton got him by the ear."

"She has him by the heart."

And a few other parts. "In any case, I retreated to literature in the grand English tradition, and that led to plays. By the time I was finally turned loose for a few terms at public school, I had pretty much memorized all of Shakespeare, and university was just an excuse to expand my repertoire."

"And you trotted out your quotes like the obnoxious sprig you were?"

"My sisters took to mimicking me, and I learned from their examples. Pause here, look at the audience there, pace a little faster with the second couplet, then slow down. Drysdale often rehearses in front of a mirror. I had no need of a mirror with my sisters to mock me."

The memories were painful now, when he hadn't allowed them

to be before. Nobody had meant any harm, but harm had been done. Home had become ever so slightly hostile to tender masculine pride, and that had set a process in motion that ended with leaving Crosspatch altogether.

Retreating still further into literature and plays.

"Dane mocked me," Rose said, shifting to lay her head against Gavin's thigh. "Minced about fretting in a falsetto about pin money and quince jellies and wheat fields flattened by hail. His favorite sobriquet for me was Miss Dramatic."

"You should have flattened him." Gavin trailed his fingers through her silky hair and along the sweet curve of her jaw. She enjoyed having her ears stroked, like a hound, and he made so bold as to indulge her. She sighed, and another weight lifted—this time from his heart.

"The drink did that," she said. "Flattened him. You asked for the worst memory... Have you ever tried to impress a lady with your love-making when you were drunk?"

Oh God. "That particular folly is part of a university education. If the lady is kind, she settles for a cuddle and tells you it happens to everybody when they overindulge. The spirit is willing, the flesh is inebriated. If she's not kind... there is no worse humiliation."

"Dane was drunk *a lot.* He wanted children—sons. It was... I was embarrassed for him, when I wasn't furious on my own behalf. He eventually stopped trying... with me. And I was relieved. The ridiculousness of a man aspiring to passion when there's no passion in him... The steps he expected me to take to overcome his indifference... Even my mother had no idea how bad it got. Timmens doubtless has her suspicions, but they are only suspicions."

"Did you consider leaving him?"

"Yes, but if I'd left, Colforth Hall would have been a ruin mortgaged to the rafters in six months. I could not have that on my conscience—not that too. Besides, I had nowhere to go, and my mother would have been mortified. Your thigh is not an ideal pillow."

Gavin snagged the genuine article from the corner of the bench.

"Try this, and consider that Dane's affliction might have been guilt as much as excesses of alcohol. He played you false apparently from early days, and not only with his London mistress. In his own mind, a lack of progeny might have been the price he paid for those pleasures. Rather than give up his pleasures, his conscience demanded that he not be allowed marital satisfaction."

Rose half sat up, arranged her pillow, and subsided. "Men think like that?"

"To call it 'thinking' might be applying too orderly and sophisticated a term. Do you need a blanket?"

The rain had picked up, though it still didn't qualify as a downpour. A summer shower that would leave an extra sparkle come morning. Gavin hadn't exactly planned a tryst for this outing, though he'd certainly been open to the possibility.

But then, they'd trysted like a pair of minks in Derbyshire, and that had not ended well.

"I will need a blanket," Rose said. "But, Gavin?"

He bent nearer, the better to enjoy the scent of her perfume blending with the aroma of the rain. "Hmm?"

"I need you too."

CHAPTER ELEVEN

Gavin's fingers went still on Rose's earlobe. "I beg your pardon?"

"I need you. I've tried not to, tried to forget you, to put aside the memories, but they won't stay aside. They keep intruding, and then your sisters adore you, or Lord Phillip gets a certain fond look in his eye when you and Lady Tavistock are off in a corner trying to have a discreet argument. These people love you because you *are* lovable."

"We weren't arguing. We were discussing whether I should fetch Grandmama, who doesn't want to be fetched and is perfectly capable of choosing her own entertainments." His fingers resumed their slow, easy stroke on her ear. "Why Lissa can't afford Grandmama the same freedoms Lissa herself insisted on from the age of seven, I do not know."

Thunder cracked above, then trailed away. Gavin's fingertips glossed over Rose's lips. "I need you, too, but I can't allow myself to... surrender as I did in the north. That wasn't wise. You said no strings and no expectations, but, Rose, there are expectations upon me, and I intend to fulfill them."

Just don't stop touching me. "To marry?"

"We'll save that discussion for later, but yes, marriage is expected of me, just as it was of Lissa and is of Di and Caro. I took you to enjoy a pint of cider in the village because that is what one does in Crosspatch when out on a hack with a guest. I endure my steward's bleatings because, again, that's what one does. My family is no longer connected to the shop as we were in my grandfather's day, but we aren't yet connected to the land. We ruralized as mere tenants on my father's watch, and only by the grace of Tavistock is my grandmother the owner of Twidboro Hall now. My job is to connect the DeWitts to the land."

Rose knew he wasn't referring to mere acreage, which could be so many shackles on a person's time, finances, and mind. "To connect your family to respectability?"

"Shopkeepers are generally respectable, but true esteem only attaches when a family has and tends to substantial agricultural holdings. Someday, that might change, but now, for the sake of my sisters, their progeny, my mother's peace of mind, and my own self-respect, the DeWitts need to polish the art of profitably minding their acres."

"It's not as easy as it looks," Rose said, sitting up. "But I like the challenge. I thought Dane would appreciate my efforts to learn estate management, but I simply made it easier for him to go larking about."

Gavin took her hand. "You said no strings and no expectations, Rose, but I still have hopes. They are like your memories. They won't stay in the wings, awaiting their proper cue. They intrude on every scene, and those hopes involve you."

She wanted to put her hands over her ears, and she wanted... *him.* "Don't propose to me, please."

"Ever? Because if you simply want another glorious tumble, I cannot oblige. We've done that, and..."

"It did not end well. I agree with you there. Why did you bring me here?"

"For privacy, to advance my hopes. To talk, and perhaps a bit more."

And Rose sensed he was being honest, drat him. He might have speculated about that *a bit more*, but he hadn't fixed his mind on seduction.

"I haven't considered remarriage," Rose said, which was only half true. Up north, with Gavin in mind, she'd all but chosen new wallpaper for the Colforth library.

"Because you've been too busy recovering from your last bout of matrimony. I understand that, and I'm not proposing now."

The rain was slowing, more dripping than precipitation, and the evening had grown cool. Gavin rose, shrugged out of his jacket, and draped it around Rose's shoulders.

That gesture—intuitive, considerate, a small gallantry—made up her mind. "I want more than a tumble, Gavin. I don't know how much more, but a passing encounter won't do for me either. We are starting afresh, and whatever we are embarking on, it's not another mad gallop."

He resumed his place beside her. "We'll be honest and careful?"

"Honest, yes, but when you get to kissing me... Careful is beyond me, Gavin. I used to be so decorous, so ladylike. You kiss me, and my dignity deserts me."

"Good. I wouldn't want to be the only one feeling winded and witless over a mere glance. Did you know, these benches fold out like the seats of a traveling coach and make a very comfortable cot."

Rose's heart took a happy, only slightly nervous leap. "I did not know that. Perhaps you could show me?"

"I'd be delighted."

~

"You saw them?" Phillip asked, joining Tavistock beneath an overhang on the terrace.

How did Phillip always manage to move so quietly? "Why do you think I asked the footmen to extinguish torches that would eventually sputter out on their own? Diana reported that Gavin was looting the Twidboro Hall pantries following his afternoon hack. Caroline saw him disappearing onto the towpath with a hamper while the ladies dressed for their evening out."

"Shame on you, corrupting the morals of Crosspatch's young ladies. Shame on our Gavin, for not being more discreet. What else did the girls say?"

Tavistock sorted through sororal effusions from Diana and quiet asides from Caroline. His sisters-by-marriage were every bit as astute as his marchioness, though he was only now realizing it.

"They like Mrs. Roberts."

"As do I," Phillip replied. "She was a friend to both me and Hecate in Hampshire, and the Earl of Nunn would have dusted off his rusty Mantons to defend her honor. Hecate has asked a few discreet questions. Mrs. Roberts did not have an easy time of it with her dashing husband."

"'Dashing' seems to be all the crack with the bachelors. Amaryllis prefers that I be steady, affectionate, hardworking, and occasionally inventive."

"Spare me." Phillip took a sip of his drink. Brandy, from the scent. "Will Mrs. Roberts break Gavin's heart is the question. She used him and cast him aside up north."

"Shied at a fence, you mean?"

"I don't know. Gavin was blessedly sparing with particulars. Said she tried to turn it into some sort of transaction. More professional entertainment. What do you make of Drysdale?"

Professional entertainment sounded... bad to Tavistock. An actor was a professional entertainer, but *not like that*. Somebody had bungled. Maybe two somebodies.

Tavistock hooked a wrought-iron chair with his boot, took a seat, and propped his feet on the table. He'd never have disrespected Amaryllis's furniture to that extent had the terrace not been dark and deserted.

"Drysdale's an actor," he said. "One expects him to be engaged in playing a role, but somewhere beneath all the smiles and politesse, a real human being should dwell. I doubt I'd like the fellow inside the costumes."

"Then why invite him and his players to join this gathering, at great expense to you and no little displeasure from your wife?"

Phillip was the sort to ponder and cogitate and pick at a problem until he'd solved it to his own satisfaction. The riddle might be how to win the hand of his darling Hecate, or it might be where to run a fence line to take best advantage of natural terrain. He was nothing if not patient and persistent.

"Why do you think I invited them here?" Tavistock asked.

"Because Gavin DeWitt is miserable and bearing up as well as he can, and we both know how that feels. We know *all too well* how that feels. Do you truly believe that confronting his old chums and hearing a few lines from the Scottish play will tempt him from the bucolic course his womenfolk have set him on?"

Phillip took the second chair, and while he didn't prop his feet on the table, he sprawled in an ungenteel manner Tavistock could only aspire to.

"Gavin could have got away with more time on the stage, even a career on the stage, had his sister not married me. She's *our marchioness* now. Half of Mayfair is already speculating about whether Diana can bag a title, and if so, will she look as high as her sister? Di isn't as hugely dowered as Amaryllis was, but she's young and lovely, and Gavin has not stinted with her settlements."

Phillip was quiet for a moment. "I want to tell you that this is more of your typical dunderheaded overreaching. That your lordly imagination has attained new heights of invention, but you are absolutely right. Had Amaryllis married Lawrence Miller, or some other prosperous local lad, Gavin could have spent the rest of his life on stage, and Diana and Caroline could have married decent chaps who weren't too high in the instep, provided Gavin came home occasionally to rusticate."

Phillip took another sip of his drink. "Gavin has been moping about Crosspatch like a man pining for a long-lost love, and missing the stage might well be part of it. How does Drysdale fit into your plans?"

Phillip *would* circle back to that. "I wanted to show dear Gavin what he's giving up. I wanted him to rethink his decision with some relevant comparisons nearer to hand. I was all full of plans and resolve in France. Go home to London, take a proper English wife, settle down, be fruitful and dunderheaded. When I finally returned to Town and faced the reality of executing those plans... My thinking shifted."

"And God be thanked for that. But why Drysdale? Gavin abandoned the Players, and I doubt the parting was as amicable as he claims."

As did Amaryllis, now that she'd met Drysdale, and Tavistock trusted her instincts utterly. "I tried to hire the East Anglia bunch, but they had summer commitments. Drysdale got word I was looking and contacted me."

"Bold of him," Phillip said. "But then, *audentis fortuna iuvat* and all that. Nevertheless, Drysdale is a lesser light as a thespian. Gavin is the genuine article—younger, better looking, wealthy. A dabbler with talent from Drysdale's perspective. At the very least, Drysdale has grounds for jealousy. Whatever else is true, you've enlivened the gathering considerably."

Phillip had refrained from scolding. Kind of him. "Thank you as always for your unwavering support, dearest brother."

"You know you have it, but Gavin has been a friend since long before you became the local Marquess of Malt. In his way, he has been as solitary as I was, but without my adorably retiring nature. He resorted to charm, stories, and dramatic recitations to draw us all near. That's not the same as being close to the man himself."

Tavistock desperately hoped that Mrs. Roberts was drawing close to the man himself. Amaryllis vowed that Gavin's worst affliction was not boredom or resignation to unappealing duty, but rather, a lonely heart.

A condition with which Tavistock could sympathize. "If I'm not to spend a night on the dressing closet cot, I'd best find my wife and stay close to her. You'll keep an eye on Drysdale?"

"And on Gavin. What of Mrs. Roberts? She has a prior acquaintance with Drysdale, too, and I saw him casting speculative glances her way on the pall-mall court."

Tavistock rose, feeling old in his bones. A change of weather could do that, as Mr. Dabney would no doubt agree.

"I think we can trust to Gavin's good offices to keep an eye on Mrs. Roberts."

"And perhaps his hands and occasionally his lips on her as well." Phillip saluted with his brandy. "'I drink to the joy of the whole table.'"

"Shakespeare?"

"Of course Shakespeare, you heathen. I take it your lady wife has been apprised of your motivations where Gavin and the actors are concerned?"

"Amaryllis put it together without even a hint from me. Took her a night's sleep, but she rose in the morning with that I-want-a-word-with-you-sir look in her eye. She agrees with me that our marriage has curtailed Gavin's options."

"Gavin likely doesn't see it that way. Guilt curtails his options. Haring off without a backward glance, trusting the wrong brood of vipers, youthful arrogance... But you wouldn't know anything about that."

Tavistock cuffed Phillip half-gently on the back of the head, because, as near as he could tell, that was expected between brothers. "Go find your dear Hecate. Maybe she can kiss some manners into you."

"I live in hope. You'll leave the terrace door unlocked?"

"I can't expect Mrs. Roberts to climb in a window, can I?"

Phillip rose and stretched. "She'd manage. Let's hope she can manage Gavin, because so far, nobody else has done a proper job of it."

Leaving Gavin to manage himself, all alone, without reinforcements. Tavistock knew how that felt too, and went posthaste to find his darling wife.

To yield to mere desire was in the character of the fool. Gavin realized this as he pulled off his boots and stockings, and Rose arranged pillows on the makeshift bed. Desire, like playing the fool, called for some technique and experience, a good sense of timing, and a bit of dash, but the role could be shed along with the costume once the curtain came down.

He'd surrendered to desire with Rose in Derbyshire and hoped all the complicated emotions would sort themselves out eventually.

Months of taking on more challenging parts, followed by months of galloping all over the shire hadn't sorted anything out, except that he'd missed Rose more than he missed the stage, and he didn't understand how he and she could have been at such cross-purposes up north.

"You look so pensive," Rose said, sitting on the bench-bed and bending to unlace a boot.

"Let me do that." He knelt before her as he had on many other occasions and dealt with her footwear. Garters and stockings next, and while his mind was still trying to parse the significant questions —*what am I doing? how is this different from before?*—his body reveled in the feel of Rose's muscular calves, her sturdy ankles, her hand glossing over his hair.

"You were always so considerate," she said. "I treasured you for that."

He brushed her skirts up and kissed her knee. "I tried to be, until you knocked me witless and wanton. I treasure you for your passion." And for the notion that she'd let herself go *like that* only with him.

Her words—*I need you*—rang in his imagination as the herald of joy, but *don't propose to me* lurked as a warning. He was auditioning for the role of suitor—again—but this time, both he and Rose acknowledged his aim.

That was an important step forward, but by no means an assurance of success. *Don't bungle this. Don't overplay the moment. Don't think too much.*

"You're sure, Rose, about this much at least?"

"If you walk out that door now, Gavin DeWitt, I will trip you flat with or without the assistance of enchanted trees, and I will personally drag you 'full fathom five' into the cold depths of the Twid and wish you to perdition."

This time of year, the Twid hadn't any such depths. "I'm not going anywhere." Yes, he was stuck in Crosspatch Corners, mired in family duty, and bound to social expectations, but at that moment, he was also exactly where he wanted to be. A paradox to ponder later.

Rose unknotted his cravat. "You will soon join me in this bed, if you please. I know exactly what allowing you to remain on your knees can lead to."

"Pleasure, yours and mine, and then more pleasure."

"Shocked sensibilities, unspeakable intimacies, me sprawled flat on my back and yet dizzy. You've haunted me, Gavin DeWitt."

He rolled up her stockings and considered indulging in those same unspeakable intimacies, then set that option aside for a time when he could claim more patience and less uncertainty.

"The haunting was mutual, Rose Roberts. You visited a few unspeakable intimacies on me too."

She scooted sideways and stood, giving him her back. "You can have no idea what a relief it was to be intimate with a man and have my expectations so wildly exceeded that I barely believed the experience was real."

Gavin got to his feet and dealt with the hooks at the back of her dress. "Your wiles are considerable, Rose. If Dane couldn't satisfy himself with you, he was a bungling idiot. You were never the problem."

She turned and wrapped her arms around him. "Thank you. You

showed me the truth long ago, but the words are still comforting. I asked the midwife awkward questions, I read French novels, I tried medical treatises... Dane was convinced that if I'd only try harder, and stop nagging, and act more wifely..."

"Dane knew damned good and well he was at fault, and now you know it too." Gavin did not want to discuss Dane the Dimwit, but if Rose needed to air the topic, he could at least listen. The poor sod had literally come to grief on the side of the road. He'd landed in a ditch he'd dug for himself, one filled with gin, brandy... *and guilt.* He'd willfully neglected and disrespected his wife and the home she'd made for him.

Gavin hadn't intended to visit any hardship on his family when he'd left Crosspatch. Just the opposite. He'd meant to spare the ladies his restless, frustrated presence and *do something* in pursuit of a dream.

Another point to consider some other time. He held Rose for the space of three slow breaths, an actor's tool for settling the mind.

"I know Dane was to blame for at least part of the problem." Rose kissed Gavin's cheek and then wiggled free of her dress and jumps. "Thank you for that, and I will thank you as well to get out of those clothes."

Subject changed, and none too soon.

She assisted him to undress. Playing minor roles, changing costumes a half-dozen times in a night, the assistance of a competent dresser was sometimes a necessity.

Rose was an exceedingly talented *un*-dresser. She delivered little brushes and pats as she unbuttoned Gavin's waistcoat. When she started on his shirt, she ran her fingers beneath his collar, pausing at his nape, an exquisite caress. The patience she brought to unfastening his falls nearly cost Gavin his composure, and when she extracted his rampant member from his underlinen, her touch was sweet torment.

She'd been a curious lover, intent on exploring him inch by inch.

He wasn't up to such heroics at the moment. "If you start with your mouth, Rose, I will demand turnabout."

She straightened, wrapping her fingers around his shaft. "I lack the fortitude for your sort of turnabout just now."

"Thank the merciful powers." He peeled out of his breeches and underlinen and tossed them on the otherwise neat pile of clothing Rose had created near the door. "To bed with us."

He climbed onto the cushions first. Rose liked to be on the outside of any bed that abutted a wall, a preference doubtless based on all the times she'd left her husband snoring off his latest overindulgence.

Rose settled on the cushions and remained sitting while Gavin lay on his back. "The rain has stopped."

"For now. We will have to make our own thunder and lightning."

She eased down beside him, and Gavin rolled to his side, the better to behold his lover. They were good at making thunder and lightning, but as Rose scooted closer and hiked a leg over his hips, he realized a part of what was different about this time.

He'd wanted to impress her—before. He hadn't been keeping score exactly, but he'd been keeping count, gloating a little every time she'd yielded to desire first, mentally strutting when she'd demanded a nap between rounds.

A fool, albeit a besotted fool.

Now, he wanted to *make love* with her, not provide her with a mutually enjoyable performance. Thunder and lightning, *and love.*

She anchored a hand in his hair and urged him within kissing range.

"You could simply ask," he said, brushing his lips over her brow. "'Gavin, might you indulge me in a few of your exceedingly delightful kisses?' 'Gavin, have you some caresses to spare?'"

"Gavin, use that mouth for a better purpose than twitting my shyness. We don't all enjoy your penchant for dialogue. I haven't... That is, not since... One doesn't find much opportunity in Hampshire for..."

He gathered her close. "Nor in Crosspatch. Nor even when passing through London. No opportunity at all, not since I was with you."

In the meager light of the lantern, they smiled at each other, and Gavin saw how he should go on. Slowly, carefully, joyfully, as if it were their first time, because in a sense, it was.

Kisses blended into caresses, until Rose straddled him and tossed her chemise in the direction of the door. That occasioned another shared smile, more tender and wicked than the previous version.

"Such bounty," Gavin murmured, levering up to worship her breasts with his mouth and hands. "Such exquisite, beautiful, lovely..." Lines from the sonnets drifted through his mind. *I in thy abundance am sufficed, And by a part of all thy glory live.*

Then, even the Bard, with all his skill and insight, was insufficient to the moment.

Rose crouched over Gavin, her breasts brushing his chest in a manner doubtless intended to drive him mad.

"Another time, sir, we can tarry over the preliminaries," she said, "but just at this moment..."

"Right. Another time, soon. For now, let us seize the night and seize each other." He shifted his hips, and Rose went still.

"Seize away." She braced her hands on his shoulders. "Though slowly, please."

He tried to oblige her, but as soon as he'd gained the first inch, Rose shuddered.

"Damn you, Gavin DeWitt. That feels..." The shuddering went on, even as Gavin held still.

"Marvelous?" he whispered, his control threatening to unravel. "Astounding? Fabulous?"

"Hush, you beast." She hung over him, panting, then began to move. "I've missed you."

She had always known exactly how to *ply* him. "Missed the pleasure?"

"Not only the pleasure. The pleasure is part of it. I've... missed... *you*."

One moment, he was a man in possession of some self-restraint, a generally capable lover intent on pleasing his lady before indulging his own needs. The next instant, his will was obliterated by welling delight. He thrashed and bucked like the beast she'd named him and endured an unbearable intensity of sensation, even as he lunged for more.

Withdrawing in the name of honor had never been such a near and difficult thing.

By the time he'd subsided onto his back—and Rose had stopped laughing—he was winded, ebullient, and wrung out.

"Need a nap?" she whispered. "I certainly might, because I am not finished with you, Gavin. I need at least the rest of the night to settle my humors."

I need you. His first instinct was to keep the words to himself. So was his second and his third. And yet... He was an aspiring suitor, and if Rose was to send him packing, he wanted to know his fate now, rather than after another night of unfathomable bliss.

"What I need," he said slowly, "is the truth, and your trust, and some courage."

She levered up, brushed his hair back, and rummaged under the pillows for the handkerchief he always tucked in such a location.

"You also need some tidying up." She dismounted, tended to him and to herself, and tossed the linen aside. "What are you going on about, Gavin? I am not at my best at the moment—some handsome bounder has stolen my wits—but neither have I any engagement more pressing than a restorative nap."

She was back on her dignity, despite not wearing a stitch.

"Let me hold you," Gavin said. "Please. I need to ask you a difficult question, and yet, I am loath to vex you."

Rose lay on her side, facing him, and allowed him to draw her near, tucking her nose into the crook of his shoulder. "You do vex me, Gavin. I'm all at sixes and sevens. I thought I had put the past aside and could manage a fresh start, but I've missed you so, and you aren't the dashing blade I've tried to paint you, or not merely that, and..."

"I know. We cannot build a new foundation without first clearing away some rubble. So tell me, Rose. When we became lovers up north, why did you leave me that money?"

She lifted her head and, as the lantern began to gutter, fixed him with a frown. "What money? I never left you any money. That was the problem, or so I thought."

She wasn't angry. Her words bore caution, hurt, and not a little bewilderment, almost as if...

"Tell me what happened," he said, shifting over her. "Leave nothing out. Spare no one, least of all me, and take your time."

She hugged him, and then she began her tale.

CHAPTER TWELVE

"Lady Rutherford's house party wasn't the respite I'd hoped it would be," Rose said, making herself concentrate rather than gloss over painful generalities. "I was free of mourning and free of London, but nothing could free me from the memories. Then I looked up from a dull bit of verse, and there you were."

Gavin kissed her nose. "I went barreling into the music room, thinking to review the lines I was most in fear of bungling, hoping to find solitude. I found so much more than mere solitude."

Rose put a hand on his chest and applied the slightest pressure, and he was gone. He listened to her with his body and his mind. How she adored him for that.

"We became enamored," she said, sitting up and wedging a pillow at her back. "Or I became enamored and then... besotted. I had hopes, Gavin. I hadn't gone so far as hoping for remarriage, but I'd thought myself lost to hope in all regards. My lot at Colforth Hall would be contentment, gratitude, hard work, and rural friendships. A good if stultifying and lonely life. You upended my expectations, and I tossed my common sense to the wind."

He situated himself beside her and took her hand. "As did I."

Rose was glad the lantern no longer burned, glad Gavin could not distract her with his smiles and knowing glances. She could be braver in the dark. More focused.

"You know most of the rest," she said. "We became lovers, and that was magnificent, but I awoke alone. I knew we could not completely abandon propriety and dressed with particular care for breakfast."

"You wore your hair half up, half down. I thought you were taunting me." He took her hand and kissed her fingers. "What did you think?"

Rose cast her mind back to that awkward, difficult meal. "That you'd spurned me. You were perfectly, frigidly correct to me. When I invited you to begin the day with a stroll in the garden, you declared that pressing correspondence demanded your attention, then I saw you sitting on a bench among the daffodils, staring at nothing. Clearly, I had given offense, or I had seriously misjudged you."

Gavin rubbed his thumb over her knuckles, a sweet little gesture that had once meant he was thinking through a knotty dilemma.

"Gavin?"

"You are correct that we could not become oblivious to propriety. I thought to join the other lucky fellows stealing about the corridors before the sun rose. To catch a nap and awaken to the joy of my lover's countenance across the breakfast table."

"What happened?"

"I rose from the bed, kissed your slumbering cheek, and found a considerable pile of coins among my effects in the dressing closet. Because I had undressed with some care, I knew for a fact the money hadn't been there the previous night."

Rose shook her hand free of his. "You thought I *paid* you?"

"The evidence of such insulting generosity was right before my eyes."

"Gavin... I never left the bed. How could I...?" Darkness was no ally now. "Why would I *pay* you any more than you would pay me?

That wasn't... By all the biblical plagues, I did not leave you any money."

"And yet, the money was there. Not on the bedside table, not on your vanity. Tucked discreetly into the folds of my cravat. I returned the coins to your jewelry box, dressed as best I could, and concluded that you'd given me my congé."

"I had not."

"But I became distant and correct, Rose. You thus concluded that I had given you *your* congé. Somebody saw what was blooming between us and sundered a growing attachment on purpose."

"It's worse than that," Rose said, straddling his lap and cuddling close. "I asked Mrs. Drysdale what could have put you in such a standoffish mood. She told me that actors are proud and mercurial, and they expect to be paid for *all* of their performances. The house party was proving less remunerative than you'd been led to believe and she implied that you were pouting. I concluded that you expected me to compensate you for the attention you'd shown me."

Gavin held Rose loosely, his hands trailing patterns on her back. "Oddly enough, she spoke the truth. Drysdale promised we'd each earn generous vails. Instead, we were to content ourselves with a few weeks of room and board plus free rehearsal space."

"Was she misleading me, or was I reading too much into ambiguous words?" Rose thought back to a hasty, quiet exchange and couldn't decide, but Gemma Drysdale had had no reason to bear her ill will.

"Who left me that money?" Gavin murmured. "The dressing closet could be accessed from the corridor, but somebody had to have known I was finally, at long last, sharing your bed."

"We didn't make a secret of our attraction."

Rose lapsed into silence, and despite Gavin's gentle caresses to her back, she could feel him mentally parsing the same questions that bothered her.

Who benefited from wrecking a budding romance?
Who would be so bold as to intrude on a tryst?

Was the whole sorry business some sort of joke? A misunderstanding? A combination of the two?

"I don't like it," Gavin said. "You were hurt and insulted, and I was furious."

"You were hurt too."

He hugged her. "Devastated, but allow me the fig leaf of outrage."

"Then I was outraged too."

His hands went to her shoulders. "The other guests were busy with their own intrigues. That leaves staff and the theater company, but the staff hadn't a small fortune to waste on a nasty whim."

"So somebody among Drysdale's Players didn't want you forming an attachment to me."

"Or somebody among the other guests—who were more likely to have spare coin—didn't want you forming an attachment to me."

The idea that she and Gavin had been manipulated made Rose bilious. "What did it matter to Drysdale if you developed a fondness for me? Actors are not exactly rarities. He hired you; he has probably hired a handsome young fellow every few years. The better talent moves on to London, Dublin, or Edinburgh and must be replaced."

Even as a part of her mind began reviewing the guest list—as best she recalled it—Rose's body was very aware that she was wrapped around a naked Gavin DeWitt, whom she'd missed very much and who had *never played her false.*

"The situation wants thought," Gavin said, kissing her on the mouth. "Calm, logical thought. A systematic—Rose, what are you about?"

She brushed her thumb over his nipple. "We can think later, and we will. For now, I am too happy to untangle plots and point fingers at villains."

"That is not my finger pointing at you."

"I know. I left you no money, you never sought payment. We are entitled to make up for lost time, Gavin."

She could *hear* him smiling in the dark. "A lot of lost time. Kiss me."

She kissed him, and more than kissed him, and got in two good naps before an insistent robin woke her. Gavin was already dressed and munching a biscuit, and a hint of gray light framed the gazebo's window on the Twid.

"Do not," he said sternly, "look at me like that." He held out the biscuit. "We'll have to make a dash for the side door as it is."

Rose sat up and scooted to the edge of the cot. "Will you skip your ride this morning?" The biscuit was good—buttery and cinnamon-y.

"Not a chance. Roland needs the gallop, and I think best on horseback. We have a deal of thinking to do, Rose. Another biscuit?"

"Are there more?"

"And cider. I put the canteen in the river about an hour ago. It should be coolish." He passed over a flask. "I left the sandwiches for the beasts."

He would. "You are different this morning."

"Happier, more at peace, and exceedingly determined. Your biscuits." He passed over two.

"Perhaps we should let sleeping dogs lie, Gavin. Maybe the money was a prank gone awry, a bet between the bachelors I was ignoring." How could he look so damnably delectable with his hair tousled, his shirt unbuttoned, and his eyes shadowed with fatigue?

He collected his stockings and boots. "Do you believe that?"

Rose ate her biscuits and took a mental inventory. "Gemma Drysdale might have been speaking in the general case about remuneration for services rendered. Another guest might have been pranking you. Somebody in the theater company could have been making a nasty statement about our liaison, but you say you were paid a goodly sum. That speaks to malice and an agenda."

"You didn't notice the money in your jewelry box?" He rose and shrugged into his waistcoat, doing up a few buttons.

"I rarely open my jewelry box. Timmens selects what I'm to wear, and she likely thought I'd had a good night at whist."

Gavin held out a hand. "*That* good?"

Rose stood with his assistance and allowed herself to hug him. "Timmens believes the Quality are all prone to vice and venery. She has no frame of reference for polite gaming stakes. I had some money with me for travel expenses and vails. One pile of coins looks very like another."

"God, you feel good." He'd muttered that against her hair. "You look good. Luscious, rosy, rumpled, tumbled. Please heave me into the Twid, lest I become incoherent with desire."

"I love it when you finally lose all that self-possession, but the sun will rise on us cavorting like otters, and then the whole village will be scandalized, along with all the guests."

He gave her a squeeze. "Very well. We appease the jealous gods of decorum for now."

Rose had to count to three—twice—to marshal the resolve to leave his embrace. She was soon dressed and trundling along the towpath, hand in hand with her lover, heart light, mind for once at peace.

"I need a nap," she said. "Another nap, thanks to you, but when I awaken, and when you have ridden your demon colt all over the shire, we must talk."

"Right. Talk, think, ponder, and plan. I thought it a sorry coincidence that Drysdale should pop up here in Crosspatch, but perhaps it's an opportunity."

Rose dragged him back when he would have marched across the gray mists of the park. "A kiss for luck."

The kiss became very lucky, and then Gavin was escorting her—properly, of all the inanities—up the garden walkway. He parted from her only after ensuring the terrace door was unlocked.

"Until luncheon," he whispered very near her ear. "Dream of me. And, Rose?"

"Hmm?"

"Keep an eye on Lady Iris. Something about her bothers me. When we were playing pall-mall..."

"She pretended to not watch us until you caught her at it. Then she did that silly little wave when she's not a silly woman."

"I have the sense I've seen her before, but I can't place her."

"As do I. You'll be careful on your gallop?"

"For you, yes. I will be careful." He kissed her again, and Rose lingered in the shadowed doorway, watching his retreat until he disappeared into the soft mists of the new dawn.

"Your colt's stride is more relaxed," Phillip said, nudging his gelding to fall in step beside a sweating Roland. The hour was still misty early, though the birds along the towpath had long since been awake. "He's gained enough muscle and wind to enjoy the gallops."

Gavin thumped his mount on the shoulder. "Roland has always delighted in a hard run, and he's growing up. My boy will be ready for some competitive outings when the weather cools. I'm loath to turn him over to a real jockey."

DeWitt was more relaxed, too, less... bleak. An evening frolic by the Twid was ever useful for restoring the spirits.

"Phillip, may I ask you a question?"

"You excelled at asking questions when you were a lad. Now you're all manly silences and churchyard platitudes."

"I bored the village witless for years with my recitations, and they were all too kind to tell me to shut my gob. I'm repaying their consideration with some self-restraint. If somebody were intent on parting you and Hecate, how would you respond?"

Phillip adjusted reins that needed no adjusting. Herne was to be trusted under saddle in all particulars, unless an inviting mudpuddle tempted him from proper deportment. Mudpuddles turned an otherwise sane equine into a frolicking foal.

"I expected a question about schooling a horse over jumps, not amatory tactics."

"Mrs. Roberts and I became close shortly after we met. Somebody schemed to separate us or cause trouble between us. They succeeded, though Rose and I are sorting out particulars only now."

"Rose."

"Yes, Rose. If fate is kind and the lady willing, I hope to offer her the role of Mrs. Gavin DeWitt."

"A prudent man would allude to rushing fences and misjudging footing in the face of such a pronouncement. She tossed you into the ditch before."

They came to the turnoff for Lark's Nest, and yet, Phillip rode on.

"She never left me that money, Phillip. Somebody else schemed to injure my dignity, and Rose and I never discussed it. She took my hurt pride for an inexplicable rejection, and then she misconstrued some remarks made by another member of the company. Possibly."

"Dunderheadedness on every hand. Mrs. Roberts is an attractive, comfortably well-off widow. You doubtless had competitors for her attention, whether you noticed them or not. You were the centerpiece of Drysdale's budding hopes for a London tour, and allowing you to be distracted by a wealthy widow was not in his plans."

"I was no such thing."

"Mrs. Drysdale has arrived, and I had the good fortune to partner her at whist last night. She's looking very much forward to renewing her acquaintance with you."

"Gemma Drysdale had little enough use for me before, and I lived down to her expectations. I left the company just when Drysdale was considering allowing us to take on the shorter tragedies. She said I'd abandon them as soon as I'd learned a few roles, and she was right."

And yet, Gavin didn't sound engulfed in remorse for having fulfilled her worst predictions. "She spoke glowingly of you. Said you had real talent and deserved a better stage for your abilities."

"If she's at Miller's Lament, the other ladies will have arrived at Twidboro Hall."

Gavin had always been a clever lad. "You went directly to the stables from your bed this morning?"

"In a manner of speaking. Stop dawdling. Herne will grow fat and lazy if you don't keep him moving."

Ah, young love. Such an *energetic* affliction. "Drysdale might well have meddled between you and Mrs. Roberts. You were competition for him on the stage and doubtless made the actors who'd been with him longer discontent. They either resented you or took your part against Drysdale's less ambitious plans."

"This has occurred to me. Drysdale likes being center stage, which isn't the same as having the talent to occupy that spot. He and I need to have a frank and private discussion."

Phillip's money was on Gavin, who had the advantages of home turf, personal integrity, a smitten heart, and loyal reinforcements, did he but know it.

"And yonder he comes," Phillip said. "The man himself, almost as if he heard his cue. I'll leave you to state your business to him. Shall I take Roland to the grooms?"

Twenty yards up the path, Drysdale was ambling along as if lost in thought. Another unconvincing performance.

"That will suit," Gavin said, bringing Roland to a halt and swinging down. "Tell the stable lads Roland was an exceedingly good boy. I'll see you at lunch." He passed over the reins, touched a finger to his hat brim, and strode forward like a man with a purpose.

Drysdale didn't check his progress to wait for Gavin, meaning Gavin had to hustle to catch up. That, of course, was deliberate posturing from Drysdale, and Gavin wasn't in the mood to humor the man—to continue humoring him.

He paced along behind Drysdale about four feet back, scraping his boot against the path from time to time for added effect.

"I can do this all day, DeWitt. Let's cease with your puerile games."

"I can do this until the Twid meets up with the Thames miles on, and I have. Many a time. The going always gets a little muddy when the local streams debouch into the Twid, but if one knows the way, the mud can be avoided."

"How symbolic."

Gavin halted and stuck his nose in the air. "'We'll talk, you and I, about what I'm doing here. For now, I'll be providing the entertainment, just as I was hired to do.' I am not entertained by innuendo and strutting."

Drysdale turned. "You always were a good mimic."

Gavin had acquired that skill while reciting verse in the snug of the Crosspatch Arms and from performances given before his siblings. Both undertakings had imparted some common sense to him too.

"You learned that I usually exercise my colt along the Twid early in the day, and so you take the first morning constitutional of your long and storied life. You planned to accost me. I'm well and duly accosted, and my sisters expect me for breakfast, so talk."

Drysdale smiled, adopting the air of the tolerant senior diplomat. "I like your sisters. Miss Caroline will be an original, and Miss Diana will cut a swath in Town. They have provincial charm atop a good education and fine prospects."

Gavin had started the day with a heart full of joy and determination. He'd had a phenomenal ride on Roland and was already looking forward to seeing Rose at lunch. Drysdale's mention of Di and Caro put a blight upon all that sparkling wonder.

"My family is not your concern."

"For two years, they weren't your concern either. A man who will turn his back on his loved ones is not a fellow of sound morals. Despite his great wealth, he's also apparently inclined to the occasional bit of thievery. I should know. He used my troupe to disguise—note the irony—his larceny."

The Twid, swollen with the previous night's rain, was in lively good spirits, the morning sun brilliant upon the waters. Off in the distance, old Fortinbras bayed a welcome to the morning stage, and yet, Gavin had the sense that evil fairies had transported him from his home surrounds.

"I am not a thief, and you had best explain yourself."

Drysdale studied the water, his expression one of philosophical resignation. No wonder he stuck to the lighter fare—the tragic airs were not his forte.

"The rest of the cast supports you," he said. "I've questioned them all closely, and while they recall you roaming the Derbyshire venue freely and at curious hours, they don't condemn you."

"What on earth would they condemn me for?"

"Immediately following our Derbyshire engagement, you took a notion to decamp. I was adding repertoire, shifting parts, and varying our route all to accommodate your whims, and yet, you turned your back on that opportunity. Why? Because you stole the funds I was paid at that house party, and you stole a certain necklace sitting in the same vicinity. That's why you quit Drysdale's Players for no apparent reason. Admit it, DeWitt. There is no other reason for your sudden departure."

A broken heart was a reason—and none of Drysdale's bloody business. "I stole nothing, and I had no need of stolen funds. I have no motive, the entire troupe had the same access to these alleged treasures as I did, and *you* are always in need of coin."

Drysdale clearly hadn't expected a logical challenge to his accusations. He stalked off, pivoted, and would likely have shaken his fist at the sky—one of his favorite bits of stage business—had an audience been present.

"You wealthy young wastrels will commit felonies for a lark." He marched back, stopping just out of pummeling range. "Half this village will attest to the difficulties your womenfolk were in as a result of your thespian adventures. For all the world knows, you *did* need coin, and you should not have repaid my generosity with betrayal."

Drysdale's accusations raised myriad questions. Where had this necklace come from, if it even existed? Had the coins nestled in Gavin's cravat been the missing sum? If larceny had been committed, who was at fault? What could Rose add to Gavin's meager recollections of the other house-party guests?

At the moment, none of that mattered. "You expect me to repay the missing money? Am I also to compensate you for this mythical necklace?"

"You are to return the necklace, you dolt. A piece like that is priceless, and I would not accept the money without the necklace, in any case."

"How can I return a necklace I've never seen?"

"If you can't recall the sight of a rope of rubies set in gold, you are blind as well as arrogant."

"Sorry. We don't see much in the ruby line here in Crosspatch Corners. If you can prove I owe you money, I will happily repay a reasonable sum, but I left your troupe without collecting the wages due me, and I gave you three weeks' notice so you could shift any needed rehearsals. I will consider this distasteful topic closed."

"No, you will not." Drysdale took a step closer, then apparently thought better of increasing his proximity. "Between Gemma and me, we can manufacture enough testimony to see you transported at least. If that doesn't get your attention, then consider the damage I can do to your sisters' prospects when I pass through my London haunts. A word or two about mental instability in the DeWitt lineage, weak character *even for an actor*, and recent financial difficulties will work wonders."

Gavin's fist in Drysdale's paunch would work wonders too. "My brother-by-marriage is a *marquess*, Drysdale. Do you really believe spreading rumors backstage at third-rate houses will be sufficient to counter his influence?"

"Most certainly. Tavistock will take your part out of loyalty and because he sympathizes with a man who's short of coin. If you doubt I can affect your sisters' prospects, and you're happy to risk a trip to the Antipodes—or the gallows—then at least have a care for Mrs. Roberts's reputation."

A fist to the gut was too good for such a scoundrel. "Mrs. Roberts is well above reproach in all particulars and has no part in your schemes. Why even mention her?"

"She wanted no parts of you by the time we left Derbyshire. Perhaps you stole more from her than her trust and her time? Maybe she simply tired of your charms and is ready to work her wiles on the next unsuspecting bachelor. Widowhood can turn some women up so wonderfully frisky, but Society expects discretion from those ladies all the same."

The roar of the river blended with a roar building in Gavin's soul —of outrage, determination, and disgust. He instead drew upon the civility that a budding respected squire should be able to muster in all circumstances.

He bowed politely. "If you've finished reciting your lines in this farce, I'll be on my way. I know of no missing necklace. I stole nothing from you or from anybody else. I wish you the best of luck with the remainder of your engagement at Miller's Lament."

Petty tactics, to break the taboo about wishing an actor luck with a performance, but satisfying. Gavin strolled off, intent on taking the side path that led to Twidboro Hall.

"I'll give you one week, DeWitt," Drysdale called. "If you have to retrieve the damned jewels from London, that should be sufficient time, but don't try my patience any further. When I mutter to my London confreres about your light fingers and the poor character of the women you pursue, my animosity will be unquestionably sincere."

Gavin ambled along until he reached the turnoff to Twidboro Hall. From the tail of his eye, he saw Drysdale thirty yards up the path, gazing at the river and affecting the pose of the sad contemplative.

What bloody necklace was he pondering—if such jewelry even existed—and who was the true thief?

One thought swam to the surface of the miasma of dread and rage in Gavin's mind: Rose could not be associated with any of this and most especially not with Gavin himself. Not until the whole sorry business was resolved.

CHAPTER THIRTEEN

"You barely spoke to Mrs. Roberts at luncheon." Diana leveled her accusation at her favorite brother in the whole world, who was also, at the moment, her unfavorite brother in the whole universe.

"You hurt her feelings," Caroline said, unnecessarily, but Caro was tenderhearted and had caught on to Gavin's odd behavior before Diana had.

Gavin came around the billiards table and pretended to study the rack of cue sticks. He'd taught them both how to play, and many a winter afternoon had been less boring as a result. Even Lissa and Mama had occasionally taken turns.

"This is what you dragged me up here to discuss? My deportment? I am one of a handful of men participating in this inane gathering. As much as I esteem Mrs. Roberts—very much—I cannot become her personal escort. If you'll excuse me, I am due to meet with the steward at the Arms. Roland and I will go for our hack thereafter, and I will see you at supper."

"You are always meeting with the steward," Diana countered. "Lissa convened with him regularly, too, but she didn't hare off to the Arms to do it."

Gavin snatched a cue stick and arranged the three balls on the table—white, red, and spot. "I am not haring off."

"Yes," Caroline said. "You are. It's what you do. We don't mean you are leaving Crosspatch again. We mean you always have an excuse to go elsewhere. You must hack out on Roland—twice a day, Gavin, every day, rain or shine, without fail. You must meet with the steward. You must call on Vicar. You must see to the accounts. You used to have time to be our brother."

Diana could not have launched such a salvo with just that blend of pique and wounded pride. Perhaps Caro harbored thespian tendencies too.

Gavin set his ball to the left of the spot. "We grow up, Caroline. Diana is poised for her come out. You will soon follow in her footsteps. I have more on my mind than teaching you lot birdcalls."

Gavin could be testy or a touch ironic, but he was never, ever mean. He wasn't being mean now. He had the same holding-on-by-a-thread look in his eyes that Lissa and Mama had had the whole time he'd been gone. Something or someone had rattled him badly.

Not Mrs. Roberts. She'd been rattled as well, by Gavin's exquisite —and slightly distant—good manners.

"Gav, *what's going on?*"

He chalked the tip of his stick. "Why does anything have to be going on? Anything other than the oddest house party in the history of the entire blighted institution? The usual unbridled curiosity of the neighbors? The equally predictable long-windedness about an approaching harvest that will arrive whether we discuss it or not?"

Caro let forth a harrumph worthy of Grandmama on the subject of Prinny's financial excesses. Give the child credit, she otherwise held her tongue, another masterly tactic borrowed from Grandmama's arsenal.

"I'm sorry," Gavin said, eyeing the table and looking very gloomy indeed. "I am out of sorts, and I do apologize for my short temper."

"You are haring off again," Diana said. "Retreating into good manners and masculine condescension. If you don't nip away to the Arms—and to some of Mrs. P's best summer ale—you will claim it's time to ride a horse who could use a day off every now and then."

Gavin winced. "I'm conditioning Roland. He's done too much resting in his short life."

Caroline pushed her specs up her nose. "You are not your horse, Gav, which is fortunate, or we'd never be able to close a window when you were in the room."

That shot provoked a wan smile. "I am not my horse, but I am the de facto manager of Twidboro Hall. Why don't you two enjoy a game?"

He proffered the cue stick, and a year ago, maybe even six months ago, Diana would have taken the bait and been pleased to indulge in a generally male and grown-up diversion.

"Why don't you tell us what's the matter, Gavin DeWitt? We're your sisters. We want to help."

He put the cue stick on the table. "I know you are my sisters. I wouldn't have it any other way, but I really must be going."

Caroline sent Diana a look, part exasperation, part panic. Very well. Diana would haul up the sororal artillery.

"Be off with you, then," Diana said, taking up the cue stick. "We won't bother telling you that we saw Lady Iris rifling Mrs. Roberts's effects as we went down to lunch. Mrs. Roberts's room has the best view of the Twid on that side of the house, and we meant to peek out her window to see if you were coming up the path. Lady Iris was in the dressing closet."

Gavin was no longer eyeing the door. "Go on."

"We thought she was a maid," Caro observed. "She was going through the drawer at the bottom of the wardrobe, like a maid counting linen. We didn't see her at first, and she apparently didn't see us. She wore a mobcap and long apron, which struck me as very odd accessories to an afternoon dress."

"The bell had rung," Diana added. "Why wasn't she on her way down to the buffet?"

Gavin had gone very still, staring at the neat trio of balls on the table, the red ball waiting, waiting, for the opening shot.

"Lady Iris was loosely disguised as a maid, and she was rifling Mrs. Roberts's linen?"

"When she noticed us," Diana said, "she held out a rolled-up pair of stockings, smiled like a guilty schoolboy, and said, 'Found them!' As if one pair of summer stockings would stand out from all the rest. Then she was out the door that opens onto the corridor. She said nothing about it at luncheon."

"She wasn't wearing the apron or mobcap at luncheon either," Caro said, walking around the whole table, as Gav had taught them to do when preparing for a game. "She did go on without ceasing about the medicinal properties of green tea, as if anybody cares to know about that."

"Precisely the point." Gavin took the cue stick from Diana and passed it to Caro. "Any sane person would avoid becoming the audience for such a discourse and forget entirely that Lady Iris had been late to the meal."

"She was," Diana said, pleased that Gavin was thinking about something besides ledgers, summer ale, and his flatulent horse. "Not horribly late, but slipping into the line when some of the guests were already seated."

Caroline positioned her ball on the right side of the table. A wise choice when the afternoon sun was pouring through the windows facing the left side.

"Lady Iris is good at slipping in and slipping out," Caroline said, gaze on the table. "She left the library last night as the tables were forming for whist."

Gavin looked thunderous at that news. "Where did she go?"

Caro looked up from the table. "Upstairs. But the ladies' retiring room is on the main floor."

Diana had forgotten that part. "She came back with a shawl. Does it take twenty minutes to fetch a shawl?"

Caroline bent low, the cue stick in position. She resembled a cat preparing to pounce. The crack of one ball hitting another resounded through the afternoon's peace.

"Good job," Gavin said, offering the first genuine smile Diana had seen from him that day. "You got your hips into it."

Caroline grinned. "I had a good teacher. What is Lady Iris up to, Gav?"

"I suspect she's either looking for stolen goods, or she's planning to purloin somebody's treasures. Ladies will occasionally hide valuables someplace other than their jewelry boxes."

"Because," Caroline said, "jewelry box locks are notoriously easy to pick."

Gavin's brows twitched down. "Who told you that?"

"You did. Honestly, Gav, are you going all elderly and decrepitated on us?"

"He's in love," Diana said, because no good brother should go untwitted. "Though he wasn't acting very lovable at lunch."

"I am... preoccupied."

Caroline twirled the cue stick like some sort of performer at Astley's. "You hurt Mrs. Roberts's feelings."

"I am sorry for that, and I will make amends. For right now, I want the two of you to promise me something."

Caroline left off threatening the breakables. "We don't make promises lightly, brother dear."

"I don't make this request lightly. Be careful of Drysdale. Don't share your meals with him. Avoid his escort in the garden. By no means allow him to pry into family business. If he tries to strike up a conversation, be as boring as Lady Iris on the subject of her herbs."

"I'll quote Wordsworth," Caroline said. "I've got pages and pages of him off by heart, all rhyme-y and sweet. I can make a regular hash of it all too. Maybe I should do some Shakespeare for him."

She'd clearly surprised Gav with that one. "When did you take up memorizing the Bard?" he asked.

"When you disappeared."

Gavin caught Caroline in a hug. "I'm never disappearing again. I thought we'd established that."

Caroline tolerated the embrace with patient long-suffering and stepped back at the first opportunity.

"So where are you off to now?"

"I must have a very frank and very private talk with Mrs. Roberts."

Mission accomplished. "Be off with you." Diana waved a hand toward stage left. "Caro and I will avoid Mr. Drysdale's company. Our regards to Mrs. Roberts."

Gavin headed for the door. "If she's still speaking to me."

"Gav, dearest, if Mrs. Roberts won't speak to you, neither will we." Diana blew him a kiss and took up a cue stick.

Gavin bowed and slipped out the door.

"You didn't leave me much in the way of shots," Diana said. "Shall we play to eight points?"

"We shan't play at all." Caroline had drifted to the window, but was standing a good foot back from the panes. Lurking, in other words. "Keeping an eye on the Drysdale creature isn't the same as accepting his escort, is it?"

Diana put the stick back on the rack and went to the window. "Why no, brilliant sister and observant sister of mine. Not the same thing at all." She joined Caroline at the window, also keeping back a foot or so. "Dear me. Mr. and Mrs. Drysdale seem to be out of charity with each other."

The couple were on the path that led to the river, and Mrs. Drysdale was apparently delivering a hearty dressing down to her spouse. He countered with a hand raised to the heavens, followed by a finger shaken at his helpmeet.

"They are actors," Caroline said, "but this conversation is dramatic even for thespians."

"She's upset with him. Mrs. Pevinger gets the same exasperated air with Mr. P when he offers a free pint to the winners on darts night."

"How could you possibly know that?"

"Because Tansy P and I are friends, and... Good Lord, she's having the last word." Mrs. Drysdale was storming off in the direction of the house, while her husband remained on the path, his expression one of bitter exasperation.

~

Rose was bitterly exasperated, bewildered, and... overreacting. "I'm fine," she informed her reflection in the vanity's folding mirror. "Gavin was preoccupied, and it's not as if we can be lost to all decorum."

Though they had been. For a few, luscious hours, they had been lost to everything but shared pleasure. If anything, intimacies with Gavin DeWitt were lovelier than ever, which should not have been possible.

His touch was magic, soothing and tender, then naughty and bold, then...

"I'm fine," Rose said again, trying for some calm. "I shall be fine. Gavin has a lot on his mind."

The words were out of her mouth, the same futile phrase she'd used to excuse Dane's relentless neglect of her and his home.

The bedroom door opened, and Timmens bustled in. "Oh, there you are. Been looking high and low. Let's get you into a proper walking dress, shall we? The company will leave for the village in thirty minutes, though when has a gaggle of Society ladies ever done anything on time?"

Timmens marched straight for the dressing closet while Rose remained on the vanity stool. Two hours of Lady Iris's herbal sermons, Miss Peasegood's incessant prattling, and Lady Duncannon's braw, bonnie tippling would send Rose straight to Bedlam.

"I'm not accompanying the ladies on their walk. I needn't change."

"Nonsense." Timmens emerged with a burgundy velvet frock

that was far too hot for a summer afternoon, though it was hemmed for walking. "The fresh air will put some roses in your cheeks."

Rose assayed her appearance in the mirror. Her cheeks were quite rosy enough. "You can put the dress away, Timmens. If I were to hike into the village to buy hair ribbons I don't need and swill cider that could fell a dragoon, then I wouldn't wear half mourning to do it."

"You are a widow." Timmens's tone presaged tempests of the sulking variety. "This is a lovely dress. Your late spouse brought the velvet home from London himself, if you'll recall. I thought you might be missing him."

I should sack her for her meanness. Rose had attributed such thoughts on previous occasions to passing exasperation, the irritability that accompanied months of enforced mourning rituals, the annoyance any employer might occasionally feel toward an outspoken employee. Timmens was loyal, if irksome, and she was mostly competent.

I should sack her had nearly become *I shall sack her.* But one did not sack servants of long standing when far from home, and Timmens was not responsible for Rose's present upset.

"I had plenty of opportunity to miss Dane when he was living, and that was his choice. Put the dress away, Timmens, and leave me some privacy. I am inclined to take a nap."

Timmens drew herself up, the dress folded over her arm. "Best not, ma'am. You get all out of sorts and inside out with your days and nights when you start napping."

And who had urged naps on Rose without ceasing as the best medicine for grief? Rose had complied, simply to have some solitude in the middle of the day.

"Very well. I'm for the library, then. The company of a good book appeals. I'll select my own ensemble for supper. You may do as you please with your afternoon."

Timmens looked as if she'd continue the battle, then her air became martyred. "I'll tend to the mending, then. Enjoy your book, ma'am."

Rose's wardrobe needed no mending, though perhaps Timmens had taken to tearing her own hems. The maid retreated into the dressing closet and commenced banging drawers open and closed, one of her favorite tactics for continuing a disagreement.

And that was all just... *fine.* Domestic service was demanding and not very remunerative, and Timmens had got on well with both Mama and Dane, and Timmens wasn't the true problem.

Rose took herself out into the corridor and aimed for the library, which was likely to be deserted. Lord Tavistock had purchased a quantity of books while on the Continent, and Rose had yet to investigate his collection.

"The problem," Rose muttered to the gryphon carved on the outside of the library door, "is that I am falling in love again—or maybe I never really fell out of love—and Gavin acted just as politely chilly at luncheon as he did up in Derbyshire. And that..."

His behavior had hurt her. The distant politeness had bewildered her, frightened her, and reminded her all too well of how Dane's shifting moods had racked her nerves. Jolly one moment, morose the next. Abjectly apologetic, then snide and dismissive.

The memories, combined with her present shaken nerves, made a bilious combination. Perhaps some poetry...

"Except that I never cared for ruddy poetry."

"Mrs. Roberts?" Lady Tavistock, looking composed and kindly, had appeared with the exquisitely bad timing of the concerned hostess, and Lady Phillip was at her side. "Are you well?"

I'm conversing with a wooden gryphon. What do you think? "Just debating a minor point of philosophy. I'm—"

"You look a tad disconcerted," Lady Phillip said. "Even good company can become tiresome when one is accustomed to solitude."

She spoke from some sort of experience, and her words were meant kindly, but Rose wanted nothing so much as for her hostesses to *go away.*

She'd often wanted Dane, Mama, and Timmens to go away. When Dane had gone away—always at the busiest times of year for Colforth Hall—she'd wanted him to *stay away*. She did not want Gavin to go away, but in some regard, at luncheon he had.

"I thought I'd find a good book," Rose said, pushing open the library door. The space was blessedly deserted and flooded with afternoon light. "I am a voracious reader, and an outing into the village doesn't appeal just at the moment."

"This has to do with my dunderheaded brother, doesn't it?" Lady Tavistock said, accompanying Rose into the library. "He was all Mayfair manners at luncheon, and yet, he kept looking at you when you were pretending not to look at him."

Lady Phillip closed the library door and began a circuit of the room, twitching at beautifully arranged bouquets of sweet peas or straightening candles that needed no straightening.

"Men can be the very devil," she said. "My own dear Phillip included. He is the best of fellows, and I adore him without limit, but he has been slow to accept that a wife is for confiding in."

"Tavistock has come a long way," Lady Tavistock observed. "I daresay I have as well. Gavin is still very much a work in progress."

"Might we discuss Lord Tavistock's books?" Rose asked. "I understand young Caroline is a bibliophile."

Rose's hostesses did not so much as glance at each other, and yet, they seemed to be acting in concert.

"A wonderful collection," Lady Tavistock said briskly. "Gavin has the better library of plays. If you like, I can take you over to Twidboro Hall while Lady Phillip accompanies the ladies into the village."

Somebody was having an argument around the side of the house. The words were indistinct, while the bickering tone was unmistakable. That dispute meant Rose could not snatch a random volume and flee to the garden, and Lady Phillip just happened to be blocking her path to the door.

"We can venture to Twidboro Hall another time," Rose said. "I'll content myself with some damned Wordsworth for the moment."

She realized she'd cursed only when a silence of several eternities' duration greeted her words.

"I'm sorry. I'm a bit out of sorts. If I can manage a few hours to myself, I'm sure I'll be fine. I don't actually care for poetry."

Lady Tavistock crossed from the hearth and gave Rose the sort of look a mother aimed at a docile child turned up inexplicably cranky.

"You don't care for Wordsworth at all, do you?"

The compassion in her ladyship's eyes, the complete lack of judgment, shattered something old and brittle in Rose's soul.

"I abhor his every rubbishing rhyme. Perhaps I need a nap, or one of Lady Iris's t-tisanes. I'll come around, I'm sure. I'm just... I'll be..."

Lady Tavistock held out her arms. "You are not fine. You are not fine at all."

Rose went into her ladyship's embrace and commenced bawling as if her heart was breaking. Lady Tavistock, who was a few inches taller than Rose, wrapped her in a fierce hug and spoke past Rose's shoulder to Lady Phillip.

"Find my dunderpated, hen-witted, bumbling excuse for a brother, please. He has much to—"

The door swung open. To Rose's undying mortification, Gavin stepped through.

"Has anybody seen Mrs. Rob... Rose. What's wrong? You're crying. Who has made you cry? I'll blacken both his eyes and boot him from the property."

He advanced, handkerchief at the ready, and his very fierceness made Rose cry harder.

"You have," she said, wrenching herself from Lady Tavistock's hug. "You have, you wretched bounder, and I am *not fine*, and that is your fault, and I am ready to pack my bags and leave you to your stupid male moods and whims, because *I have had enough*."

She was being unfair, of course. She was heaping on the present moment an entire marriage worth of misery, plus the detritus of the debacle in Derbyshire, and all the uncertainty that came from last night followed by Gavin's performance at luncheon.

"I'm tired of being fair," Rose added. "It's a rubbishing lot of work for no reward. I'm tired of being a proper widow, tired of even the servants feeling entitled to judge me. I'm exhausted and not in the mood for your intrigues and machinations, Gavin. If you mean to apologize, do so—you owe me an apology—but I want answers, too, and no more of your passionate odes one minute and ignoring me over the dessert tray the next."

"Badly done," Lady Tavistock murmured.

"Phillip noticed it at once," Lady Phillip said. "You were not subtle, sir."

Rose dabbed at her cheeks with Gavin's handkerchief, which bore the light, woody fragrance she associated with him, and with unforgettable intimacies. She wasn't about to return it to him, despite her present anger.

"I'm sorry I hurt your feelings," Gavin said, directing the words solely to Rose. "I wasn't aiming for a subtle performance at the buffet. I am also sorry I could not explain what I was about earlier, but if you can stand to listen, I'd like to explain now. I *need* to explain, and if we could send the ladies off to the village with Mama and get Tavistock and Phillip in here immediately, I'd appreciate that as well."

Lady Phillip marched from the room, while Lady Tavistock studied her brother. "This is serious, isn't it?"

Gavin reached for Rose's hand. "Deadly serious, and that was before I found the woman I love in tears."

CHAPTER FOURTEEN

"I'll explain to Mama that she must lead the next charge on Pevinger's ladies' parlor," Amaryllis said. "I won't be gone long." She aimed a look of sororal doom at Gavin, then left him alone with Rose.

Who hadn't withdrawn her hand from his, but neither had she accepted his apology.

"Drysdale wants something I don't have," Gavin said. "I learned of his ambitions only this morning. He is conspiring against me and my family, despite the DeWitts' connection to Tavistock and his lofty circle. My theatrical past has risen up to haunt me exactly as Grandmama and Mama feared it would."

Rose dabbed at her eyes with his handkerchief. "How can Drysdale hurt you, Gavin? He's a jumped-up strolling player, mediocre at best, and hardly well connected."

Gavin led her to the reading table, lest he take a wing chair and pull her into his lap. Such nonsense would doubtless earn him a ringing scold, but he treasured even Rose's scolds.

"I've underestimated him," Gavin said, holding an end chair for Rose, then taking the seat at the head of the table. "He has cronies and familiars in London, and some surprisingly well-placed families will allow the occasional younger son to frolic among the thespians."

Rose tucked Gavin's handkerchief into a pocket. "To say nothing of the company kept by opera dancers who rub shoulders with seamstresses who are married to the fellows in the orchestra, one of whom might also have a post as an organist at St. Somebody's, and so forth. I spent enough time in Town to realize it's a series of connected villages. I found the complexity unappealing. Hard to know who somebody truly is when he's a carousing rake one evening, a churchyard dandy the following Sunday, and the next MP from some banker's home village the day after that."

Some banker's pride and joy had much to answer for—a challenge for another time. "You have it precisely, and Drysdale is threatening to use those connections to see to it that Diana's come out is a disaster."

Rose stood and paced the length of the windows. "You want to tell yourself he couldn't possibly do that. He's being outlandish, and nobody would be stupid enough to listen to him, but gossip doesn't work like that. Gossip seeps up from the servants' hall like rising damp. It creeps down the flue like coal dust. It wafts around the churchyard like the stink from the river when the wind is just right. The people who matter would hear of your family's failings not from Drysdale, but from trusted sources."

"You truly do not care for London, do you?"

She stood at the window overlooking the garden, her figure lonely and dear. "I feel toward London as you likely do toward the countryside. The shires have many fine qualities, you are connected to some lovely people there, but it's simply not right for you."

"I wouldn't go that far."

She aimed a look at him over her shoulder. Analytical, dispassionate, not the look of a woman in love. "You tell yourself that you'll manage here in Crosspatch Corners, that there's nothing truly wrong. That a vague discontent is hardly worth noting, much less dwelling on, and you have much to be grateful for—all true. And yet, somewhere more honest than your mind—your heart perhaps—knows differently. You aren't fine at all."

Gavin rose and drew her away from the windows. "I haven't been right since I left you in Derbyshire. Lately, I've wondered if that, rather than a life limited to my own perfectly lovely village, is what's plaguing me."

Rose considered him. "I am beset, too, Gavin, and I am part of your past. I want a future with you, one free of intrigue and the sort of posturing you got up to at lunch. You've summoned your in-laws because you seek to warn them, don't you?"

"Of course I must warn them. I'll let Mama and the girls know what's afoot as soon as Phillip and Tavistock have been informed."

"And then?"

And then loomed a series of possibilities, all of them vexing. "Drysdale maundered on about a necklace, and he claims I also owe him money, a sum greater than the amount I found among my clothes in Derbyshire. I can repay him the money easily."

Rose shook her head. "He'll come around, again and again, his entrances exquisitely timed to cause you embarrassment and worry. Until it's Caroline's turn to make a come out, and then Diana will have a daughter, and so forth. He truly is a plague, Gavin. Dane had creditors like that, but fortunately, what he owed them were debts of honor, so claims of interest were only so much attempted bullying."

"These creditors harassed you upon Dane's death?"

"Like vultures flapping around a carcass. I'm convinced Dane spent time in the country mostly to avoid his duns. He'd sell a couple of hunters, pawn some of the Roberts family jewels, and then he'd be off again. He had no respect for Colforth Hall. Considered it a ball and chain, but without an heir to consent to breaking the entail, he was stuck with it. My sole redeeming quality was my ability to squeeze money out of the place. My settlements stated that the property came to me if we had no children—and thank heavens and Mama's solicitors for that."

Gavin took her hand, then slid an arm around her shoulders.

"Dane was a disgrace. I love my family and my home, Rose. I'm not Dane. I'm also not a natural fit with the role of country squire."

She curled into his embrace, and for a moment, all the menace and mayhem Drysdale threatened slid away.

"You are a better fit than you think. You love time spent in the saddle. The neighbors are all fond of you, your sisters adore you, and your land prospers."

Gavin bent his head and spoke near Rose's ear, lest she mistake his words. "I love you. I love your ferocious passion and your abiding sense of respect for the land. I love your laughter and your tender heart. I loathe that I gave you occasion for tears. Am I forgiven?"

Rose rested her forehead on his shoulder. "Drysdale threatened me, too, didn't he?"

Gavin considered lying, then mentally kicked himself for even entertaining the notion. This was Rose—his Rose—and her acumen was another reason he loved her.

"Yes, and he had a front-row seat to our affair in Derbyshire. He'll make you out to be the merriest widow ever to disgrace her husband's memory."

Rose was quiet, and Gavin could feel her thoughts whirling like a mill wheel. "It's worse than that, isn't it?" she said. "Many a widow has enjoyed her freedom. Society grants her that latitude, provided she's discreet. You mentioned a necklace. Will he accuse me of stealing it when he's done blaming you for its disappearance?"

A queasy dread had Gavin stepping back. "He... could. He said the players would connive to provide enough testimony to see me transported, or worse. If he's willing to go to those lengths, he's probably holding the threat of criminal charges against you in reserve, but you're right. He will get there eventually." While Rose had made the leap nigh instantly.

"Tavistock would tell you to take a repairing lease on the Continent."

"Tavistock would tell *us* to take that repairing lease."

"I cannot abandon Colforth Hall as harvest approaches. You have reinforcements here, Gavin. Tavistock, your family, Lord Phillip... They will all manage your interests in your absence."

"Tavistock took a repairing lease on the Continent, and it nearly ended in disaster. I larked off to join Drysdale's Players, and that, too, nearly ended in disaster. I am loath to retreat this time, Rose."

"Thieves and threats, harvest bearing down, villains skulking about in the hedges, and missing necklaces nobody has seen... This would make a fine stage play." She returned to his embrace. "Don't ever snub me like that again, Gavin. I don't care if the hounds of hell will turn on me should you show me any favor. You cannot employ that tactic with me ever, for any reason."

She fit in his embrace perfectly. Always had. "I might have to. Drysdale can ruin you and me both. Your best bet is to leave here, enraged with me, letting all and sundry know that I am the last man you will ever spare a thought for, unless it's to pray for my doom."

"And then highwaymen will hold up my fleeing coach, and Drysdale will be their leader, and you will thwart them, and all will come right before the curtain comes down, except this isn't a comedy, Gavin. Transport ships leave regularly for the Antipodes, and I'm sure a fair number of their passengers are innocent of any crime save bad luck."

Gavin held her, breathed with her, and considered her words. Running wasn't an option. Paying Drysdale off wasn't an option. Ignoring his threats wasn't an option. How to end the play so the villain got his just deserts, and virtue was rewarded?

"The first thing we do," he said, "is expand the cast. Your thinking and mine are the same in that regard. Increase the forces on the side of right. Then we add to the confusion and befuddle our foe, until he either surrenders or flees the scene."

"He needs to flee the country, Gavin. I'll not have that man lurking in the wings of our life."

"Neither will I." The library door opened to reveal Tavistock, flanked by Lord Phillip, Lady Phillip, and Amaryllis. "Our reinforcements have arrived. Friends, have a seat. We have much to discuss."

Tavistock settled his wife at the foot of the table while Lord Phillip held a chair for his Hecate.

"We're not wandering into the village to swill cider and be gawked at by our neighbors?" Lord Phillip asked.

"Not today," Gavin said.

"Mama will escort the ladies," Amaryllis said. "We are guaranteed a bit of privacy, but not for long. Gavin, enough theatrics. What on earth is going on?"

"We have a thief in our midst," he said, "possibly two thieves. Caroline and Diana caught Lady Iris going through Rose's wardrobe, and her ladyship was minimally disguised as a maid at the time."

Rose, who'd resumed her corner seat, thumped a fist on the table. "That's where you saw Lady Iris before, Gavin. She was a maid up in Derbyshire. Wore her hair under a cap, often had a smudge of ash on her cheek. Her spectacles sat ever so slightly crookedly on her nose."

Gavin wanted to blow Rose a kiss. "You're right, and we noticed the smudge and the glasses and were distracted from the fine features and lovely eyes. The rest of you, lend me thine ears, because Drysdale is threatening to bring charges against me, destroy Rose's reputation, and ruin Diana's chances in Town unless I can produce a certain ruby necklace, which he claims I stole in Derbyshire."

That announcement inspired a babble of *how dare he* and *brood of vipers* and *deserves a proper hiding*. Gavin let the expostulations fly for a moment, then waded in with further explanations.

"That ruby necklace—if it exists—doesn't belong to Drysdale," Tavistock said at a lull in the exchange. "If he got his hands on a piece like that, he'd be pawning it on Ludgate Hill and buying himself a little manor house, not racketing about from market green to village crossroads to spa town."

Lord Phillip wrinkled his nose. "He stole it first, you mean, and then somebody stole it from him?"

"My vote goes to Lady Iris," Rose said. "She's more than a bit peculiar. She's skulking and lurking, and now that I think about it, somebody might have stolen my pearl earbobs in Derbyshire. I am lamentably careless with my jewelry—none of it is worth much—but I liked those earbobs. Bought them for myself in London."

"We need a plan," Amaryllis said. "I'll not have Miller's Lament's first house party become an object of scandal. Drysdale must be sent packing, and before he can cause any more trouble. Tavistock?"

The marquess, who'd once again propped an elbow against the mantel, straightened. "Thief-taking is not in my gift. Phillip?"

"I have a few ideas, but I'd like to hear what DeWitt has up his sleeve. He knows Drysdale best, and he's our greatest thespian talent. If the matter takes some playacting or dramatics, DeWitt is our best hope of prevailing."

"I agree," Rose said, "but I'd certainly like to take a supporting role."

"As would I," Lady Phillip said. "I played the part of the money-obsessed spinster for years, and nobody suspected I'd rather have been spending my time making mint jelly."

"My favorite," Phillip murmured, "and whither thou goest, and all that, though I doubt I'm much of an actor. Lady Tavistock?"

"If I can be of any use... I always did fancy our local theatricals. Gavin, for once, you may tell me what to do, but don't get carried away. I am still your sister."

Was this what Gavin had sought when he'd wandered from home? A loyal troupe? A band of brothers—and sisters?

"The plan," he said, "wants refining, so all ideas are welcome, but I thought we'd bait our trap with some of Tavistock's sparkly tat. I assume the Vincent family has some impressive jewels..." He spoke, he listened, he revised some details, and then revised a few more.

By the time Gavin was once again alone in the library with Rose, the game was well and truly afoot.

～

Trevor, Lord Tavistock, beamed at Miss Peasegood as she recounted her aunt's goddaughter's best friend's court presentation. Miss P

treated Tavistock to a word-for-word rendering of the exchange with
the sovereign and his aging mama and a plume-by-pearl description
of the young lady's attire.

The longer Miss Peasegood held forth, the more the part of the
slightly tipsy, ornamental, aristocratic host bearing up loyally under
the tribulation of his wife's social ambitions felt like Tavistock's reality, rather than a part he played for the sake of the larger drama.

Ye gods, the woman could talk. "But what of your own presentation?" Tavistock asked. "Surely that day was more memorable than
some distant acquaintance's experience?"

Miss Peasegood blinked, she sipped her punch, she sneaked a
glance at the formal parlor's mantel clock. "The whole business was
so long ago, my lord, and the details fade. Tell me, where did you and
the marchioness meet?"

Miss Peasegood had apparently never been presented. Interesting. "Not far from here, as a matter of fact. I was on the last leg of my
journey out from Town, and she was enjoying a pleasant afternoon
hack." Until Roland had bolted and dumped her into the nearest
ditch. "Ah, Mrs. Drysdale, Mr. Drysdale. Greetings. We were having
the most fascinating discussion of all things fashionable, and Miss
Peasegood has turned the topic to the happy day I met my
marchioness. How did the two of you meet, if I might indulge some
natural curiosity?"

He smiled at them fatuously, suggesting he'd been at the punch
too enthusiastically. In truth, Tavistock did not give a malodorous
equine flatus how the Drysdales had met, but Gavin, in rapt discussion with Lady Duncannon over by the mantel, had yet to signal that
the next stage of the proceedings could commence.

"We met in a production of *Twelfth Night*," Gemma Drysdale
said. "I was wardrobe mistress in addition to playing a few of the
smaller roles, and dear Hammond had a propensity for destroying his
costume."

"She stitched me back together." Drysdale patted the hand Mrs.
Drysdale had wrapped around his forearm. "My Gemma is still the

best theater seamstress I know, and we never lose a prop or a prompt book, thanks to my dear wife."

"I love Viola's speech," Miss Peasegood said, apparently still focused on *Twelfth Night*. "When she's realized what a great lot of confusion she's caused as Cesario and has no earthly idea how to sort it all out..."

I left no ring with her: what means this lady?
    Fortune forbid my outside have not charm'd her!
    She made good view of me; indeed, so much,
    That sure methought her eyes had lost her tongue.

"A wonderful speech," Mrs. Drysdale said, sparing Tavistock from devising a means of stopping the juggernaut of Miss Peasegood's discourse. "Women can have a much lighter touch with humor than men, don't you think?"

Over by the mantel, Gavin finally brandished his pocket watch.

"I will trust you ladies to sort through that profound topic," Tavistock said. "Drysdale, you might appreciate the art we have hanging in the library. Let's leave the ladies to philosophize for a moment or two, shall we?"

The Drysdales exchanged a look, which to Tavistock's eye looked minatory from the lady and slightly annoyed from her husband, though both spouses were smiling.

"The library art is nothing special," Tavistock said when he and his guest had gained the corridor, "but the decanters offer something more substantial than punch. You are my alibi, Drysdale, and I expect you to be duly impressed with the Constable over the mantel."

"I've always fancied Constable. Such vision, such subtle symbolism."

"Oh quite, if one prefers a countryside done in unrelenting shades of brown. Greenish brown, bluish brown, creamish brown, brownish brown. I vow I do not recognize the countryside he paints. Perhaps England was plagued by incessant drought in his youth. I do recognize a good brandy when one comes my way."

Drysdale smiled. "A marquess after my own heart."

Tavistock opened the library door and recalled Gavin's advice. *Don't act if you can instead emphasize the parts of true life that fit best with the role.*

"Do you know how tiresome being *the* marquess becomes in these surrounds?" Tavistock asked, going straight to the sideboard. "I might as well be one of the hyenas in the royal menagerie, I'm such an oddity. The local folk are very dear, but also prone to gawking. I've trotted out the '98 to fortify my nerves for the duration of the gathering. Do join me."

The vintage in the decanter was good, but hadn't a patch on the real '98. Tavistock was saving that to share with Amaryllis on their first wedding anniversary.

He poured two servings, nosed his portion, and lifted his glass. "To successful performances."

Drysdale returned the gesture. "To successful performances. Speaking of which, what did you make of young DeWitt's foray into the theater? Not quite the done thing, was it?"

"My years foraying about on the Continent weren't the done thing either." Tavistock knocked back his drink, which had been half the size of Drysdale's serving. "Young fellows can benefit enormously from kicking over the traces, or so my marchioness claims. Between us, though... She's very relieved DeWitt has put all that behind him. We have hopes he'll take a wife soon, though Diana's come out must take precedence."

"Miss DeWitt is all that is lovely, I'm sure, and there's a younger sister, too, I believe?"

"Caroline. Wonderful child, but a *girl* child. She's at that awkward age between birth and maturity. Believe I'll have a bit more. Will you join me?"

"I'm still working on my first. Wonderful vintage." Between sips,

Drysdale appeared to take a subtle inventory of the library's appoint-ments. The Constable over the mantel was the usual bucolic scene with a sky worthy of the Low Countries—the clouds were also a bit brownish. The opposite hearth sported a severely sunny depiction of Venice by Canaletto.

Tavistock didn't care much for either piece—no *personality*, despite the accomplished technique. The library also held his books, though, and that made the chamber a storeroom of treasure indeed.

"Would it surprise my lord to know that young DeWitt parted from the Players on less than cordial terms?" Drysdale asked, perusing the atlas open at the standing desk.

"DeWitt doesn't say much about his time away, and we don't pry. By damn, this is good brandy."

"I suspect DeWitt of larceny," Drysdale said, taking out a quizzing glass and peering more closely at the map of Crosspatch Corners. "Stole some baubles and more than a bit of coin. We couldn't prove anything, but I could not let it be suspected that we harbored a thief."

Tavistock retrieved a key from under a bust of Aristotle and began opening and closing the drawers of the desk sitting before the Constable hearth. "Now see here, Drysdale. I'm a peer, and you are not a peer, so talk like that can't be dealt with over pistols or swords, but you mustn't go insulting my brother-by-marriage under my own roof. Where in blazes...?"

"I meant no insult, my lord. More of a warning. Has my lord misplaced something?"

"Why would I need a warning?" Tavistock locked the desk, replaced the key, and went to the sideboard. There, he retrieved a key from beneath a bottle of calvados and repeated the opening and closing of drawers and cabinets, making a good deal of noise in the process.

Who knew playing the fool could be so diverting?

"Some people can't help themselves," Drysdale said gently. "They see something pretty, and they must have it. The issue is not one of necessity in the sense you or I would use the term, but of a wounded soul hoping to come right by nefarious means. The noose means nothing to such wretches. Then too, they usually excel at purloining what they fancy, so the noose isn't truly much of a threat to them."

Tavistock set the key back under the calvados and straightened. "What are you prosing on about? DeWitt is not a thief. Growing up in this village, he couldn't so much as sneeze in the stable at noon without the vicar praying for his health before sundown. He'd have no opportunity to steal even an apple from the livery, much less perfect the art of appropriating... What did you call them? Baubles? And a bit of coin?"

"More than a bit. I intend to have reparation from him while I'm here, my lord. I want you to know that."

What Drysdale apparently wanted Tavistock to know was that Gavin should be suspected of hanging felonies. That Gavin was not to be trusted, much less respected. Perhaps Drysdale was a better actor off the stage than on it.

Tavistock extracted a key from under a candlestick on the mantel and crossed to the cabinet that held the maps, a piece of furniture much like a clothespress, with myriad wide, flat, shallow drawers on rollers. En route, he purposely brushed too close to the reading table, pretended to stumble, and came up cursing.

"If you have business with DeWitt," he said when he'd finished airing his French vocabulary, "you needn't burden me with the details. He's an adult, a man of means, and much respected locally. I merely caution you to discretion." Tavistock unlocked the mechanism at the side of the cabinet. "Bloody furniture. Footmen move it about every time they beat the carpets."

Drysdale sipped his drink and pretended to study the Canaletto. "And if my issues with DeWitt should involve the law?"

Tavistock rubbed his thigh. "The law? One supposes you have proof and witnesses and such?"

"An entire acting troupe has reason to wish DeWitt had never crossed our path. I have witnesses."

But not proof. "Thespians are known for their ability to dissemble. They support themselves with it, in fact, meaning no offense. Testimony alone won't get you very far when our magistrate is the estimable Mr. Pevinger, as counseled by his formidable wife and daughters. Ah, here we are. My darling lady tells me where she puts them, but always when I am balancing the ledgers or seeing to my correspondence." Tavistock held up a string of emeralds, letting them wink and twirl in the last of the slanting evening light. "I'm having the piece replicated in amethysts. Not as valuable, I know, but a lovely complement to her ladyship's complexion."

Drysdale had given up any pretension of admiring the art. "You keep your emeralds *in the library?*"

"More than emeralds, though much of the collection remains in Town. We haven't a safe, and installing one would insult the servants. My wife was raised in these surrounds, and insulting the servants is apparently the eighth deadly sin. Damnedest notion I ever heard this side of *liberté, égalité, et fraternité.*"

"The usual approach would be to keep those goods in a jewelry box, my lord." Drysdale had sidled across the room and was goggling at the open drawer. Amaryllis had put together a pretty display on maroon velvet. Two parures and various other adornments in precious and semiprecious stones, gold to the left, silver to the right.

"A jewelry box?" Tavistock tucked the emeralds into his breast pocket. "If you were a maid intent on lifting a fetching brooch, where would you look, Drysdale? You'd look in the jewelry box after popping the lock with a hairpin. I grasp—begrudgingly, but I do—the business about not insulting the servants, but neither will I forgo all caution. Domestics are only human, and these goods, as you call them, would tempt many a weak character. The marchioness and I compromise by keeping the jewels under lock and key but in an unlikely location. Where did I leave my drink?"

He locked the case, replaced the key under the candlestick, and retrieved his brandy from the sideboard.

"Does DeWitt know where the jewels are kept?" Drysdale asked, resuming his perambulations about the library. The question insinuated that DeWitt *should not* know where the jewels were kept.

"Of course. Those trinkets are available to all the ladies in the family, including the marchioness's mother and grandmother. Lord Phillip knows as well. The younger girls have seen the collection, and I believe Diana has tried on a few of the simpler pieces in anticipation of next Season's folderol."

"And you intend to execute your duties as host with emeralds gracing your pocket?"

"I'll take this necklace upstairs to my wife's dressing closet. She has a final fitting tomorrow for the formal ensemble she'll wear at Friday's supper. For the setting to become entangled in the lace of a decolletage would be catastrophic, apparently, though I might find the spectacle entertaining—don't tell my wife I said that. As the master of this household—in name at least—I alone have responsibility for transporting the jewels to and fro about the domicile. Besides, I need to visit the retiring room. That punch is worse than ale for inspiring regular trips to the jakes."

Drysdale's expression went momentarily blank before he recovered his mask of genial reserve. "Mrs. Drysdale is looking very much forward to Friday's supper."

"While I look forward to the end of this house party, just between us gents." Tavistock finished his second half brandy, pretended to trip on the edge of the carpet, and parted from Drysdale at the foot of the main staircase.

He made his way to the study, where a safe had been installed some fifty years past. The time in the library had been enlightening, insofar as Drysdale had announced his ill intentions toward Gavin. The true revelation had been on a different subject entirely.

Acting was whacking good fun. Playing a role, hitting just the right notes to make the part credible without overdoing the whole business... Gad, what fun. Far more diverting and challenging than counting turnips or thumping through another Roger de Coverley at the quarterly assemblies in Crosspatch Corners.

No wonder Gavin DeWitt had run off. His family was trying to turn him into the Marquess of Mangel-wurzels, and he'd had sense enough to flee that fate for a far more appealing venture on the stage.

CHAPTER FIFTEEN

Supper, a semiformal meal, went by fairly quickly. Gavin was absorbed with amplifying the role he'd created at lunch. The jilted suitor trying manfully to hide his injured pride, while manfully upholding his duties as one of few gentlemen present and manfully consuming a trifle too much wine.

The details—surreptitious glances down the table, tiny conversational lags, a lack of interest in excellent fare—were drawn from his final days in Derbyshire and came all too easily.

Rose, for her part, had lapsed into sniffy disdain toward him while engaging with her neighbors in overly bright conversation about camphor and chamomile, as best Gavin could overhear. Tavistock had sauntered back into the parlor before supper and winked heavily at Amaryllis, the signal that the trap in the library had been baited.

All's well that ends with Drysdale on a transport ship.

"Ladies," Amaryllis said from her end of the table, "we would in the normal course withdraw to our tea at this point, but we would leave the gentleman bereft, I'm sure."

"We few," Tavistock said, gesturing grandly toward his marchioness. "We bereft few."

He was either a natural thespian or slightly foxed. Perhaps both. His quip had half the table—those who knew their Shakespeare —smiling.

"I'd thought to gather us around the pianoforte," Amaryllis said, "but the tuner's horse threw a shoe, and thus we must improvise. I hoped my brother might entertain us with a few sonnets and recitations."

The piano at Miller's Lament had been tuned the day before the first guest had arrived. Amaryllis, in true big-sister fashion, was up to something. The script called for Diana to entertain the guests, but Diana was merely looking at him expectantly.

"Please do," Lady Phillip said. "We'd love to hear your rendering of the Bard's verses. I'm sure the Drysdales would enjoy your perspective on say, Sonnet 18?"

"Oh, do," Gemma Drysdale said. "But not No. 18. I always thought your handling of No. 23 inspired. 'As an unperfect actor on a stage, who with his fear is put beside his part...' You have the nuances with that one."

Gavin looked to his mother, who occupied the place beside Lady Duncannon to Tavistock's right. Mama had shown increasing unease with his theatrical tendencies as he'd been growing up, and she had been adamant that Gavin *put all that behind him.*

Amaryllis had apparently decided otherwise, for at least the next half hour.

Did he *want* to offer up those sonnets to this audience?

Well, yes, because Rose was among their number. "A few verses, then," he said, rising. "No dramatic parts, though. Those take a certain shift in mental focus that eludes me after such fine sustenance and libation."

"He means food and drink," Tavistock said, getting to his feet and offering his arms to Lady Duncannon and Mama. "Our Gavin forgot to mention the intoxicating effect of such lovely company. To the music room, my friends."

In the general crush to leave the dining room, Gavin tried to elbow his way to Rose's side. Rose took hold of Drysdale's arm and stuck her nose in the air.

"Please let's do gain the corridor, Mr. Drysdale. A dining room can grow so stuffy by the end of the meal, don't you think?"

Drysdale countered with some remark about heat on a well-lit stage, while Lady Iris gave Gavin a sympathetic look and took his arm.

If Gavin had been directing the action, he could not have asked for a better sequence of cues, lines, and stage business. Ah, well. A bit of improvisation, then.

The folding doors between the music room and family parlor had been pulled back, the resulting space adequate to accommodate all the guests. Drysdale took a seat near the door to the guest parlor, while Gavin paced up and down before the pianoforte as if rehearsing his lines. He'd come upon the sonnets as a boy of fourteen, and they'd captivated his adolescent imagination as only artful references to love could interest a lad of that age.

The verses were old friends, and how fitting that they should come to his aid in the present circumstances.

"Do the summer's day one," Lady Duncannon said. "We aging beauties take comfort from those lines."

"I see no aging beauties," Tavistock said. "Only vintages approaching their prime."

"I second No. 18," Lady Phillip called. "'Shall I compare thee to a summer's day?' I have some lovely memories of summer days. I do believe that one is my favorite."

Gavin obliged, and reciting for an audience of mostly ladies gave the poetry a different scope, gave him, in the role of lover, a different perspective. They were, all of them, worthy of such rhymes, or should regard themselves thus.

Gavin laid a hand on the piano, paused, and directed his gaze to Rose, who sat in the shadows near the great harp. "'So long as men can breathe or eyes can see. So long lives this and this gives life to thee.'"

Somebody sniffled. Rose began to fan herself languidly. Drysdale had slipped from the room.

Fast work. If Gavin hadn't known better, he'd have said Drysdale's exit was right on cue.

"Do the gentlemen have a request?" he asked. "Lord Phillip, have you a favorite?"

Phillip asked for No. 102, a fitting choice given his retiring nature. The Bard made the point that like a nightingale that waxed lyrical in spring and became silent over summer, mature love could be quieter than the first throes of infatuation—quieter, deeper, and sweeter.

Lady Phillip had taken her husband's hand before Gavin had rendered the closing couplet—and Lady Iris had discreetly followed Drysdale out the door.

As a nod to the fellows, Gavin moved on to No. 61, a lesser-known treasure that compared true love to insomnia. By the time he'd finished No. 116—"Love is not love which alters when it alteration finds"—an obligatory item on any menu of romantic sonnet, it was time to bring the curtain down.

"One more," Gavin said, "of my choosing, in honor of the present company." He let his gaze travel around the room, resting only briefly on Rose. "Attend me, friends, for the Bard speaks from my heart."

When, in disgrace with fortune and men's eyes,
   I all alone beweep my outcast state,
   And trouble deaf heaven with my bootless cries,
   And look upon myself and curse my fate...

· · ·

Handkerchiefs were dabbed against cheeks. Lord Phillip kissed his wife's knuckles, and Mama was blinking at the carpet. Gavin focused on Rose, whose fan lay in her lap, and tried to will her to meet his gaze.

Haply I think on thee, and then my state,
(Like to the lark at break of day arising
From sullen earth) sings hymns at heaven's gate;
For thy sweet love remember'd such wealth brings
That then I scorn to change my state with kings.

Gavin expected a polite patter of applause and got only silence. For the space of two heartbeats, he fretted that he'd disappointed his audience, then Amaryllis rose from her chair by the hearth and threw her arms around him.

"That was wonderful," she said, hugging him tightly as the other guests began clapping. "Wonderful, magnificent. You've ruined us for any other version of the sonnets. Ruined us utterly."

Rose was smiling—breaking role, shame on her—and Gavin smiled back over Amaryllis's shoulder.

"Well done," Phillip said, passing Gavin a brandy when Amaryllis had retreated. "Exquisitely done. One suspected, but the proof overwhelms all doubt."

What proof? What doubt? Before Gavin could ask, Phillip had withdrawn to make himself useful serving drinks and passing around tea.

"You've improved," Gemma Drysdale said, taking Phillip's place. "I did not think that possible—your talent approaches genius—but you were born to bring those sonnets to life for the very audience that can appreciate them best. Drysdale will pout for a fortnight."

She departed on that puzzling speech, and Gavin was confronted with his mother.

"I know you don't approve," he said quietly, "but the whole business was in aid of a larger scheme. I'll explain it to you on the way home, and we must bring Diana and Caroline into our confidence as well."

Mama took the drink from his hand, set it aside, and gave him the sort of look he'd usually earned as a youth when he'd failed to wipe his boots for the twentieth time in two days.

She hugged him, and while Amaryllis's embrace had been firm and dear, Gavin was reminded that his mother hadn't hugged him since he'd come home. Not once, not even half a hug.

"I was wrong," she said. "A gift like yours cannot be buried in Crosspatch Corners. I was wrong, and selfish, and your father would scold me for thwarting your dreams. He loved No. 29 the best, too, you know. Trotted it out whenever I was c-cross or testy. Sometimes he'd just look at me, and I'd hear him reciting in my head. I still hear him, when I'm melancholy and missing him. I still do."

Mama was weeping, something else that hadn't happened since Gavin had come home. He held her, realizing just how great the burden of her sorrow had been—and still was—and how an only son disappearing God knew where had increased that burden.

"I'd forgotten about Papa's ear for poetry," he said, passing Mama his handkerchief when she stepped back. "He was very good with limericks, too, wasn't he?"

"Oh, he was. And he could be so naughty. Brilliant, with verses too scandalous for pen and paper. Not too scandalous for his wife, though. I do miss him."

When Mama had dabbed at her eyes, Gavin passed her his drink. Rose watched the whole business from a corner, and Gavin wished more than anything that she could join the conversation.

"I understand why you left," Mama said. "Grandmama and I have discussed it endlessly. This is what it was like for you, wasn't it?"

A few of the guests were drifting toward the terrace. Tavistock murmured something to a footman, then slipped out the door, the footman with him.

"I beg your pardon?" Gavin said, leading Mama to a love seat. "What *it* was like?"

"Mostly ladies as far as your eye could see, or so you must have felt. Caroline and Diana bickering constantly, my incessant haranguing about marital prospects, Grandmama haranguing me to stop fussing, and Amaryllis pretending she wouldn't mind another London Season, though we knew she dreaded the prospect. A lot of female drama for one young man."

Well, yes, but her synopsis left out a few particulars. "Not female drama. Family drama, and maybe I was simply adding to it by leaving. Or hoping my absence would be felt more keenly than my presence had?"

Mama studied her brandy. "Possibly. The fact remains that you have a gift. Diana and Caroline will manage. Amaryllis has already begun campaigning on their behalves." Mama drew herself up and looked him square in the eye. "Go back to the stage if you choose to."

Lovely words. Words he'd never thought to hear, except... He didn't choose to. Not now. Not exactly.

Gavin was fumbling for how to discreetly explain his change of heart to Mama when Tavistock came into the music room, Lady Iris and Hammond Drysdale marching before him like prisoners headed for the dock.

The crowd had thinned considerably, and still, Rose remained in her shadowed corner, agog with... awe, love, hope, determination. Gavin's recitations had, in addition to impressing her, fortified her.

Dane hadn't loved her; she hadn't loved Dane. She'd tried to, though, while he hadn't been worthy of her efforts. He'd been worthy of her care, of the food, clothing, shelter, and company she'd provided him, but not of her heart.

His criticisms, snide jokes, infidelities... Nasty comments before the staff, homecomings that were always put off, resources squandered that should have been put by to keep the Hall sound in the bad years...

Why had she wasted her time resenting Wordsworth when she could have been nourishing herself with Shakespeare?

Tavistock returned in the company of Mr. Drysdale and Lady Iris—when had *she* left the audience?—and the entire trio looked too grim for such a pleasant evening.

If that meant the marquess had caught the blighters red-handed, so much the better.

Gavin whispered something to his mother, then assisted her to her feet.

"Miss Peasegood, Lady Duncannon," Mrs. DeWitt said, "let's catch a peek at the marquess in leading strings, shall we? The gallery has several portraits of him in his misspent youth and one of Lord Phillip when he was still in dresses. Tavistock's curls were adorable."

Lady Iris was busy glowering at the darkness beyond a window. Miss Peasegood and the countess had no choice but to accept Mrs. DeWitt's invitation.

"I'd like to see that," Gemma Drysdale said. "The marquess before Society got its paws on him."

Rose expected Tavistock, the host, the peer, the largest specimen in the room, to thwart her. Instead, Gavin merely shook his head.

"You will stay, if you please. You will want to hear what's said."

"Don't order my wife about, DeWitt," Drysdale drawled. "The exercise is pointless in the first place and insulting to me in the second."

Rose emerged from the shadows. "Mrs. Drysdale will stay. She has been present for the whole drama, and she deserves to see the final act. Shall we be seated?"

If the marchioness objected to Rose taking on the authority of the hostess, she hid it behind a slight smile. Not only did Lady Tavistock take a chair herself, she patted the place beside her on the love seat, and like a loyal hound, the marquess was immediately settled next to her.

Lord and Lady Phillip occupied a sofa, Lady Iris sat alone, and the Drysdales took wing chairs at opposite ends of the parlor hearth.

Gavin indicated that Rose might be comfortable on the piano bench, a front-row seat as it were.

"Let the play begin," Rose said.

Gavin remained on his feet. "A prologue is in order. Early last year, I met Mrs. Roberts at a house party in Derbyshire. I was present as one of Drysdale's Players, hired to entertain, make up numbers, and improve the scenery. I became enamored of Mrs. Roberts, and on an occasion of parting from her, I found a heap of coins—a small fortune—among my effects. I put the coins in her jewelry box and said nothing about it to anybody."

"Must you?" Drysdale shot his cuffs. "Every fellow has youthful indiscretions, DeWitt, but there are ladies present, at least one of whom might appreciate some delicacy."

"I would appreciate the truth more," Rose said. "Carry on, Mr. DeWitt."

"The discovery caused a misunderstanding between Mrs. Roberts and myself, one we've sorted out, though we are left with questions. Who intruded on a very private moment to put the money where it should not have been, and why?"

"A prank, perhaps?" Gemma Drysdale suggested. "The Players are no respecters of privacy or decorum. You hadn't been with us that long, and practical jokes were to be expected."

"Pranks involving enough money to keep the Players in hot meals for an entire winter?" Gavin asked.

Mrs. Drysdale sent a curious look across the room to her husband, who was absorbed with fiddling with the lace at his cuffs.

"Interesting," Lady Tavistock said. "But how does this ancient business have any relevance now?"

Her ladyship knew exactly how, but she, too, had a role to play.

"Drysdale accosted me shortly after his arrival at Miller's Lament," Gavin said. "He accused me of stealing both money and a ruby necklace. I'd never seen such a necklace, but Mrs. Roberts reminded me that our hostess in Derbyshire had had a portrait done, and in that portrait—which graces her formal parlor—she's wearing rubies."

"The Versailles Rubies," Lady Iris said. "A gift to her great-grandmother from the Sun King, passed down from mother to daughter, and one of few treasures your hostess was able to take with her from France. She promised her mother she would never sell or break up the necklace, but somebody took it while the house party was in progress."

"That somebody was not Mr. DeWitt," Rose said. "He had ample means of his own, little opportunity, and no motive. Was that somebody you, Lady Iris?"

Her ladyship looked, for once, less than beautiful. Her mouth was grim, her eyes shadowed with fatigue. The fashionable original so relentlessly preoccupied with her herbal was a role, apparently. No surprise there.

"I believe Lady Iris blames herself for the necklace's disappearance," Gavin said. "She was placed among the maids and footmen to help keep the valuables safe."

"And I failed," Lady Iris spat. "I failed, and I promised I would rectify my error. The necklace hasn't surfaced in any of the usual underworld locations. No new creations of spectacular rubies have come on the market. The Ludgate jewelers haven't heard a whisper in all the time since the necklace went missing, and Paris, Amsterdam, Milan, Saint Petersburg, Rome, even Prague haven't either."

"Which leaves investigating the guests?" Drysdale asked. "You suspect DeWitt just as I do."

"Which leaves," Gavin said, "investigating everybody. Going back over the notes, again and again. Lady Iris and her friends have doubtless been snooping about all up and down the Derbyshire guest list in the months since I came south. Am I the last possibility?"

Lady Iris opened her mouth, then shut it, then appeared to reconsider. "You were."

"Though, of course," Gavin said, "if you, yourself, had taken the gems, then this diligent investigation would provide the perfect ruse for hiding your larceny."

Her ladyship crossed her arms and tried for imperial disdain, to no avail.

"Nosing about while maundering on about failure would be the perfect distraction," Drysdale said, slapping his knee. "By God, DeWitt, you do have a brain."

"But I still don't have an answer," Gavin said. "If her ladyship was the thief, why did she bother following you into the library, Drysdale? Why were *you* trying to open the map cabinet when Tavistock joined you there?"

Tavistock crossed his legs at the knee, Continental-fashion. "I switched the keys," he said, sounding perilously sober. "DeWitt explained to me how the sleight of hand works. Drysdale was trying to use the desk key to open the map cabinet, while Lady Iris lurked in the darkest corner, half concealed by curtains. If Drysdale merely wanted to admire the gems again, why not light even a single sconce?"

A silence stretched, while Gavin took up the place beside Rose on the piano bench.

"I took nothing," Drysdale said. "So what if I wanted another peek at an amazing display? Anybody would have been impressed."

"You weren't merely impressed," Gavin said. "Tavistock was also careful to let you know that many others had access to that hiding place. My entire family, the marchioness, Lord Phillip, and his wife... We all know about the map cabinet, and you knew we know and could thus be suspected if an item went missing. You were tempted."

"I took nothing," Drysdale said again, "and I have no ruby necklace. I suggest we search Lady Iris's effects for starts and perhaps Mrs. Roberts's apartment in an abundance of caution."

Oh dear. He ought not to have said that. Rose could feel the shift in Gavin, feel the leap of anger, stayed only by the firm hand of self-discipline.

"The difficulty for you, Drysdale," Gavin said softly, "is that you knew the rubies had been taken. The owner knows, her professional snoops know, and the original thief—that would be you—knows. The riddle remaining is who stole the rubies from you?"

"He's right," Lady Iris said. "Lady Rutherford was keen to keep the loss private. At first, she wanted to believe she'd misplaced the gems, and she refused to implicate her own staff. The authorities know nothing. The local magistrate wasn't even informed. She had contacted us before the house party for extra security, and she continues to rely exclusively on us to this day."

"Us?" Tavistock asked.

"The Mayfair Blossoms," Lady Tavistock said. "They apparently have something of a reputation if one knows where to ask."

"I have no necklace," Drysdale said, "and I was a victim of thievery as well. The entire sum paid to me for our efforts in Derbyshire went missing and has never been recovered. Our door at that house party had no lock worth the name, and you know, DeWitt, how casual the Players are about privacy. You took that money on a lark, just to see if you could."

"Drysdale, cut line," Gavin said patiently. "You accused me of taking both and claimed the valuables were in close proximity. You were caught trying to steal from Tavistock not thirty minutes past. Regarding the necklace, you had motive, means, and opportunity. If you admit the specifics of your crime, we might be able to track down the second thief."

Rose had been watching Gemma Drysdale throughout the conversation. Gemma's expression remained one of mild curiosity, despite the noose tightening around her husband's neck, setting Rose's imagination to work on the question of *how*.

How would anybody in a close-knit troupe living in one another's pockets hide anything of value, much less a distinctive necklace? Who among all the Players would have had that much privacy, that good a hiding place?

Who knew precisely where Hammond Cicero Drysdale would never bother searching?

"Let's have a look at the Players' store of props," Rose said. "The costume jewelry in particular. I'm sure we'll find a very fine ruby necklace among the paste and pinchbeck, won't we, Mrs. Drysdale?"

"Gemma?" Drysdale's bewilderment was real. "Gemma? What is she saying?"

Gemma looked at her hands. She looked at the clock. She looked at her husband. "Mrs. Roberts is saying that you were going to get us all hanged." She rose and crossed the room to the great harp, taking up a study of its elaborately carved pillar. "I meant to return the necklace, but the opportunity never presented itself, so I thought to put it in Mrs. Roberts's jewelry box—she would notice such a fine piece among her widow's collection—but she had... company. I had to improvise. I suppose we've reached the part where I go mad or drink poison."

Gavin went to the sideboard and poured a tot of brandy. "Or we've reached the part where you tell us the rest of the story, and we listen as open-mindedly as we can."

"I don't understand," Drysdale said, looking old and confused. "I don't... Gemma, I don't understand."

She sipped her brandy. "You never have, Hammond. You've never even tried to understand."

Gavin's imagination had painted Drysdale as the lead in some sort of deep scheme—stealing the necklace, realizing Lady Iris was on to him, and then pretending to lose the necklace while pointing an accusing finger at innocent parties.

In the alternative, Drysdale might have been in league with Lady Iris.

Lady Iris might have been diligently framing Drysdale for her own ends.

Rose's conjecture—that Gemma Drysdale figured centrally in the drama—made all the sense in the world, with the benefit of hindsight.

"As Drysdale's wife," Gavin said, resuming his seat beside Rose, "you had two problems. Your husband was a thief, and I was outshining him on the stage."

"The connection isn't as simple as you think," Gemma said, tracing a vine carved into the rosy maple. "You inspired Drysdale to think beyond our humble sphere, to get ideas. He could stage a few of the lesser tragedies with you to lead the cast. He could aspire to longer works, because your memory is apparently limitless. His ideas cost money. Hammond's ideas always cost money. You were a problem precisely because you are so talented, DeWitt."

Drysdale watched her caressing the wood as if he'd never before in all his born years beheld her. "You stole the necklace."

She closed her eyes and steadied herself against the harp, unwittingly adopting the signature pose of the tragic heroine.

When Gemma turned her gaze on her husband, her expression was full of banked rage. "Let us be very clear, Hammond: You stole the necklace from its rightful owner and after our hostess had so generously paid us. Lady Iris does not make a very convincing maid, and there were a couple of footmen who always seemed to be lurking in alcoves with nothing to do. I realized that if our effects were searched, we would be bound over for the assizes before you could say, 'Out, damned spot.'"

"You stole the money too?" Drysdale asked.

Gemma took the stool beside the harp. "Can a wife steal from her husband when she's considered nothing more than a legal afterthought to his personhood? I hadn't planned to take the money, but when I went to put the necklace in Mrs. Roberts's jewelry box, I had the sum in my pocket, lest somebody else relieve you of it. I saw that Mrs. Roberts had company, and that was a solution to my other problem."

"Meaning me," Gavin said. "My ability was inspiring Drysdale to greater feats of greed and folly, so I had to go."

"You had to go," Gemma said. "Not only was Drysdale getting wild notions about touring the great capitals, you were nobody's fool.

We knew you came from means, and you'd see what the members of the troupe might miss—new sets, new wardrobes, scripts, props, handbills, advertisements... It all costs money. A lot of money, and that's in addition to keeping the Players fed, decently clad, and housed. If you asked the wrong questions, if you heard the wrong rumors up from Town... you could send us all to the Antipodes."

Gavin thought back to Gemma's quiet presence with the prompt book, her silent appraisals in rehearsal, her apparent dislike of him.

Not dislike, but rather, fear.

Rose took his hand. "You worried about another possible consequence if Mr. DeWitt remained associated with the troupe, didn't you?"

Gemma's smile was wan. "That his talent would be forever buried in the shires?"

"That he'd be found guilty by association, and a good man would be branded a criminal because *your husband was a selfish idiot.*"

So that's how Rose had solved the riddle—the ghost of Dane Roberts had pointed squarely to Hammond Drysdale.

"The Players and I know what Hammond is and what he isn't. He's not the world's greatest thespian. He never will be. But that troupe is his life. He would do anything to keep us together and performing. Anything. DeWitt was a recent addition to our numbers, with no idea what a mare's nest Hammond could make of things."

"But, my dear," Drysdale began, pinching the bridge of his nose, "I don't take these risks for myself. I only did it—"

"Do not"—Rose's voice would have cut marble—"imply that you steal, lie, and break your word for the sake of others. If you could not be the great hero onstage, then you'd be the great hero in your own mind. Misunderstood, unappreciated, nobly bearing up under the slings and arrows of outrageous fortune while nevertheless having a jolly time on precisely your own terms. Be glad your wife hasn't taken up the art of the horsewhip."

Rose's warning inspired a flurry of glances, between Lord and Lady Phillip, Tavistock and his marchioness, and Drysdale and his wife. Even Lady Iris was regarding the supposedly quiet widow respectfully.

"You have a flower name," Lady Iris said. "I told Delphine and Zin that you have a flower name."

"As does my marchioness," Tavistock said. "Back to the matter at hand. Was it you, Mrs. Drysdale, who left the coins among DeWitt's effects? Were you trying to incriminate him?"

"I was trying to put him in disgrace to a sufficient degree that he'd be glad to leave the troupe. I expected Mrs. Roberts would see the money sitting among DeWitt's clothing. She should have been suspicious of its origins when Drysdale reported that his funds had been stolen, and she should have been further concerned when she found a heap of rubies in her jewelry box. The only party with access to her quarters who might have purloined the coin and the necklace was Mr. DeWitt. She should have suspected him of theft, though I doubt she'd have turned him over to the authorities."

That plan was not exactly outlandish, but neither was it very astute. But then, Gemma Drysdale's perspective was that of a woman much disappointed by the man in her life. That Gavin might waken first, and take offense at the coins, hadn't occurred to her.

"The necklace never made it to my jewelry box," Rose said. "What happened?"

Gemma ran a hand gently over the harp strings and graced the air with the soft whisper of a glissando. "I was startled."

"Mr. DeWitt startled you?"

"With a perfectly lucid rendering of the opening lines of *Romeo and Juliet*. 'Two households, both alike in dignity...' I nearly screamed I was so surprised."

"Instead, you fled with the necklace?"

"And I have been fleeing with the necklace ever since, though when Drysdale mentioned this gathering, I hoped my luck had turned. I meant to hide the necklace among the effects of one of the guests and hoped Lady Iris would learn of it. They all seem so chummy, with their flower names and disguises and roles."

Roles. Well, yes. Gavin would ponder that puzzle later. "Where is the necklace now?"

Gemma plucked a minor chord. "Mrs. Roberts has the right of it. The necklace has been hiding in plain sight, among the props with a lot of paste. I've never let anybody wear it for fear Drysdale would recognize the piece."

"As well I might." Drysdale rose. "If Lady Iris will take charge of the necklace, then it only remains for somebody to repay me the coin I was parted from in Derbyshire. All's well that—"

"Don't attempt the merry exit," Gavin said, rising. "Your stupid greed caused untold suffering to many victims, and while you can return the gems, you cannot undo misunderstanding, shame, or hurt feelings. You cannot wave away the pain Lady Rutherford, a decent and generous woman, endured because she could not protect a family legacy from your ambitions."

"You've caused me more than a spot of bother too," Lady Iris muttered. "I say we summon the magistrate."

"I say," Rose countered, "your ladyship accepted an invitation under false pretenses, and more to the point, you've bored half the company witless with your herbal blathering. If that's not an offense against the king's peace, it's certainly a violation of the rules of hospitality."

Lady Iris had the grace to look chagrined. "I am sorry. My interest in herbs is genuine, and I've been tracking that necklace for months. Do as you will with Drysdale, but I am determined to retrieve the necklace."

Do as you will... Gavin thought of all the miles he'd galloped hoping to elude despair, all the letters he'd tried writing to Rose, only to toss them into the fire. He thought of Rose, confidence at low ebb, grieving a failed marriage, then faced with the prospect of a fickle suitor...

"DeWitt," Tavistock said, "what shall we do with yonder thief?"

The most precious loss Drysdale's scheming had caused hadn't been the blasted necklace, or Lady Iris's time and effort, or Gavin's budding theatrical ambitions, or even Gemma Drysdale's peace of mind.

The most precious loss had been Rose's self-esteem, though she'd regained it and then some.

"Mrs. Roberts," Gavin said, "the decision is yours."

Rose and Gemma exchanged some sort of silent communication. "If Gemma sought to profit from her husband's larceny, she would be kicking her heels in Rome, the necklace long since broken up and sold in parts. She chose to stay by Drysdale's side, to continue protecting him from his own folly. I'd like to hear what Drysdale has to say to her."

"So," said Lady Tavistock, "would I."

"The jury of the distaff are unanimous," Lady Phillip said. "Drysdale, this had better be the most convincing speech of your life."

CHAPTER SIXTEEN

Rose wanted nothing so much as to kick Hammond Cicero Drysdale from Berkshire to the Borders, and she was feeling none too charitable toward Gemma Drysdale either. And yet... to be tied to a man whose ambitions exceeded his abilities, a man convinced of his own victimhood, a man loyal only to his own pleasures...

Drysdale wasn't Dane, but they shared an immature version of honor that came perilously close to self-delusion. She had wanted to believe that Gavin was different, but her faith in a nascent romance had been eclipsed by too much experience with disappointment.

That, and by the Drysdales' marital drama.

"Drysdale," Gavin said, "you have the floor."

The actor remained in his seat. "I never planned to steal that necklace."

Gemma snorted.

"What I mean is, I had popped into a random sitting room to retie the garters on my knee breeches and realized I was in the private sitting room of the lady of the house. The appointments were old-style and ornate, and that made me curious about the bedroom, which proved to be just as lavishly decorated. The ceiling mural alone had likely cost a fortune, and the bed hangings... I digress."

No grand gestures accompanied his discourse, which was fortunate for Rose's temper.

"I was agog at the surrounds," Drysdale went on more quietly. "Heartbroken, in a sense, to think that one person enjoyed all that comfort and beauty, while my players often shivered in their cots. I know the way of the world, but the world used to appreciate theater, music, the arts. Now... traveling troupes are a dying breed. Every market town has its assembly rooms, every goosegirl can lisp a few lines of Sheridan. The gentry can pop into Town for some professional entertainment, and John Bull otherwise can't be bothered to waste what little coin the nobs allow him."

As opening monologues went, Rose was decidedly unimpressed with this one. "You did not steal that necklace to improve the lot of the poor, Mr. Drysdale. You are lucky half the maids weren't sacked because of your larceny."

"The maids are sacked, madam, because quite often, they're guilty of larceny, not that I blame them. I didn't steal the necklace to fritter the proceeds away in a London gaming hell."

Drysdale couldn't know how close his comment came to a hit, given Dane's proclivities. "What did you plan to do with your stolen goods?"

"Exactly what Gemma foresaw. New sets, new costumes, decent rooms for the summer at a northern spa town. Time and energy to tackle the more ambitious theatrical works. If the troupe could develop a circuit of those spa towns, then a school for the dramatic arts might not be too big a stretch in a few years. I may not be directly descended from Thespis himself, but I am a fair director and a better teacher."

Gavin, Rose noted, did not contradict Drysdale's claim.

"Hammond," Gemma said tiredly, "how many trinkets and spoons did you intend to steal before you gave up on that dream? A noticing footman, a sharp-eyed maid, an innkeeper with a dim view of actors... You put us one accusation away from ruin, time and again. A spoon isn't worth your life."

"And what if," Drysdale said, sitting up straighter, "that spoon stood between us and utter failure, Gemma? Yes, I have dreams, but the players need to eat. They need shoes and scripts. Spoons go missing all the time."

Rose had heard enough. "If I were a jury, Drysdale, I'd convict you of blind arrogance in addition to thievery. What you need is sponsorship, and you are too proud and dunderheaded to ask for it."

"Hammond Drysdale wouldn't ask Saint Peter for admission to heaven," Gemma said. "I've tried telling him that good theater has always been appreciated in Merry Olde, but he won't even try to find us a patron. He claims that's the difference between actors and beggars. We have our pride, they have their occasional crust. He has yet to explain why that makes acting the better choice."

"It's not a choice," Drysdale said with some of his old hauteur. "The stage is a vocation. One cannot refuse the call of his art any more than a warhorse can ignore the drums presaging battle, and whom would I ask to sponsor us? The Players are the provincial hacks all of London disdains, no matter that our comedy is better than theirs and our actors more versatile than that lot in Drury Lane."

"If you're so accomplished," Rose said, "then don't look for sponsors, look for investors."

Lady Phillip whispered something in her husband's ear. Lord Phillip kissed her cheek.

"I might know some interested parties," Lady Phillip said. "We'll want budgets, estimates, and schedules. Records from the past few years' performances. A list of the troupe's repertoire, the current members' abilities, assets and liabilities, that sort of thing."

Drysdale looked to his wife. "Gemma manages the books, if that's what you're asking about."

Why did Gemma not leave her idiot spouse at the nearest crossroads? But then, Rose knew why.

Drysdale was her husband.

"Mrs. Drysdale." Lady Phillip rose with her spouse's assistance. "You and I will meet after breakfast. Good night, all. The evening has been... interesting."

Lord Phillip bowed and escorted her ladyship from the room.

Tavistock rose and extended a hand to his marchioness. "The hour grows late, and I'd classify the evening as equal parts diverting and taxing. Drysdale, I am not content that you should find financial support as the sole consequence of your mischief. That's going a bit too far with the quality of mercy, if you ask me. I leave the matter in the hands of those in a better position to decide your fate."

Lady Tavistock departed on her husband's arm.

"I'm retrieving that necklace," Lady Iris said, "and I don't intend to wait until breakfast to do so. Mrs. Drysdale, if you'd oblige?"

Gemma rose. "I can't wait to get rid of the wretched thing. Drysdale, I don't believe Mr. DeWitt and Mrs. Roberts are done with you. Neither, for that matter, am I."

On that ambiguous observation, she and Lady Iris departed, and Rose was left with her hero and the villain. She was tempted to tell Drysdale that no investments would be forthcoming—Lady Phillip would support her decision, and Drysdale could bestir himself to look elsewhere for his coin—but the Players had been Gavin's first step toward independence. But for them, Rose would never have met the man who meant so much to her now.

"We will conclude our discussion after breakfast, Drysdale," Rose said. "You can spend the night in contemplation of your sins. Gemma could have at any point turned you over to the law, claimed ignorance of the whole matter, and seen you onto a transport ship. She'd have been left with the Players and her freedom. She apparently wasn't willing to sacrifice you to have them. One concludes such devotion is based on virtues I have yet to see you exhibit. Mr. DeWitt, if you'd light me to my room?"

"Drysdale, good night." Gavin held the door for Rose and accompanied her into the shadowy corridor.

Gavin took a carrying candle down from a sconce, and they walked along in silence as far as the top of the steps.

What had just happened? Rose began to make a list in her mind.

Gavin had been exonerated of all wrongdoing.

Drysdale's blackmail scheme had been thwarted.

The Players might well be on their way to more solid financial footing, and...

Something else had transpired, something that left Rose feeling a little winded and a lot pleased with herself.

Gavin set the candle on the third stair. "You were magnificent. I would never have put together that whole business about Gemma and the money and the—"

Rose threw herself into his arms and held on tight. "I want to kick him, Gavin. I want to kick him where he will never recover from the blow."

"Then take his Players from him. He deserves at least that."

"Do you want his Players?" The answer mattered to Rose, though she could see the notion was an utter surprise to Gavin.

"No, I do not," Gavin said slowly. "I do not and never did. I want you. I'm very clear on that."

"Good," Rose said, taking him by the hand, "because I want you as well. The love nest on the Twid will do nicely, though I suppose we'd best raid the kitchen for some comestibles first, and you'll have to help me change into an old walking dress."

Gavin bowed. "Your devoted servant and dresser, madam. I should change into riding attire, and as it happens, I have some here."

"I can help you with that." She retrieved the candle and took Gavin's hand. She could help him with a lot of things, in fact.

Gemma Drysdale was a woman imprisoned by loyalty, convention, and pragmatism, and Rose well knew how that felt. She also knew what it was to be fettered by guilt.

All that was in the past, though. Having seen Drysdale for the whining, scheming, dishonorable pestilence that he was—that he chose to be—and having Gavin's unshakable support and devotion, Rose Roberts also knew what it was to be *free*.

Wordsworth's poetry landed with a soft plop on a placid stretch of the Twid, bobbed for a moment on the surface, then left only concentric ripples expanding across the moonlit water.

A whimsical variation on *Hamlet*'s graveyard scene popped into Gavin's head. "Alas, poor Wordsworth, I knew him, Horatio." He squeezed Rose's hand, hoping to lighten the moment.

"Not Wordsworth," Rose said, leaning against his side. "I commend to the bottom of the Twid the old Rose, the one who could not speak up for herself, the one who was *fine* when her heart was breaking and *fine* when she should have been furious. I still want to kick Drysdale, but I no longer want to kick myself."

"Ah. A good feeling. Do you want to kick me? I should have known you would not cheapen what was between us with an offer of coin." Gavin had certainly been kicking himself over that error.

Rose, to her credit, was quiet for a moment. "The ladies in your life have been less than supportive, Gavin. I'm sure some part of you was expecting that I'd let you down too. I don't need or want to kick you, but perhaps you need to pitch something into the river too?"

Gavin wasn't about to toss his family into the water. He loved them dearly, for one thing, and for another, they could swim like porpoises. Rose was right, though. The DeWitt ladies hadn't supported him, hadn't even *seen* him, really, but that had apparently changed.

"Maybe I'm the one who needs a dunking. Can you swim?"

"Yes." Rose headed up the bank to the towpath. "Don't tell anybody, but I was raised in the country after all, and summers do get so wretchedly hot."

Gavin began a mental list of adventures he and Rose would share. A midnight swim in the Twid, a mounted race across the countryside with her on Roland, a night at the opera in the finest box to be had... and many, many quiet walks wherever Rose sought to lead him.

"What will you do with Drysdale?" Gavin asked.

"I don't know yet. I'm more focused on what I'll do with you in the next several hours."

"I have a few suggestions." He caught her again by the hand and drew her in for a kiss, which turned into a long, lusty, and mutual indulgence.

"I do believe," Rose said, marching off several minutes later, "you'd be more comfortable without your clothes, Mr. DeWitt."

"These hot nights," Gavin murmured, catching up with her. "Such a tribulation."

They reached their trysting place, and Gavin soon had himself and Rose free of every stitch. Her lovemaking acquired a strategic quality, full of self-restraint on her end while she drove Gavin witless with her caresses and kisses.

She had him on his back, which was lovely and maddening and exactly where he wanted to be.

"You will regret this obstreperousness, madam." He stroked her hips and knees, and she retaliated by using the end of her braid on his nipples.

"Will I? Will I regret it any time soon, or do you propose to lecture me—finally."

He'd taken himself in hand, found his destination, and begun the joining. "You're in a hurry now?"

"I'm in... transports. Do that again."

He kept the rhythm slow and sweet, like the soft summer night that gave them such lovely privacy. Rose began to pant gently. She stopped tormenting him with her braid and crouched close enough to kiss him.

"Rose?"

"Hmm?"

"I do love you. I have from the first moment I saw you reading in the... Not fair, madam." She'd pinned his hands beside his head. "I want to touch you."

"What do you call this?" She gave a little fillip with her hips. "A wave from across the ballroom?"

"Diabolical woman." Gavin could break her hold easily, but relished the novelty of Rose in charge of every particular. She apparently liked it, too, because she dallied with him until he could not have quoted the Bard to save King Henry's army at Agincourt.

"Diabolical man." Rose began to shudder, and a moment later, Gavin was shuddering right along with her. The satisfaction was cataclysmic, overwhelming every sense and dissolving Gavin into a sparkling sweetness suffused with joy and love.

"No handy quote?" Rose murmured drowsily a few minutes later. She breathed with him, rising and falling on his chest as if he were the Thames and she a one-woman pleasure barge.

"I love you. Not very original, but profoundly sincere."

She kissed his chin. "Love you too. Have forever. I'm falling asleep."

She dozed off as Gavin stroked her back and marveled at the wonder of Rose Roberts. She deserved a proper proposal, bended knee, a pretty bauble—rubies, perhaps?—and a lovely little monologue about happiness and fate and...

Gavin's eyes grew heavy as he composed an offer of marriage in rhyming couplets. His caresses slowed, and soon, the tide of love took him gently out to sea.

Rose woke aware of a pleasant soreness in novel locations and of Gavin's arm wrapped around her waist. Some inconsiderate bird insisted on greeting the day, though the merest hint of gray suggested sunrise was still a good hour off.

She and Gavin had time yet for one more... serious conversation.

"You 'wake?" Gavin gently brushed a bristly cheek against her shoulder, and temptation blinked awake as well.

"Dozing." Rose linked her hand with his. "We should be dressing soon."

"Clothes. Bah. It's summer. I might even let Roland have a day off. I'm told horses and people both benefit from rest."

"What do you benefit from?" A version of this question had vexed Rose even in sleep. What did Gavin need to toss in the Twid? What dream would inspire him to his greatest accomplishments?

"The past few hours have done me a considerable power of good," Gavin said, rolling to his back. "You see before you—or you would if you rolled over—a man awash in delight. Words fail, Rose. And the notion that I must present myself, coherent and properly attired, at my sister's table later today... I don't want to leave this place, where I've made such lovely memories with you. I don't want to think, don't want to"—he paused to yawn—"make small talk. I'm composing the most impressive, moving, sincere proposal in the history of romance. Consider yourself warned."

"If you offer me that proposal now," Rose said, "I will render you the standard you-do-me-great-honor rebuff, Gavin."

He half sat up and leaned over her as she lay on her side. "Rose? Did somebody put a pile of coins among your clothes? Have I bungled? Is there some impediment I must remove?"

"You have not bungled." She rolled to her back to face him, and that was a mistake. Gavin was luscious with a morning shadow of beard, hair tousled, eyes alight with tenderness and concern. "I bungled. I made Dane's happiness, his approval of me, the center of my world. Trying to please him, to appease him, to win a smile from him, became my unrelenting challenge. You aren't happy here in Crosspatch Corners."

He drew back. "I'm not miserable, but we don't need to bide at Twidboro Hall. I can move to Hampshire, if you'd rather."

"Where you will do what? Be the grudging squire at Colforth Hall rather than the grudging squire here in Berkshire? I heard you deliver those sonnets, and I agree with Gemma Drysdale. You were good in Derbyshire. Knew all the lines, rendered the gestures so they felt genuine, had ferreted out the nuances and the humor and humility. You are better now. You are..." His own word came back to her. "*Magnificent,* and when you were reciting those old sonnets, Gavin..."

His gaze had grown guarded.

"I think you were happy," Rose went on. "You brought every person in the room with you, and those ladies are not a sentimental bunch."

"What are you saying?"

"I have had one discontented husband. Hammond Drysdale is a discontented husband. The species wreaks mischief, and I have learned my lesson. Your talent is too rare and precious to be ignored by me and certainly by you. I must continue to steward Colforth Hall—harvest will soon arrive—and you must find a way to respect the talent that brings you such joy, even if your family objects."

"They apparently don't any longer, not as they once did."

"Then the hesitation is yours, Gavin, and I will not be the reason you remain restless and... incomplete."

He left the bed, looking angry and splendid in the altogether "I will be much more incomplete if you swan off to Colforth Hall and leave me here galloping about on a horse who's more than ready for his first race course."

"You are more than ready. Resume acting, if that's your pleasure. Try your hand at directing. Become the patron Drysdale must impress if his troupe is to rise above obscurity. *Use your gifts,* Gavin. Will Roland be content to while away his years in some shady paddock now that he's become the fastest horse in the shire?"

"I am not a horse."

"You are not a jovial squire, or not only that. My worst fear is that five years from now, I will be your devoted wife, and you will be my darling husband, but when I ask you how you're faring after a day with the tenants and the steward, you will say you are *fine*—splendid, even—when you're bored, frustrated, exhausted, and resentful."

He pulled on underlinen and riding breeches and paused, shirtless. "How could anybody mistake you for anything other than a dragoness in her prime?"

"I mistook myself for a failed wife and a bewildered widow. For the sake of my dignity, please put on a shirt."

Gavin grinned and twirled, finishing with an elaborate court bow. "You aren't indifferent to me."

Rose got off the bed, pulled her chemise over her head, and tried for a glower. "I love you. I want to spend the rest of my life with you, but if I haul you away to my Hampshire lair now, I fear we'll leave precious treasure behind. You deserve to be happy, Gavin."

"I deserve to be married, to you, and while you've given me much to think about, I don't want to take over Drysdale's troupe. He's right that he knows that bunch. He's a competent director, and he can get the best out of them. Where did I...?"

Rose handed Gavin his stockings. "I'm not sure what to do with Drysdale. On the one hand, I think Gemma longs to be free of him. On the other, he's not truly evil. Merely weak and vain." Dane had been merely weak and vain. Toss in a dash of arrogance and an unrelenting fondness for the bottle, and the combination became stale very quickly.

Gavin pulled on boots and stockings and assisted Rose into her dress. "Shall I decide his fate?"

"What would you advise?"

"He and his troupe will perform, gratis, for all of Hecate's sailors' homes every year without fail. They will perform at Chelsea on the same terms, if invited, and for other audiences of your choosing. Drysdale thrives on a challenge, and bringing some laughter and joy into those lives should motivate him to do his best."

"And also remind him of how fortunate he is. I like it." She passed Gavin his cravat and was smoothing his hair—or pretending to —when the baying of a hound pierced the morning stillness.

"Fortinbras," Gavin said, kissing Rose's cheek. "The coach will be pulling into the Arms within a quarter hour. That dog is more accurate than any clock. Shall I see you back to Miller's Lament?"

"You're anxious to get on your horse?"

"Roland will be saddled and waiting for me, but that's immaterial."

The horse who had kept Gavin sane over some very difficult months would never be immaterial to him. "You're angry?"

This time, he kissed her cheek. "No, but I am in imminent peril of begging you to marry me. I appreciate that you're correct—I love the theater, I love its history and wisdom, its power and frailty. That has been true since I was a boy. I love you, too, and I'm not sure what you're asking of me."

Rose was asking him to love himself and his own dreams with the same passion he brought to his care for her. Not a small request, as she well knew.

"Think on the puzzle, then, while I see to harvest at Colforth Hall and wait for letters from the man I adore."

He kissed her on the mouth. "My family might think I'm running off again if I resume my interest in acting."

One more kiss and Rose would be doing the begging. "You were not running away from them. You were running toward a dream."

The dog howled again, and Gavin went still. His gaze became distant, and for the longest moment, he did not move.

"What?" Rose asked, willing herself not to touch his hair again. "Something troubles you."

"Drysdale will run away." Gavin grabbed his coat and gave Rose a thorough smacker. "Drysdale is doubtless planning to be on the morning stage. If he gets to London, we'll never find him."

"Gavin, what are you...?"

"I'm off for a rousing gallop. I love you."

"I love you too," Rose called after him as he loped through the door and took off down the towpath at a brisk jog. "So very much."

She sat on the bed and munched on a cinnamon biscuit,

wondering if she'd just been an enormous fool, or truly wise. Gavin hadn't really put up much of an argument, and he certainly had not begged her for her hand.

"I cannot have another discontented husband," she said, finishing her biscuit. "I cannot ever again be a wife made unrelentingly anxious by her husband's personal discontent." She tidied up and left the hamper on the balcony, then locked the door with the key above the lintel.

She'd no sooner made her way to the towpath than a thundering streak of horse and rider pounded past. Ye gods, they made a magnificent picture in the predawn mists. Rose blew a kiss in their wake and half hoped Gavin would let Drysdale escape.

Then Gavin would have to step in with the Players, and that might solve several problems at once.

"But is that what would make him happy?"

She trundled up the towpath and was soon in her bedroom, dreaming of Gavin reciting those wonderful sonnets, just for her, and also for a packed theater of misty-eyed women.

Gavin knew all the shortcuts, and more to the point, Roland knew them. Once the horse sensed that the objective was to gain the London road, he needed no guidance. Gavin's job was to give the beast his head and let him do what he loved to do.

Roland took two stiles in foot-perfect rhythm, streaked across a pasture, splashed through a tributary to the Twid, and cleared the streambank in a single mighty bound.

You were made for this. A ditch, a ha-ha, and one more stile, and Gavin was on the London road, the stage a quarter mile ahead and kicking up a cloud of golden dust.

Gavin applied a hint of leg. "Go, boy. Catch him for me, for Rose, and for the Players."

Roland's terrific speed increased yet more, until Gavin was

galloping directly behind the stage. The travelers up top waved and began to cheer him on. A small boy stuck his head out the window and nearly lost his cap when the coach careened around a curve.

The coachy was apparently not inclined to pull to the side, which meant more strategy was in order.

On the next broad, sweeping curve, Gavin sent Roland across the field that the thoroughfare bordered. Roland not only made short work of the whole distance, but also cleared the stone wall on the far end as if he were merely beginning his morning romp.

They landed on the road mere yards ahead of the cantering coach horses. Gavin aimed his mount down the center of the lane and refused to give way.

"Git yer wretched arse off the King's Highway, ye ruddy gobshite!" the coachy called. "Ye be interferin' with the Royal Mail."

That expostulation inspired the outside travelers to more cheering.

Gavin put some distance between himself and the coach, then swung Roland around to halt such that the road was thoroughly blocked between venerable stone walls. The coach rocked to a halt amid more profanity from the coachman.

"You are abetting the flight of a suspected felon," Gavin called. "Put Hammond Drysdale out, and you can be on your way."

"Are ye oot of yer bluidy mind, Mr. DeWitt?" The guard, a crusty old Scot with whom Gavin had shared an occasional pint, laid his pistol across his knees.

"I am on the king's business. Hammond Drysdale is suspected of thievery and attempting to flee justice. Put him out, and I'll trouble you no more. He's probably disguised as a bearded old man who's hard of hearing."

A short conference took place up on the box, and one of the rooftop passengers passed another a coin.

"Drysdale!" the guard called. "If ye be aboard, show yerself."

The summer sun began to crest the tree tops, one of the coach horses stomped impatiently, and the dust of the road drifted lazily in the morning air. The buffoons on the roof began to stomp and pound on the coach. After a few moments of that nonsense, the coach door swung open, and Drysdale half stumbled, or was half pushed, from the vehicle. A satchel was pitched out after him, nearly hitting him in the breadbasket.

"Thank you," Gavin said, shifting Roland to the verge. "Mr. Drysdale and I will return to Crosspatch Corners. I appreciate the assistance."

"I appreciate that colt," the coachy said. "Likes o' him deserves to run at Newmarket. He'll win ye a tidy packet." The coachy called to his team, cracked the whip above their heads, and rolled off in a fresh cloud of dust.

Roland curvetted and tossed his head, clearly ready to give chase once more.

Gavin thumped his mount on the shoulder. "Good boy. Well done. You are a credit to Crosspatch Corners and to your dam and sire."

"He's worth some coin if you can keep him sound," Drysdale said. "Why the great drama, DeWitt?"

Gavin swung down and took his time loosening Roland's girth and dealing with the stirrups.

"I gave chase because you were running away." He took the reins over Roland's head and began walking in the direction of the village, a good mile up the road. "Come along, Drysdale. The sun will grow hot if you think to tarry."

"The morning will be comfortable for a while yet." Drysdale peeled off the false beard and bushy eyebrows he'd been wearing, wadded them up, and tossed them into the ditch. "Wretched stuff is itchy." He used his handkerchief to wipe away the remains of the glue. "Has your lady decided to have me arrested?"

His tone was jaunty, his smile winsome, and Gavin realized that Hammond Drysdale was a fine actor—off the stage.

"Has *your* lady decided to be quits with you?" Gavin asked, setting a modest pace.

"I'm sparing her the effort." Drysdale collected his satchel and fell in step. "When I joined Gemma last night, she was already in bed and sharing the mattress with a vast silence familiar to disgraced husbands. I spent a few hours dozing and thinking in a chair, then decided to, for once, do the right thing."

"Disappear into London?"

"Leave Gemma in peace. We're not married, you know. She uses my name for propriety's sake, but she refused my ring. She deserves better, and with me out of the way, she can find it."

While Drysdale avoided any uncomfortable interviews with the magistrate. How noble of him. "Gemma is devoted to you. If she's turned down your proposal, then you're not doing it right."

"I assure you, DeWitt, when it comes to marital enthusiasms, I can acquit myself—"

"Not that part. You are a discontented husband, or you would be if she ever agreed to marry you. She needs you to sort yourself out. You steal because you think she wants you to build some grand histrionic legacy, but you're wrong. Gemma just wants you to be yourself and to appreciate her."

Roland balked, snorted at nothing, then resumed walking.

"Now you're the sage of Berkshire?"

"I'm a man in love, and not only with the theater. This path will take us to the Twid." Gavin would have turned down the indicated track, but Roland chose then to prop, stand very tall, then lower his head.

He repeated that maneuver until a rabbit hopped across the path, which occasioned a sidewise shy that devolved into a surreptitious swipe at the grass.

"Walk on, horse," Gavin said, tugging on the reins. "If you ever tire of racing, you can hire yourself out as a sentry."

Drysdale came along as well and without any nonsense. Perhaps he truly hadn't wanted to decamp for London.

"Word of advice from an old thespian, DeWitt. You don't fall out of love with the stage. If it's in your blood, you will starve, steal, beggar yourself, and worse for an opportunity to give Falstaff another go. You'll wait hours in the cold for a chance to audition for a part as one of the witches, and you will fall asleep more nights than not with a script pressed against your cheek."

"All of which tells me that Drysdale's Players need to find their next venue. Since returning to Crosspatch, I've corresponded with a brother and sister who've recently opened a theater in Bristol. A general expression of goodwill from one who appreciates... that sort of thing." The sister had even written back. "I can't say I know them, but through Tavistock's step-mother, there's a distant connection."

And writing to the managers of a provincial house had been more appealing than enduring the steward's lectures.

"The Merchants? I've seen the place. Splendid appointments, modern design, and not too high in the instep."

"They aren't trying to compete with London. They're offering lighter fare and doing a good job of it. Miss Merchant strikes a hard bargain, from what I've heard, but she allows her brother a free artistic hand with the place. I think you and he would understand each other."

"Ah, but will Gemma allow me to make the attempt?"

Gavin was betting that yes, she would. "She took on the threat of the noose rather than let you bear the risk you'd brought on yourself. That should give you considerable pause. At the turnoff for Miller's Lament, you will give me the satchel, and I will pass it along to the most discreet footman I can find. When the guests are at lunch, he will unpack it for you. You will tell Gemma that you've been for a dawn constitutional along the river, and you have a profoundly sincere apology to offer her."

"For pity's sake, DeWitt. I tried that last night. She refused to hear a word of it."

"No, you did not. You tried to wheedle and explain and excuse what you've done. Don't quote a lot of poetical blather. Tell her if she casts you aside, you will be lost, and you are bloody sorry for your dunderheadedness."

"You rehearsed that speech with Mrs. Roberts?"

"Not yet, but I'm considering it."

They plodded along in an odd kind of commiseration. "Why do we pay money," Drysdale mused, "to watch drama on the stage? All this haring about, lurking behind curtains, the marquess playing me for a fool, the lady thief-takers, or whatever they are, nearly getting caught in their own snares, while the course of true love runs no straighter than the course of yonder river. Jolly good entertainment, as long as it's not your life."

Phillip was probably entertained, but then, he was a philosopher at heart. "Who is the fool in this play?"

"That would be me, I suppose. Trying to be clever, convinced you were my nemesis when, in fact, my dear Gemma's loyalty and clear thinking were thwarting my schemes."

"You will be a fool if you can't patch it up with Gemma."

"And you," Drysdale said as they reached the path to Miller's Lament, "if you don't make Mrs. Roberts your bride, young man."

Gavin took the satchel. "You needn't state the obvious. I'll see you at lunch."

Drysdale winked and saluted. "'Once more unto the breach, dear friends, once more.'"

Roland lifted his tail and fragranced the morning breeze with *le parfum d'un cheval en bonne santé.*

CHAPTER SEVENTEEN

"Drysdale seems more jubilant than repentant," Rose observed as Gavin accompanied her up the main staircase on the final day of the house party. "I am not feeling jubilant."

Gavin patted the hand she'd wrapped around his forearm. "I'll come see you within the month. I'm hoping absence makes you desperate to become my wife."

Gavin's demeanor was not that of a lovesick swain, but rather, of a man confident of his objective. Rose took heart from that.

"You will see a woman desperate to finish harvest before exhaustion and inebriation fell every tenant and his family. The weather has been perfect, and that never remains the case for long."

"These two weeks have been perfect." Gavin drew her into an alcove at the top of the steps, and Rose went with him willingly. He excelled at small gestures of affection—a touch on her shoulder, a hand on her arm when he whispered some endearment during one of Diana's sonatas. With the more serious displays, Gavin had become nothing short of genius.

Rose endured lavish and tender kisses and the most perfect of embraces with no witnesses save a bust of some old Roman statesman.

"You torment me," she said, stepping back.

"I'm getting even for last night. If you don't want to leave, Rose, then don't. Come bide with us at Twidboro Hall for the next week. Your stewards and tenants are doubtless competent to get matters under way without you."

"Why are women always cast as temptation's minions?" Rose left the alcove, and Gavin came with her. "You fellows can give a good account of yourselves in that department when you're of a mind to."

"Consider my inspiration."

He was in the most devilish mood, while Rose felt weepy and uncertain. Widow-ish, and that would not do *at all*.

"I have the last of my packing to do," she said as they approached the door of her apartment. "You will see me off?"

"Though it will break my heart, I will of course see you off. My sister would go very spare with me if I were to turn up dunderheaded at this stage. She wasn't trying to marry me off, you know."

"The marquess and Lord Phillip were certainly investigating that possibility."

"They are good, simple fellows. Marriage has filled their respective cups with joy. I was not thriving here in Crosspatch. Ergo, I would benefit from a wife. As it happens, I agree with them, provided that wife is you."

Logical romance. What had the world come to? "Will you go to Bristol?"

"Not for some time. I, too, have a harvest to oversee, and Drysdale and the Merchants will sort themselves out more easily if I'm not making an inspection tour on behalf of Lady Phillip's investors."

Rose wrapped her arms around Gavin's waist and leaned against him. "I hate the word 'harvest.'"

"No, you don't. You excel at managing Colforth Hall, and you enjoy it. I excel at the theater, and I enjoy it. You insist I investigate those possibilities, and I insist you delight in running the whole business down in Hampshire."

Rose straightened. "I do enjoy it. Colforth Hall has sound bones. The tenants are hardworking and conscientious and the land good and generous. You will come see me?"

"Thirty days hence. I promise, and I keep my promises, Rose."

Gavin was not Dane. Rose would likely be reminding herself of that eternal verity for some time, hopefully with less and less frequency.

She took his hand, lifted the door latch, and drew him through the sitting room into the bedroom. They had time for other and further expressions of a fond farewell, if they—

"Timmens." Rose's maid was at the jewelry box. A large trunk sat open at the foot of the bed, Rose's black shawl folded neatly atop the contents. "I thought you'd be down in the Hall making your good-byes."

"Most has already gone," Timmens said. "That lot out from Town wasn't very friendly anyway. Putting on airs, talking posh."

"You are from London," Rose said.

"I'm from Hampshire now, ain't I? P'raps Mr. DeWitt could summon us some footmen to haul this trunk down to the coach?"

Gavin walked around the open trunk to prop a hip against the windowsill. If he was appalled by Timmens's bit of cheek, he gave no sign of it, but Rose wasn't in the mood for her maid's uppish crotchets.

"If there are footmen to be fetched," Rose said, "you will fetch them. I don't suppose you've found my bracelet?" The wretched thing had gone missing at some point before the final formal dinner. Rose might have suspected Drysdale, except that Gemma would have murdered him in his sleep for even considering the notion.

"That clasp was none too reliable," Timmens said. "The marchioness will probably find the bracelet in some coal bucket, mark my words, madam. I'll just be off to find those footmen." She popped a curtsey at Gavin that had something of rudeness to it and flounced through the bedroom door.

"A moment," Gavin said. "Timmens, you can set my mind at ease regarding one bit of old business."

She turned in the doorway. "Sir?"

"You were with Mrs. Roberts in Derbyshire."

Timmens's chin came up. "I been with Missus for better than five years. She doesn't go anywhere without me."

"And Mrs. Roberts tells me that she also trusts you in matters of petty cash. You paid the vails in Derbyshire?"

Whatever he was on about, Rose knew that measured tone, that gentlemanly reserve. Gavin was in deadly earnest, regardless of his objective.

"How can I recall back that far?" Timmens said. "That was ages ago, and what do a few pence here and there matter when some flighty actor is putting Missus's reputation at risk?"

"What about a few pounds?" Gavin said evenly. "What can you recall about many pounds left in Mrs. Roberts's jewelry box?"

Timmens took a few steps forward, as if she'd shake a finger directly in Gavin's face, then stopped and speared Rose with an exasperated look. "Will you send me to fetch them footmen, or am I supposed to stand here, being insulted to my face while you keep mum? This 'un ain't never been nothing but trouble, and here he is again, stirring up more trouble."

Gavin pushed away from the windowsill and walked a slow circle around Timmens. "I hear no insult... to you. I hear a reasonable question, but I have yet to hear a reasonable—much less respectful— answer. Mrs. Roberts is your employer, and you will not disrespect her."

"Timmens handled the vails," Rose said. "In London, in Derbyshire, everywhere, until today. I gave the butler a tidy sum this morning and asked him to use his discretion in its disbursement."

"I coulda done that," Timmens said. "You had no need to take that on yourself, missus."

Gavin ceased his perambulations just behind Timmens's left shoulder. "In Derbyshire, you found a small fortune in Mrs. Roberts's jewelry box, didn't you, Timmens?"

"I'll not stand for this," Timmens said, crossing her arms. "Missus, you'd best call him off, or you'll regret it."

That was a threat. The old Rose, the one who'd tried to read Wordsworth, would have done anything to smooth over the moment.

"You stole from me?" Rose asked.

"*He* left that money in your jewelry box," Timmens said, chin jerking in Gavin's direction. "Making a common strumpet of you, he was. You were fair gone on him, and he treats you like that. Nobody else coulda done it. Of course, I took that money."

An odd sensation enveloped Rose, of having had the same discussion at many points in the past and of hearing the words clearly for the first time.

"You committed this substantial act of larceny *for me?*" Rose asked almost pleasantly.

"I couldn't let him treat you like that, and it's not as if I don't work hard."

Gavin made another slow circuit around Timmens. "Mrs. Roberts, exactly how much jewelry has gone missing?"

"Not that much. A locket, a bracelet, earbobs, a few rings, some nacre hairpins, a pair of silver shoe buckles..." Quite a lot, actually, one or two pieces at a time.

"Widows are forgetful," Timmens said. "Everybody knows that. And those actors were underfoot in Derbyshire, or Missus wouldn't have crossed paths with you. Actors are beggars reciting verse. One of them doubtless took the bracelet, because they earn even less than a lady's maid does."

"Everybody knows that too?" Gavin asked, starting another circuit of Timmens's person. "I wonder, then, why a mere maid can afford this gold chain about her neck."

He delicately lifted the clasp of a slender chain peeking above the collar of Timmens's dress.

"You leave me alone," Timmens shrieked, wrenching to the side.

Gavin held fast to the chain, which broke when Timmens jerked away. He held up the broken links and the locket dangling from them. "I believe we'll find the late Dane Roberts's miniature inside, and I suspect that coin, jewelry, and trust were not the only valuables Timmens purloined from you."

He pried open the locket while Timmens glared daggers at him.

"I earned that locket," she spat, her tone venomous. "He promised me we'd be together, promised me that he'd set me up in Town. She wanted babies of him, and he pitied her too much to leave her."

"*I* wanted babies?" Rose's voice sounded oddly calm to her own ears. "I wanted babies?"

"Sons. Every woman wants sons. You left him no peace on the matter. You never treated him right, never gave him the respect he was owed. You never understood him, how delicate his nerves were and that he drank because you drove him to it. I loved him, and *he loved me.*"

Rose felt the absurd urge to laugh, except that in Timmens she saw another woman trying to convince herself that she was—after her fashion—*fine.* Lovable, valued, desired.

"Timmens, Dane was a sot by the time he came home from public school. He was all but drunk when he proposed to me, and if you believe for one moment that I wanted to bring children into a household headed by a chronic inebriate... Give her the locket, Mr. DeWitt. She's right—she earned it."

Gavin obliged. "Shall I summon the magistrate?"

"Wot? You'll bring the law on me after all I've done for you, Missus?"

Timmens even had Dane's ability to become the tragic victim in dramas of her own creation. "I will write you a character. You can keep your treasures as severance, and I never want to see you again. Mr. DeWitt, if you'd see that Timmens is on the afternoon stage at my expense, I'd appreciate it. She had best never set foot back in Hampshire."

Gavin went to the parlor door and bellowed for a footman. A stout young blond fellow soon appeared.

"Please take Miss Timmens to the servants' hall and ensure she remains there until somebody can get her to the Crosspatch Arms. She's to be seen onto the late stage, inside fare, along with her belongings and a packed hamper. Pay her fare to any British destination outside Hampshire. And I do mean put her *bodily* into the coach."

"Very good, Mr. DeWitt."

"He loved me," Timmens spat. "He loved *me*."

Rose had spent the first few months of her widowhood trying to convince herself of the same lie, then giving up the exercise as both vexatious and impossible. She said nothing, and Timmens was soon gone from sight.

Gavin wrapped her in a hug. "I'm sorry."

His embrace was balm to the body and soul, but upon examination, Rose did not find herself much injured.

"I'm not. Timmens doubtless did me a great favor by humoring all of Dane's imagined injustices and supporting his fantasies."

"She did more than that."

"Oh, very likely. Dane had a mistress in Town. Why wouldn't he have a mistress at home? The irony is, he was an awful lover. Seldom able to... complete what he started. I dreaded intimacies with him and prayed that I did not conceive. I got Colforth Hall from the marriage —though admittedly my settlements are why the Hall is still standing —but what does Timmens get? A broken heart, coach fare, and some trinkets."

"Then I'm glad your prayers were answered, because you are right: A man who will betray both wife and leman and set the leman to betraying the wife all over again does not deserve the honor of fatherhood."

Gavin would be a wonderful father. That thought surprised Rose as none of the previous drama had.

"Timmens delighted in making me feel inadequate and diminished. I knew that and put up with it because I felt sorry for her. I still do."

"I do not. You were more than gracious, to the late lamented sot, to Timmens, and to Drysdale. Part of me wants to see them both bound over for the assizes, but the playwright in me..."

Playwright? "Yes?"

"Happy endings are more satisfying." Gavin led Rose to the bed and sat beside her on the mattress. "We are not of noble houses in Verona or princes of Denmark, but Mr. Dabney is the king of his livery stable, and Mrs. Pevinger is the queen of the Crosspatch Arms. We all know what it is to see dreams die, to lose loved ones, to struggle, to long for justice. The tragedies are all very interesting and useful as cautionary tales, but most audiences are more appreciative of laughter, hope, and love."

"I am more appreciative of those qualities. I had tragedy enough —and farce enough—in my first marriage. How did you know to suspect Timmens?"

"A bit of acting advice from Drysdale. He once said that when possible thievery arises, the audience knows who's guilty and who is falsely accused based on the moment after the alleged thief is discovered. If the person cast in that role will, even for an instant, look about as if assaying the house for support or condemnation, then the audience knows that party is guilty. That small display of self-preservation, rather than embarrassment, humor, cool unconcern, gives the thief away to the observers, but the action needs to be very small. So subtle, the audience won't be able to say how they know they behold a thief, but are certain of their conclusions."

"And Timmens gave herself away with such a look?"

"She gave away enough that I suspected, then I saw the gold clasp at her nape and heard again how disrespectful she could be. Her insubordination escalated when a maid with nothing to hide would have been relieved to leave us some privacy."

"Well, thank you. I might have gone years tolerating her behaviors out of misplaced pity and loyalty. Good riddance."

More good riddance. Good riddance to guilt, to regrets, to widowish tears, and—the realization came to Rose like birdsong on a beautiful morning—to lying about being *fine.*

She sat side by side with Gavin, holding hands and marveling at her own good cheer. She was soon to get into the coach, and she wouldn't see Gavin for weeks, but she was nonetheless confident that they had a future, and a happy one.

She got off the bed and locked the door. "This is not an ending, Mr. DeWitt, but given that we have time, and that I am in very fine spirits, I hope you will tarry with me a few minutes longer."

Gavin remained with Rose behind that locked door for nearly two hours.

Early autumn in Hampshire was a spectacular canvas of ancient hedgerows in their seasonable glory, fat sheep, gamboling foals, and harvest crews singing and sweating their way through one ripe field after another. What Hampshire lacked in forests, it more than made up in magnificent rural vistas.

"Lots of room to gallop here," Gavin said, patting his mount on the shoulder. "But let's keep it to a canter, shall we?"

He turned the horse through the Colforth Hall gateposts— dragons couchant—and started up a stately curving lime alley. When the carriageway straightened, the Hall presented itself on a slight rise at the end of a long, luminous stretch of golden foliage.

The effect was magical, imbuing Rose's home with an ethereal glow despite its generous proportions. Rose had described the place in one of her thrice-weekly letters as a cross between a cozy manor and a stately residence, but she'd clearly been viewing her home with a modest eye.

"A ruddy palace in miniature." Twidboro Hall would fit comfortably in the northern or southern wing of the edifice, to say nothing of what wings might be projecting behind the façade.

Colforth was up to Rose's weight, in other words, and while that should have given a hopeful suitor pause, Gavin was pleased. Colforth was worthy of its owner, as Gavin hoped to be worthy of her.

He'd brought his horse to a halt at the foot of the steps, and as he dismounted, the front door flew open.

"That is not our Roland," Rose said, making short work of the terrace stairs. "What have you done with your horse, Gavin?"

She wrapped her arms around him, and all equine thoughts flew from Gavin's mind. "I've missed you so, Rose Roberts. Missed you until I ache with it." He followed up that ringing statement of the obvious with a protracted kiss, and devil take any gawking neighbors, servants, horses, or grooms.

Rose stepped back all too soon. "I've missed you too, sir. Has my nose flattened for being pressed against the glass watching for your arrival?" She touched the tip of her proboscis and smiled up at him.

"You are lovelier than ever. All of Crosspatch Corners sends their regards and hopes you'll visit again soon." The lectures from their rubbishing lordships had been endless. "I carry letters from Diana and Caroline and standing invitations from the marchioness and my mother."

"My correspondence has exploded since I was in Berkshire," Rose said as a groom approached from the downwind side of the house. A stand of maples obscured what was doubtless a sizable stable and heaven only knew how many other outbuildings.

"As has mine. A certain loquacious coachman got to expounding about Roland's speed all up and down the London road. Roland has acquitted himself splendidly in his opening meets. He's being called the Second Eclipse, but more to the point, our boy is having a grand time." Also earning much more than the predicted tidy packet, bless him.

Half the proceeds had gone to investing in the Players, the other half to Lady Phillip's sailors' homes.

"Be warned," Rose said, linking arms with Gavin, "I intend to have a grand time with you. I have missed you dreadfully."

Gavin mounted the steps beside her and paused before the front door. "I'm not here to frolic, Rose."

She looked him up and down, and Gavin could see the joy in her eyes dim. "Explain yourself."

He had planned to have this discussion after some pleasantries, a meal, perhaps a tour of the Hall, but that would all be so much dithering.

"I want to marry you, but you gave me a challenge to complete before my hopes in that regard can be raised. I was to reconcile my love of the theater with my responsibility to my family and my love for you. I'd like you to read something before we..."

"Don't frolic?"

"Before we decide the nature of my call."

Rose put a hand on the door latch. "You're sure we're not to frolic? That was a very frolicsome kiss we just shared in view of God, the countryside, and half my staff."

"I'm sure that I'd like you to read what I've brought for you, and beyond that, I cannot think."

The door swung open to reveal a youngish, blond butler. "Madam. I've put a tray of lemonade and comestibles in the family parlor for you and Mr. DeWitt."

The garrison had clearly been on high alert.

"Thank you, Platz. Please inform the laundry that a bath might be needed in an hour or so."

"Very good, madam. Sir, your hat?"

Gavin handed over hat and spurs and asked that his saddlebags be brought to the family parlor. Platz bowed without batting an eye at that odd request.

Rose escorted Gavin to an airy, high-ceilinged sitting room that managed to be both elegant and inviting. The ceiling fresco was all winged creatures and fluffy clouds. The walls were hung in pale green silk. The bouquet on the sideboard included delphiniums the color of Rose's eyes and trailing vines of sweet pea.

The vista beyond the open French doors included old-fashioned formal parterres and a shaded walk along an ornamental lake.

"Your home is absolutely lovely, Rose."

"I've always thought so, but the place was going to seed when I arrived. Putting the house to rights became a cause with me."

"Because you were trying to please your husband?" How many hurts had Dane Roberts done to his wife, hurts the man would never atone for?

"At first, yes. If I could just make Colforth pretty enough, grand enough, cheerful enough... but several years of diligent effort proved my theory ridiculous. From that point on, I made the house comfortable enough, pretty enough, and well run enough *for me*. You miss Roland, don't you?"

What an odd, insightful question. "Yes, but he's as happy as a hog in slop galloping his competition to flinders. The village swears Mr. Dabney is two inches taller as a result of Roland's successes."

"But your day no longer starts with thrilling gallops, and you can't philosophize to your steed on quiet afternoon hacks. What have you been doing with yourself, Gavin?"

A footman bearing a pair of dusty saddlebags appeared in the open door.

"I'll take those," Gavin said.

"You will have something to drink as well." Rose poured two tall glasses of lemonade and added a sprig of mint to each. "Traveling works up a thirst."

Well, yes. Gavin was parched and famished and saddle sore, and none of that mattered. He'd had weeks to rehearse for this moment, and now that his cue had come...

He thrust a sheaf of papers at Rose. "Tell me what you think. Be honest, and when you've read that, we'll talk."

She took the papers. "*A Crosspatch Contretemps* by Gavin

DeWitt."

"I thought about using a pen name, but that's nonsense. Either I'm proud of what I've created, or I should publish anonymously."

"I rather liked Galahad Twidham. Had both dash and charm. If you publish anonymously, everybody will—"

"Rose, please just read the damned play." He hadn't raised his voice, but it was a perilously near thing.

She passed him a glass of lemonade. "I will read it right now, and you will drink that, admire the garden, and cease fretting. If you wrote it, I will love it."

How he loved *her*. "You might not. I took some risks, but I'm open to revisions if you think them imperative." Gavin had never felt so vulnerable, so stripped of defenses, but this was Rose, and he needed her to be honest.

"Take the tray," she said, tucking herself into a wing chair. "The views from the terrace are lovely, and I am a fast reader. Give me an hour."

Gavin wanted to give her the rest of his life. He did as she bade and even made himself drink two glasses of lemonade and eat one sandwich. He *was* parched and famished, and he might—heaven help him—need his strength for a return to Berkshire before nightfall.

He sat on a shaded bench, admiring the golden beauty of Rose's home. She'd done this—restored the gardens, subdued the parklands, rebuilt the terrace—and best of all, she'd done it for herself.

A woman like that deserved...

Gavin heard a soft chortle from inside the parlor. Thinking his ears might have deceived him, he moved to a bench closer to the French doors. Ten minutes later, he heard Rose laugh, and five minutes after that, she went off into whoops.

She likes it. No benediction from heaven could have pleased him —and reassured him—half so much as the sound of Rose's merriment. Gavin waited another thirty minutes on his bench, his backside aching, his bones weary, his heart buoyant. When Rose came out, his script in hand, she was wreathed in smiles.

"Roland and his editorial flatulence will steal the show," she said. "'Halt in the king's name!'" Then she made a rude noise reminiscent of Roland at his most gaseous. "But the love scene... Oh, Gavin, you will have every lady in the house weeping for lack of such declarations in her life."

"If the men in the audience are astute, they'll be busily paraphrasing my romantic drivel and purloining daisies from the village churchyard. You like it?"

"I adore it. I gather the character of Randolph is based on your Mr. Dabney?"

Gavin escorted Rose to the shady bench and poured them another lemonade. They discussed the play, Gavin's plans for a debut at the Merchants' establishment in Bristol, and Drysdale's suitability as a director for a production in which he had inspired the role of the foolish, lovelorn villain.

"Dabney wants a sequel featuring a clever liveryman gone to London on his trusty steed, Roland. Our hero's country wisdom and fancy riding will save the day when all the Town dandies can't sit a horse because their breeches are too tight. Dabney's preferred title is *A Crosspatch Cavalier*."

"Mr. Dabney is not far wrong regarding London fashions. You are considering it?"

He had the play half-written in his head. "One project at a time. You're sure you like my *Contretemps*?"

"Very much. I wouldn't change a word of it. Have you become a playwright, Gavin DeWitt?"

She put the question playfully, but Gavin's heart had taken up a slow tattoo. He hadn't rehearsed this moment, hadn't dared.

"I will write plays," he said softly. "I should be writing plays. When I'm in the middle of a scene, trying to get the dialogue just so—sincere, entertaining, clever—then it's like a good gallop on Roland. I'm entirely absorbed. I don't hear Diana tackling her Beethoven. I forget that I agreed to meet Phillip for a few games of chess. I'm on some imaginary stage, before an audience of my own making, and,

Rose... I am having the best time. Better than all the third-act speeches in all the houses by all the leading men... I'm pursuing one of the passions I was born to pursue."

"Good." She hugged him tight with an arm around his waist. "I'm glad. I'm overjoyed, in fact. Dare I hope that another one of your passions can be pursued with me?"

"Reconcile yourself to that unalterable fact. I have a whole proposal ready, if you'd like to hear it."

She sat up. "Does it rhyme?"

"I tossed that draft out. I tossed a lot of drafts out."

"Might we discuss this someplace more private, Gavin?"

He said the first, stupid thing that came into his head. "I need a bath."

An impish light dawned in Rose's eyes. "As it happens, there's a portion of the lake not visible from the house and a fishing cottage along that stretch of the shore. I've taken to ending my day with a swim, but you mustn't tell anybody. We can accommodate two agendas at once."

Getting clean had never loomed so tantalizingly before mortal man, and yet... first things first. "Please tell me you'll marry me, Rose. I will trot out the speech, even the rhyming versions, unless you say you'll have me."

"Gavin DeWitt, I will marry you, and I will *have* you. Come along."

He came along, and by the time he and Rose returned from the lake, she was the most spotless bride-to-be in the whole of England. Gavin was equally well scrubbed and every bit as happy. A few ideas for another play danced in his head, a tale of love, fast horses, meddling family, jolly squires, outspoken ladies, and most of all, happy endings.

A Crosspatch Courtship opened in London the following year, to full houses and wild applause, and the playwright and his first critic, muse, adoring wife, and partner in mischief were both on hand to hear every last ovation.

Made in the USA
Columbia, SC
21 December 2023

29308207R00139